CE

THE PRIME MINISTER'S PENCIL

CECIL Waye was a pseudonym of Cecil John Charles Street (1884-1964), who, after a distinguished career in the British army, became a prolific writer of detective novels.

He produced two long series of novels; one under the name of John Rhode featuring the forensic scientist Dr. Priestley, and another under the name of Miles Burton. As Cecil Waye, Street also produced four mysteries in the early thirties: *Murder at Monk's Barn*, *The Figure of Eight*, *The End of the Chase* and *The Prime Minister's Pencil*. These works are now republished by Dean Street Press.

CECIL WAYE

THE PRIME MINISTER'S PENCIL

With an introduction by
Tony Medawar

DEAN STREET PRESS

Published by Dean Street Press 2021

Copyright © 1933 Cecil Street

Introduction © 2021 Tony Medawar

All Rights Reserved

First published in 1933 by Hodder & Stoughton

Cover by DSP

ISBN 978 1 913527 89 1

www.deanstreetpress.co.uk

INTRODUCTION

His birth name was Cecil John Charles Street but to his family and throughout his life he was known as John. His mother, Caroline Bill, was descended from a wealthy Yorkshire family, and his father, General John Street, was a distinguished former commander of the British Army in what is now known as Sri Lanka. At the time General Street was serving in Gibraltar as colonel-in-chief of the second battalion of Scottish Rifles. He had joined the Army in 1839 and served in China and the Crimea, including at the battles of Balaklava and Inkerman, as well as at the siege and fall of Sebastopol. Shortly after the birth of their child John and Caroline Street returned to England where, not long after John's fifth birthday, General Street died unexpectedly. John and his widowed mother went to live with her father in a house called *Firlands* in Woking, England, and in 1895, John was sent to school at Wellington College in Crowthorne, Berkshire, recognised as the school for children of army officers.

John did well in his academic studies. Perhaps unsurprisingly, his strengths seem to have been in the sciences. In 1901 he was joint winner of the school chemistry prize, and he also won the Pender Prize for an essay on a natural history subject, his being "The Scenery of Hampshire from a Geological Point of View", a title strongly reminiscent of the geological scholarship of Dr. Thorndyke, the detective created by the great mystery writer Richard Austin Freeman with whom Street is sometimes compared. In 1901, Street was awarded the Wellesley Prize, and the following year the Talbot Prize; and he also won praise for his prowess in intermural cricket matches.

At the age of 16, John Street left Wellington to attend the Royal Military Academy at Woolwich as a "gentleman cadet", joining the Royal Garrison Artillery in August 1903. On passing out from the Academy he was awarded the Armstrong Memorial Silver Medal for Electricity and Magnetism, and prizes for his work in these subjects.

Around this time, John met Hyacinth Kirwan, who was descended from Irish gentry and the daughter of a major in the Royal Artillery. They became engaged in September 1905 and were married on 24 February 1906. In March, he resigned his commission as a second lieutenant and their daughter, Verena, was born later in the same year. The family moved to Lyme Regis in Dorset, where they lived in a beautiful house, *Summerhill*, and Street worked as the manager of the Lyme Regis Electric Light & Power Company. During his time in the town, Street also served as a special juror, gaining an experience of the work of juries that would come in useful when he came to write one of his most famous detective mysteries.

On the outbreak of what has become known as the first world war, John Street – then in his late 20s and possibly inspired by his father's military record – enlisted, initially as a second lieutenant in the Royal Garrison Artillery. On 8 August 1915, as part of the special reserve, he landed in France where three months later he was wounded for the first of what would be three occasions. In 1917 Street returned to Britain and joined MI7, a branch of British military intelligence, where he worked on the promulgation of allied propaganda "behind the lines", as he described it in a fascinating study on the work of the military intelligence sections in the territories occupied by Germany.

In the New Year Honours List for 1918, Street was awarded the Order of the British Empire and that January he was also awarded the prestigious Military Cross, an honour that is granted in recognition of "an act or acts of exemplary gallantry during active operations against the enemy on land".

Street went on to write three books about his war experiences, all of which were published under the pseudonym 'F.O.O.', standing for Forward Observation Officer. The first was *With the Guns*, the story of "a siege battery involved in the battle of Loos, with chapters on artillery, its employment, evolution, observation, changing positions and communications." This was quickly followed by another book *The Making of a Gunner*, about the artillery, and a semi-autobiographical novel, *The Worldly Hope*. All three books remain highly readable, as does the short story that appears to be John Street's earliest published fiction. In "Gunner Morson, Signaller" – which was written, one imagines, for propaganda purposes – a British soldier saves a group of his countrymen from an unexpected German attack, disarming one of the enemy with a telephone and, consistent with what would become the hallmark of John Street's detective stories, killing another with a most unusual weapon, an earth pin, a pointed steel bar about two feet long used to establish an earth return for telephone circuits.

As the First World War came to an end John Street moved to a new propaganda role in Dublin Castle in Ireland, where he would be responsible for countering the campaigning of the Irish nationalists during the so-called war of Irish independence.

But the winds of change were blowing across Ireland and the resolution – or rather the partial resolution – of what Disraeli had defined as "The Irish Question" would soon result in a treaty and the partition of the island of Ireland. As history was made, Street was its chronicler, at least from the British perspective.

He wrote *The Administration of Ireland, 1920* under a new pseudonym, 'I.O.', short for "Information Officer", and then *Ireland in 1921*, the first book to appear under his own name. Both books were a success but, with the ink now dry on the Anglo-Irish Treaty, Street moved away from the promulgation of politico-military propaganda on behalf of the British state.

Other than making headlines for falling down a lift shaft, John Street would spend most of the rest of the 1920s at a typewriter. There were political studies of France, Germany, Hungary and Czechoslovakia as well as two biographical studies and English translations of a memoir of life in the French army and a celebrated biography of the Marquis de Vauban, the foremost military engineer of the late seventeenth century. His most popular book at this time was almost certainly a translation of Maurice Thiery's acclaimed biography of Captain James Cook.

As well as full-length works, Street continued to write short stories as well as articles for various outlets on an eclectic range of subjects including piracy, camouflage and concealment, Slovakian railways, the value of physical exercise, peasant art, telephony and the challenges of post-war reconstruction. He also found time to write three thrillers – *A.S.F.*, *The Alarm*, *The Double Florin* – and a First World War love story, *Mademoiselle from Armentières*. These were published under a new pen name – or should that be a pun name – 'John Rhode', which was also the name he used for a full-length study of the trial of Constance Kent, who was convicted for one of the most gruesome murders of the nineteenth century, at Road House in the village of Rode, then a village in Wiltshire.

However, while these early books found some success and *Mademoiselle from Armentières* was even filmed, the Golden Age of detective stories was well under way, and so John Street decided to try his hand.

The first challenge was to create a great detective, someone to rival the likes of Roger Sheringham and Hercule Poirot with whose creators he would soon be on first name terms. Street's great detective was the almost supernaturally intelligent Lancelot Priestley, a former academic who was, in the words of the critic Howard Haycraft, "fairly well along in years, without a sense of humour and inclined to dryness". From his first case, *The Paddington Mystery* (1925), Doctor – or rather Professor

– Priestley was an immediate success, and Street was quick to respond, producing another six novels in short order.

Priestley appears in all but five of Street's 76 'John Rhode' novels – one of which is based on the notorious Wallace case – and they often feature one or both of two Scotland Yard detectives, Inspector Hanslet and Inspector Jimmy Waghorn who would in later years appear without Priestley in several radio plays and a short stage play.

*

So by 1930, John Street, a highly decorated former Army major with a distinguished career in military intelligence behind him, had written 25 books using four names. He was 45 years old but, astonishingly, he was just getting started . . .

By 1930, the Streets were living in North Brewham, a village in Somerset where John became vice-chairman of the local branch of the British Legion, sitting on its employment committee to help ex-servicemen find work. The village was located in the parish of Bruton and from this Street derived the first of two new pseudonyms – 'Miles Burton' as whom he wrote a series of what would eventually be 63 novels. These feature Desmond Merrion, a retired naval officer named for Merrion Street in Dublin, and – in all but two titles – Inspector Arnold of, where else, Scotland Yard. There also exists an unfinished and untitled final novel, inspired it would appear by the notorious Green Bicycle Case.

The 'Burton' and 'Rhode' detective mysteries are similar but while Priestley is generally dry and unemotional, Merrion is more of a gentleman sleuth in the manner of Philip Trent or Lord Peter Wimsey. Both are engaged from time to time by Scotland Yard acquaintances, all of whom are portrayed respectfully rather than as the servile and unimaginative policemen created by some of Street's contemporaries.

However, two pseudonyms weren't enough for a crime writer as fecund as John Street and, again adopting a pun on his own name, he *also* became 'Cecil Waye' although this was not revealed until long after Street's death. For the four 'Cecil Waye' books, Street created two new series characters – the brother and sister team of Christopher and Vivienne Perrin, two investigators rather in the mould of Agatha Christie's 'Young Adventurers', Tommy and Tuppence Beresford. Curiously, while three of the 'Waye' novels are metropolitan thrillers, the first – *Murder at Monk's Barn* – is a detective story, very much in the style of the 'John Rhode' and 'Miles Burton' books.

With three series of crime books in hand, it is not surprising to find that John Street was also a founding member of the Detection Club, the illustrious dining club for crime writers founded by Anthony Berkeley in the late 1920s. In Street's words, the Club existed so that detective story writers might "dine together at stated intervals for the purpose of discussing matters concerned with their craft." Street played a lively part in the life of the Detection Club and his most important contribution was undoubtedly the creation of Eric the Skull which – showing that he had not lost his youthful technical skills – he wired up so that the eye sockets glowed red during the initiation ceremony for new members. He also edited *Detection Medley*, the first and arguably the best anthology of stories by members of the Club, and he contributed to the Club's first two round-robin detective novels, *The Floating Admiral* and *Ask a Policeman*, as well as one of the Club's various series of detective radio plays and the excellent true crime anthology *The Anatomy of Murder*.

Street was popular and he was happy to help other Club members with scientific and technical aspects of their own work. In the foreword to Dorothy L Sayers' Wimsey novel, *Have His Carcase*, she thanks Street for his "generous help with all the hard bits" drawn from his knowledge of code-breaking and ciphers. And Street also provided the technical input for *Drop to his Death*, a novel attributed to him as well as to his closest friend at the Detection Club, John Dickson Carr, writing under his 'Carter Dickson' pen name; the two were firm friends and Carr later made Street the inspiration for his character Colonel March, head of *The Department of Queer Complaints*.

Away from crime fiction, things were running less smoothly. At some point in the 1930s, Rhode's marriage failed, possibly because he seems to have had his hands permanently welded to a dictaphone – which he had come to use rather than a type-writer – but more likely because of the effect on the marriage of the loss of their daughter Verena who died in 1932 at the age of only twenty five.

During this decade, John met Eileen Waller, the daughter of an Irish engineer and a French mother, and the couple moved to Orchards, a house in Laddingford, Kent, where Street would set one of his Dr. Priestley novels, *Death in the Hopfields*, where a local journalist described Street as "the most jovial, 'hail-fellow-well-met' types of men I have ever had the pleas-ure of meeting" and revealed that Street owned a talkative parrot and collected pewter tankards, which will not come as a surprise to anyone who has appreciated the many, many, imaginatively-named public houses that pepper his novels. It was also revealed that, somewhat improbably, John Street and Eileen wove tapestries together on a large hand loom. While in Laddingford, Street also served as a school governor and he sponsored the village cricket team, acquiring for them a playing field and a pavilion.

In October 1943, John and Eileen let Orchards and moved to the remote village of Swanton Novers in North Norfolk. In 1949, after the death of Street's first wife, Hyacinth, John and Eileen married in 1949, in Yorkshire, and they moved to Stowmarket in Suffolk, where they lived in a beautiful 16th century thatched house with exposed timbers, original fire-places and flooring.

However, John Street's extraordinary career was coming to an end. The couple moved to a bungalow in Seaford in Sussex on the south coast of England and his final novels – *The Vanishing Diary* by 'John Rhode' and *Death Paints a Picture* by 'Miles Burton' – were published in 1960 and 1961 respectively

John Street died on the 8th of December 1964 in Leaf Hospital, Eastbourne. He left nearly three quarters of a million pounds in today's money. Fourteen years later his wife Eileen also died, in a Seaford nursing home.

*

John Street wrote a large number – more than 140 – of what one Japanese fan, Yoshito Tsukada, has aptly described as "pure and clever detective stories". His approach to writing detective fiction was simple, as he explained in a letter he wrote to the author of a book on the subject, published in 1934.

> "The first thing is to devise a suitable plot. Of which there is no lack. A perusal of the daily press, and of criminal records, will disclose an almost unlimited supply. Unknown correspondents are frequently good enough to send me ideas. The progress of scientific discovery naturally suggests fresh means of ingenious murder . . ."

He went on to explain how he would "complete the crime as though I myself were the criminal, trying to think of every possible precaution. I next take the opposite point of view, that of the investigator charged with inquiring into the death of the victim . . . I am myself the logician in Dr. Priestley, giving him the services of expert practising scientists where necessary."

That attention to detail led Street's friend, Dorothy L. Sayers, to describe him as "the kind of man who tries everything out on the dog in his own back kitchen (under proper safeguards, of course, for the dog)." His mission was simply to write books that invited the reader to pit their wits against him. This was exactly the kind of novel that Street himself enjoyed, as he described in an article published to accompany a radio series entitled "Thoughts of a Detective Story Writer".

"I want painstaking workmanship and accurate expression of fact. Given those two essentials, I can thoroughly enjoy myself in trying to unravel the problem before the author divulges it . . . in true detective fiction, the actual crime is of secondary importance. To the author, and therefore to the reader as well, it is merely a peg upon which to hang the subtlety of his criminal and the acuteness of his detective."

Clearly, the technique worked for, in the 1930s and 40s in particular, John Street was immensely popular and not only with the reading public. For the writer and reviewer E.R. Punshon, Street was "Public Brain-Tester No. 1" while Dorothy L. Sayers praised him warmly – here writing about *The Robthorne Mystery*: "One always embarks on a John Rhode book with a great feeling of security. One knows there will be a sound plot, a well-knit process of reasoning, and a solidly satisfying solution with no loose ends or careless errors of fact." And on the other side of the ocean, Ellery Queen included two novels by 'John Rhode' – *The Paddington Mystery* and *The Murders in Praed Street* – in a list of cornerstones of detective fiction, drawn up with Howard Haycraft. The list also included two titles each by Christie and Sayers (as well as four by Queen!) and while Street does not have anything like the same profile as these giants of the genre, he remains among the most sought after crime writers of the Golden Age. In an essential study of some of the lesser luminaries of the Golden Age, the American writer Curtis Evans described Street as "the master of murder means" and praised his "fiendish ingenuity" in "the creative application of science and engineering". And another writer on the Golden Age, Ian Godden, has suggested that Street's books were "often read until they fell to pieces, which is as good a tribute as any to their popularity and the reason why they are so hard to find today."

While Street is not without his critics, his books are thoroughly enjoyable, often humorous and consistently entertaining. He tackles impossible crimes – with murder in locked houses, locked bathrooms and locked railway compartments, even – with Carter Dickson – a locked elevator. And who else but Street could come up with the idea of using a hedgehog as a murder weapon, or conceive of dealing death by means of a car battery . . . or a marrow . . . or a soda siphon . . . or a hot water bottle. Even bed-sheets and pyjamas prove lethal in the hands of John Street. He often creates unusual and believable settings for his mysteries such as a motor show, or the work of the Home Guard, Britain's local defence force in the Second World War, or the excavation of a dinosaur, which forms the backdrop for the 'Miles Burton' title *Bones in the Brickfield*. Street also defies some of the expectations of the genre, with one novel in which Dr. Priestley allows a murderer to go free and another in which the guilty party is identified and put on trial . . . but acquitted. And his characters – though simply drawn – are engaging and at times display an emotional depth that is rarely found in detective stories of the Golden Age. As Curtis Evans has shown in his biblio-biographical study of Street's life and work, Street was in several respects far more modern in his outlook on life than many of his contemporaries, with libertarian anti-capitalist sentiments, non-judgmental references to adultery, illegitimacy, prostitution and homosexuality, and markedly different views to most of his contemporaries on Jewish people and the rights of women as well as credible working class characters that function as real people rather than stereotypes.

Today, around 60 years after his death and a century since they were first published, only a few of the 'John Rhode' and 'Miles Burton' books are currently in print but, thanks to Dean Street Press, the four 'Cecil Waye' novels – the rarest of the author's more than 150 fiction and non-fiction titles – are now available. John Street would be simply amazed.

Tony Medawar
Wimbledon
November 2020

CHAPTER I

THE telephone instrument on Christopher Perrin's desk buzzed, with the irritating note of a large and persistent bumblebee. With a muttered objurgation Perrin laid down his pen and picked up the receiver. "Well?" he asked peevishly. "What is it now?"

The voice of his secretary, Miss Avery, answered him. "I'm sorry to trouble you, Mr. Perrin," she said apologetically. "A lady has called, and is very anxious to see you. I would have asked Mr. Meade to see her, but he's out, and I don't think he will be back for some time."

"Confound the fellow!" grumbled Perrin. "What the devil does he want to go out for, when he knows I'm busy, and don't want to be disturbed? What does this infernal woman want?"

"To consult you, Mr. Perrin," replied Miss Avery with a touch of asperity. "Her name is Miss Rushburton, and she says that you know her brother."

Perrin's eyebrows lifted as he heard the name. But still, he was not particularly anxious to interview Miss Rushburton. The business of Perrins, Investigators, of which he was the head, was rapidly increasing, and both he and David Meade, whom he had recently admitted to partnership, found every moment of their day fully occupied. At the present moment he was engaged in drawing up a highly confidential report for a distinguished client. This must at all costs be completed before post time, and Perrin had several hours of hard work before him. He glanced at his watch and made a rapid calculation. Well, yes, perhaps he could spare half an hour, not a moment longer.

He would not have dreamt of making the concession for a casual caller. But Miss Rushburton merited special consideration, if only on account of her father's position. Sir Ethelred Rushburton, Baronet, M.P., was a man very much in the public eye. He was one of the leading men of the Opposition Party, and when the existing government fell, and his own party came into power, it was taken as a matter of course that he would receive an important post in the cabinet. Curiosity played some part in Perrin's decision to receive his visitor. He wondered what errand could have brought the daughter of this eminent politician to his offices in Hanover Square.

"All right, show Miss Rushburton in," he said to his waiting secretary. "And, look here, if I don't get rid of her in twenty-five minutes by the clock, come in and get rid of her. Say that the Archbishop of Canterbury is expecting me at Lambeth Palace, or anything you like."

He put down the instrument and stood up to receive his visitor. Miss Avery opened the door, and introduced her. She was a tall girl, dressed in the height of fashion. Perrin bowed, and showed her to a chair. Distinctly pretty, but rather too patently made up, was his mental comment.

"It's very good of you to see me, Mr. Perrin," she said, as she sat down. "I suppose I ought to have rung up and made an appointment. But Ozzy hasn't got a 'phone in those poky little rooms of his, and I just came straight on here when I left him, on the off chance. You know Ozzy, don't you?"

"I know Mr. Rushburton slightly," replied Perrin. "I hope that nothing unpleasant has happened to him?"

"Oh dear, no! Ozzy's all right. I left him scribbling away for dear life. He's got the idea of the century this time, he told me. In fact, he pushed me out of the door before I'd been there five minutes. But he did just find time to tell me that I'd better come round here and see you about it. So I took a taxi, and here I am."

"I'm sure I'm delighted to see you, Miss Rushburton. But perhaps it would save time if you were to tell me what it is Mr. Rushburton advised you to consult me about."

Her expression suddenly became serious. "It's a pretty desperate business," she replied. "The old man's secretary, Cuthbert Solway, has disappeared, and nobody seems to know what has become of him. He's just vanished into thin air, pouf, like that!" She made a gesture which conveyed that the man had changed into a puff of smoke before her eyes.

But to Perrin this was not very enlightening. "The old man?" he inquired tentatively.

"My respected parent," she replied calmly. "The Champion of English Liberty, as the *Daily Bugle* calls him. You've heard of him, of course. It isn't his press agent's fault if you haven't. Solway's been with him for years, and now, all of a sudden, just when I want him the most, he takes it into his head to vanish like this."

Perrin made no effort to conceal his bewilderment. "You'll forgive me if I don't quite understand," he said. "Have you come to me on behalf of your father, Miss Rushburton?"

"Good heavens, no!" she exclaimed. "Solway's disappearance doesn't worry the old man; he's got too many other things to think about, I suppose. But it's a very serious matter for me, and I want you to find him for me."

Perrin hesitated. Would it be tactful to ask outright how the absence of her father's secretary could affect Miss Rushburton? He decided that she was not the type of girl to display any inconvenient embarrassment. "May I inquire the nature of your interest in this Mr. Solway?" he asked.

She glanced at him with a puzzled expression, then burst out laughing. "Why, you don't imagine I'm in love with him, or anything like that, do you, Mr. Perrin? You wouldn't think so if you could see him. He's the driest old stick you could ever come across. No, my interest in him is purely material, I'm afraid. You see, he wangles money for me out of the old man. You mustn't tell anybody that, of course."

Perrin smiled. This interview, waste of his valuable time though it might be, was turning out distinctly amusing. "Anything you may tell me is in the strictest confidence," he replied.

"That's all right, then," she continued. "You see, it's like this. The old man gives me an allowance, but I can't possibly do all I want on it. And the old man won't increase it. He's funny that way, he doesn't seem to care how much he spends on anything that makes a show, but he grudges a few pounds extra to his only daughter. You see what I mean, don't you, Mr. Perrin?"

Perrin nodded. It struck him that as regards "making a show" Rushburton's daughter probably played her part nobly. However, that was none of his business.

"I asked Solway's advice some time ago," continued Miss Rushburton. "He looked after the old man's money affairs for him, and I knew that if anybody could help me, he could. I found him easy enough to deal with, and he promised to do all he could for me. He used to get the money out of the old man somehow, and hand it over to me. I never asked him how he managed it. And, you see, he promised to let me have a hundred pounds today. That's why I'm so anxious to find out what's become of him. You will help me, won't you, Mr. Perrin?"

"Perhaps I may be able to give you some advice, Miss Rushburton," replied Perrin noncommittally. "But naturally, I must know more about the facts, first. When you say that Mr. Solway has disappeared, what do you mean, exactly?"

"Just what I say. Ever since I can remember, Solway has lived with us at Oldwick Manor. He has his own rooms there, but he always has his meals with whoever of us happens to be there. And I don't believe that he has ever slept a single night away from the place for years and years, until now."

"When did you last see him, Miss Rushburton?"

"Last Sunday, when Mother and I went down there, and today is Friday. You see, Mr. Perrin, Mother and I are living in our Berkeley Square house for the season, but the old man is stopping at Oldwick Manor, and only comes up to London for the day. He says he's very busy just now, but what it's all about, I can't tell you. Some political stunt, I expect."

"You saw your father and Mr. Solway together?"

"I did. In fact, I had the greatest difficulty in getting a word with Solway alone. It was then that he promised to have the money for me today. I was to go down this morning and get it. I went down as arranged, but he wasn't there."

"One moment, Miss Rushburton. What were the relations between your father and Mr. Solway on Sunday?"

"The same as they always were, so far as anyone could tell. The old man always treated Solway rather as a friend than as an ordinary secretary. They got on awfully well together. So far as I know there was never the slightest difference of opinion between them."

"I see. And what happened when you went to Oldwick Manor this morning?"

"I drove down there, and the first person I saw was Pearson, the butler. Pearson is an old ally of mine, and I told him that I wanted to see Solway without the old man knowing anything about it. He told me that Solway was away and seemed surprised that I didn't know it.

"I was so astonished that I didn't know what he meant at first. I thought that Solway might have gone up to Berkeley Square to see me, and that I'd missed him. But when I asked Pearson, he told me that Solway hadn't been at Oldwick Manor since Monday. I can tell you, Mr. Perrin, I was never so amazed in my life."

"Did Pearson know anything of the circumstances in which Mr. Solway had left Oldwick Manor?"

"Oh yes, I asked him that, of course. On Sunday evening at dinner, after Mother and I had gone back to Berkeley Square, Pearson had overheard the old man arrange with Solway that he should go up to London next day. He was to go and see Lord Brimstoke, and after that to consult Doctor Hardcastle."

Perrin nodded. The name of Lord Brimstoke was as familiar to him as that of Sir Ethelred Rushburton himself. He was one of the leading lights of the financial world, the chairman of the London and Provinces Bank, and a director of a dozen important companies besides. It was easily understandable that the politician and the financier, each equally eminent, might have affairs in common. But the name of Doctor Hardcastle was not so familiar.

"This Doctor Hardcastle is a doctor of medicine, I suppose?" he remarked. "Did Mr. Solway mention that there was anything the matter with him when you saw him on Sunday?"

"Oh, no. I don't think there was anything the matter with him," she replied. "I don't suppose he went to see Doctor Hardcastle on his own account. He's a specialist in Harley Street, and the old man has been going to see him for some time. The old man has never been ill in his life, but he likes to think that he's got something the matter with his inside. It gives him an interest in life."

"I see. You think that Mr. Solway may have gone to Harley Street with a message from your father. At what time on Monday did he leave Oldwick Manor?"

"Pearson told me that he and the old man drove up together. The chauffeur says that Solway got out at the bottom of Queen Victoria Street, and that's the last anybody saw of him."

"Your father came home that day?"

"Yes, he drove back about four o'clock, Pearson told me. Shortly after dinner he rang for Pearson and asked him if Solway had come in yet, and seemed rather surprised when he heard he hadn't. He seemed fidgety all the evening, and Pearson thinks he sat up most of the night waiting for Solway. He went up to London unusually early on Tuesday and when he came back he looked very worried."

"Did Mr. Solway take a suitcase with him when he went up to London on Monday?"

"Only a little attaché-case that he always has with him. Pearson told me that none of his clothes or anything were missing from his rooms."

"Has your father taken any steps to find out what has become of his secretary?"

"Not so far as I know. I went to look for him after I had got all I could out of Pearson this morning, and I found him in his study. He wasn't too pleased at being interrupted, though he was doing nothing, so far as I could see, and asked me what I was doing down there. I told him some yarn about having come down to fetch some things I'd left behind and then I noticed that he looked quite different from when I had last seen him, positively ill, in fact. I've never seen him look like that before."

"Did he offer any explanation of his appearance?"

"I asked him what was the matter, and he told me that he felt a bit out of sorts, but that he would be all right again in a day or two, and it was nothing really. I'm inclined to believe that he's worrying about something. I expect one of his political schemes has gone wrong, or something like that. I could see that he was anxious to get rid of me, so I didn't stay long. But I did manage to ask him casually where Solway was."

"Did your father give any reason for his absence?" asked Mr. Perrin, with a faint smile.

"He didn't. He asked me what it mattered to me where he was. In fact, he got into what we call his electioneering mood. He stood up and thumped the table, and said that he'd have been somebody by now if his family weren't always interrupting him when he was busy, and asking silly questions, which wasn't bad considering that none of us had so much as seen him since last Sunday. I really can't remember all he said: you've no idea what a flow he has when he's roused. But I know he asked me how the devil he was to know where the fellow had got to. He then went on to explain how valuable his time was, and to assure me that he had no intention of wasting time in looking after other people, who were old enough and ugly enough to look after themselves."

"I gather that you got no satisfactory reply to your question, Miss Rushburton?"

"I didn't. I couldn't get a word in edgeways. He finished up by telling me that he was expecting Lord Brimstoke to lunch, and that he didn't want any chattering women to help in entertaining him. So there was nothing left for me to do but to clear out. But I did arrange with Pearson that he should ring me up if Solway turned up."

"Has Mr. Solway any relatives alive?" asked Mr. Perrin.

"I don't believe that he's got a relation, or a friend for that matter, in the world. If he has, he keeps it very quiet."

"That's rather a pity. I was going to suggest that if he had relations, they might approach the police. He may be suffering from loss of memory, or something like that. Could you give me any sort of description of him?"

"I can do better than that. I've got a photograph of him." She took a print from her bag and handed it to Perrin. It was a group taken for publicity purposes. In the foreground was the massive hearty-looking figure of Sir Ethelred, and by his side an elaborately dressed lady, easily identified as Lady Rushburton. Behind them, almost obscured by this combined majesty, stood a thin and insignificant figure, dressed demurely in black. He appeared to be of middle size, had a rather furtive expression, with eyes set close together, and was nearly bald. Beyond that, there was nothing whatever to distinguish him.

"That's Solway in the background," explained Miss Rushburton. "He's the sort of person who always is in the background, if you know what I mean. That's the only photograph of him I've ever seen."

"It will serve my purpose very nicely, thank you, Miss Rushburton," replied Perrin, laying the photograph on his desk. "What did you do when you left Oldwick Manor?"

"Drove back to town and went to see Ozzy in his rooms at the Temple. Not that I thought he'd know anything about Solway. They aren't particularly fond of one another, I'm afraid. But I wanted to find him, and I thought that since Ozzy is a barrister, he'd be able to tell me how to set about it. He wasn't any better pleased to see me than the old man had been. In fact, he gave me your address and told me to clear out."

As Perrin glanced rather ostentatiously at his watch, it struck. him that he was the third person whom Miss Rushburton had called on that day who had not invited her to prolong her visit. The gesture was not lost upon her. She rose and held out her hand. "You're a really busy man, I know, Mr. Perrin," she said ingratiatingly. "Not like Ozzy and the old man, who only pretend. But you will find Solway for me, won't you?"

"I'm afraid I can't guarantee that, Miss Rushburton," he replied as she showed her to the door.

"But I'll certainly have inquiries made, and I'll let you know as soon as I have any news." As she left the room, Perrin heaved a sigh of relief and returned to his interrupted report. The case of Cuthbert Solway would have to await his leisure.

CHAPTER II

SINCE Perrin's marriage, he had given up his rooms in Buckingham Gate and had taken a flat in Victoria Street. David Meade, admitted to partnership about the same time, had inherited the rooms, and if the two had not seen much of one another during the day they made a point of meeting after dinner.

On this particular day Mrs. Perrin had gone to stay in the country for the week-end. That evening, Perrin strolled round to Buckingham Gate by appointment. He found his partner with a sheaf of papers in front of him, and a tray with drinks and glasses on a side table.

Meade looked up as Perrin came in. "Good, here you are," he said. "Sit down and make yourself comfortable. I've only just come in. I've been busy all day on that Sandford case. I'm beginning to see daylight. The man's a rogue, I'm pretty sure of that. But I can't tell you anything definite yet."

"It won't do you any harm to take your mind off it for a bit," replied Perrin. "I had rather an entertaining visitor this afternoon. No less a person than Rushburton's daughter."

"What, Sir Ethelred Rushburton? What on earth did she want?"

"Like little Bo Beep she's lost her sheep and doesn't know where to find them, or rather him. In fact the confidential secretary to the old man—I use her own phrase—has disappeared, and she's very anxious that he should turn up again. Listen, and I'll tell you the whole sad story."

He described Miss Rushburton's visit while Meade listened attentively. "And I promised to make inquiries and let her know the result," he concluded.

"Not much difficulty about that," replied Meade. "Old Rushburton knows where the fellow is, of course."

"Exactly, that's the only point of interest about it. I may be inquisitive, but I should very much like to know what the game is. There are some rather queer points about it, at all events according to this girl's account. And I can't help a feeling of curiosity as to what these two distinguished people are up to."

Meade shrugged his shoulders. "Some political or financial intrigue, no doubt," he remarked.

"In which this chap Solway plays the part of the mysterious go-between, I shouldn't wonder. But, honestly, I don't like these intrigues. Brimstoke may be an honest man enough; I've nothing against him. But I do mistrust Rushburton. I always have. It isn't that I disagree with his political views, but he is of that type of politician who owes his success to clever boosting rather than to sound statesmanship. And in my opinion it will be a bad day for the country when he is allowed a say in the management of its affairs."

"You don't suggest that the firm of Perrins should employ its activities at the next General Election, do you?" murmured Meade.

"No, but between ourselves, I shouldn't be sorry if anything happened to put a spoke in Rushburton's wheel. I dislike the man, not personally, for I've never met him, but on principle. Mind, I'm not insinuating that this ridiculous affair of his secretary has anything sinister behind it."

"I don't suppose it has," replied Meade. "But I'm afraid I'm not the student of politics that you seem to be. Of course, I'm perpetually seeing Rushburton's name in the papers, but beyond that I really know very little about him."

"You'll find the best part of a column devoted to him in *Who's Who*. But I can tell you the principal facts to save you looking them up. He's the only son of a man who made a large fortune out of selling some patent ointment or other. You know the formula, a quantity of lard, a little oxide of zinc, and an enormous volume of advertisement. Cure anything from writer's cramp to housemaid's knee."

Meade laughed. "My dear fellow, surely you're a bit prejudiced?" he said.

"Well, perhaps I am. Anyway, the ointment was a howling success, and Rushburton found himself a very rich man when his father died. He gave up selling ointment and went in for politics instead. There's not much difference between them really. They're both forms of gulling the public. And in order to make a suitable splash, he bought a big place in Surrey, Oldwick Manor, and a house in Berkeley Square.

"His next move was to get himself returned to Parliament by the intelligent electors of Coalborough, and very soon he pushed himself into public notice. He's able enough in his own way, there's no doubt of that. He's the sort of man who poses as a popular demagogue, the guardian of the liberties of the people, and all that sort of tosh. His nickname among his friends is Ethelred the Ready, I believe. They say he's always got a plausible answer to any question that's fired at him, and he's certainly a very persuasive speaker. After a bit, a generous contribution to the funds of his party purchased him a baronetcy, and the last time his party was in power he was given a minor government job. Under-Secretary for something or other, I forget what at the moment."

"The usual rungs on the ladder of political fame," remarked Meade.

"Yes, and he'll get very near the top when the present government falls, as I'm afraid it may do. It's only the personal popularity of the Premier that keeps it going, as it is. If anything were to happen to Wedderley you'd find friend Rushburton in the cabinet within a few weeks. And that, as I say, would be nothing short of a national disaster."

"I dare say the country would survive even that," said Meade, surprised at his partner's vehemence. "But all this doesn't seem to have much to do with his daughter's visit to you. What about the rest of the family?"

"I'm coming to them. Rushburton, I fancy, never does anything without calculating the benefit that he'll gain by it. He married the daughter of some very old family. Lady Rushburton and her daughter manage the social side of the business. Ethelred the Ready, however impressive he may be in the House, does not exactly shine in the drawing-room, I'm told. Lady Rushburton I have never met, but the daughter strikes me as being the sort of young woman who knows how to look after herself. I think she sized up her father some time ago."

"I shouldn't wonder if she had. What about this brother of hers that she talks about? Ozzy, or whatever his name is."

"Osmond Rushburton? I know him slightly. He's not at all a bad fellow. There's none of the family pushfulness about him. The idea is, I imagine, that he should follow in father's footsteps. He's a barrister, but that's only a step towards entering Parliament. I don't suppose he knows what a brief looks like, and I'm pretty sure he doesn't care. He's got chambers in the Temple for the look of the thing and, oddly enough, he lives there. I've a suspicion that the family gets on his nerves."

"What does he do with himself? His sister suggested that he was busy when she went to see him, didn't she?"

"His ambition in life is to write a successful play. You'll see him at every first night studying the technique of the thing. The rest of the day he spends spoiling reams of perfectly good paper. Whether he's really got any dramatic ability, I don't know. But so far he hasn't persuaded any manager to accept his stuff."

"And he doesn't like this secretary chap, Solway, we're told," remarked Meade.

"I dare say he doesn't like any of his father's friends. Indeed, on one of the few occasions that I've spoken to him he hinted as much. But I don't suppose he's kidnapped Solway and got him hidden, gagged and bound, in the Temple. Solway is rather an interesting figure, from what that girl told me. I've got his photograph here. What do you think of him?"

Meade studied the print which Perrin handed to him. "Rushburton's got a strong face, whatever his faults may be," he said. "The sort of chap who carries through whatever his mind is set on, I should think. Lady Rushburton is an imposing-looking person too. Somehow gives the impression of being the perfect society hostess, doesn't she?"

"Oh, damn the Rushburtons!" exclaimed Perrin. "They get on my nerves, there's nothing human about them. Their every single thought or action is devoted to the honour and glory of Sir Ethelred. It's Solway I'm interested in."

"He's the bloke standing behind them, I suppose. I had a white rat once with a face just like that. I was very fond of him."

"Perhaps Miss Rushburton shares your penchant for white rats, and that's the secret of her attraction to Solway," remarked Perrin acidly. "Look at the fellow. He's as crafty as they make 'em, you can see that. What I want to know is this. What exactly are the relations between him and Rushburton? He's more than an ordinary secretary, Miss Rushburton spoke of a definite friendship between them. Is he the real brain behind the Rushburton presence? Does the Champion of English Liberty—I quote the *Daily Bugle* on his daughter's authority—dance according as Solway pulls the string? I wish I knew."

"Upon my word, Perrin, you're raising a lot of smoke out of a very small fire, aren't you?" exclaimed Meade. "The whole affair looks to me very simple. Rushburton has sent this chap away on some confidential errand or other, and doesn't want questions asked as to his whereabouts. I don't see how we can butt in very well."

"That's the obvious theory, and that's what I've been trying to persuade myself," replied Perrin slowly. "But all the same, there are some queer points in Miss Rushburton's story. I'll admit that I've only got the facts at second or third hand. But let's take them in order. In the first place, Solway goes up to London with instructions to see Lord Brimstoke and Doctor Hardcastle. Unless, of course, that conversation was definitely to mislead the watchful Pearson.

"Let's suppose it was genuine. Rushburton and Brimstoke have some deal on together. I think we can safely assume that, since Rushburton told his daughter that Brimstoke was coming down to lunch at Oldwick Manor today. I can easily understand Solway being sent with some message for them. But Doctor Hardcastle is a different proposition. A secretary is a useful invention, but there are some things he can't do. He can't, for instance, go to the barber's and get your hair cut for you. Nor it seems to me is it much good sending him to the doctor and having your pulse felt by proxy."

"No, but it may have been a case of another message, or he may have gone to fetch another bottle of the mixture as before. There are dozens of possibilities, it seems to me."

"Your experience of Harley Street specialists is limited, I can see that," replied Perrin. "They don't dish out bottles of medicine. They hand you a prescription and charge you umpteen guineas for it. For my own part, I can't imagine any message for this Doctor Hardcastle that couldn't more easily and expeditiously have been telephoned. However, we'll let the point pass, and go on to Monday evening. We're told that Rushburton evinced surprise, I think we might even say uneasiness when his secretary did not return. Next morning he went up to London unusually early, presumably to find out what had become of him. What do you make of that?"

"Why, that he didn't know until some time on Tuesday what had become of him. The way I see it is this: Solway goes up to London on some errands of Rushburton's. Something turns up which makes it impossible for him to get back to Oldwick Manor that night. He can't even communicate with his employer. But he leaves a message somewhere which Rushburton finds when he goes up to London on Tuesday."

"Very well," replied Perrin. "I can't help thinking that it is rather curious behavior on the part of a man who has never slept out of the house for years. I'll go on another step; to Rushburton's appearance today. His daughter noticed that he was not looking his usual bright self. Again, he jumped down her throat when she mentioned Solway. I can't get it out of my mind that his rather obvious worry was concerned with Solway's disappearance. The matter was on his mind, and when his daughter so tactlessly alluded to it he not unnaturally broke out."

"Which would imply that Rushburton does not know what's become of his secretary," said Meade. "If that's the case, why hasn't he taken any steps to find him? The first thing you would have expected him to do would be to send for the police."

"Yes, perhaps," replied Perrin slowly. "But what if the prospect of Solway being found worries Rushburton more than the man's disappearance? You see what I mean. A hue and cry after Solway would inevitably result in publicity: 'Famous Politician's Secretary vanishes.' I can imagine the headlines stretching right across the pages of the evening papers."

"According to you, publicity is as the breath of life to Rushburton," remarked Meade. "I should have thought he would welcome any means of keeping himself in the public eye."

"Yes, he wouldn't mind that. His troubles would begin when Solway was found. I shouldn't wonder if it was not Solway he was worrying about, so much as the attaché-case he was carrying. It wouldn't be very wide of the mark to guess that there were confidential papers in that, and I wouldn't mind betting that Rushburton wouldn't like an unsympathetic light thrown upon his private affairs."

Meade laughed. "When first I came to you, Perrin, you were always rubbing into me to verify my facts before I tried to build up a theory on them," he said maliciously.

"Much is permitted to the master that is forbidden to the apprentice," replied Perrin. "I admit that I have been allowing my imagination to run away with me a bit. But there's always the possibility that Solway has really disappeared, in the sense that Rushburton doesn't know what has become of him. And I am going to employ a few hours of my valuable time having a good look for him."

"It'll be a biggish job to get through in a few hours, won't it?" suggested Meade.

"It would be if we depended on our own resources. You must know by this time that the Yard has any private investigator beaten to a frazzle. It is only when for some reason or another the Yard cannot be employed, that people like ourselves have a ghost of a chance. But we happen to be in the happy position of being able to employ the Yard unofficially. Do you mind if I ring them up now, and ask if Inspector Philpott is in?"

Meade grinned. "Not a bit," he replied.

Perrin put his call through, and was lucky enough to find the inspector in his office. "Hullo, Philpott," he said, "Perrin speaking. I say, are you busy? It's a lovely evening. How would you like a nice walk across St. James's Park to my old rooms? There's a bottle of whisky at the end of it. It's not mine, but I assure you it's pretty good."

"I was just going home," replied Philpott. "What's in the wind now, Perrin?"

"My dear man, do you think I want to talk business at this time of night? It's a long time since I saw your manly figure, and I thought perhaps you might be able to find time to come round and have a drink with Meade and me."

"Very good of you, Perrin, I'm sure. All right, I'll be with you in a quarter of an hour or so."

From that moment Perrin dismissed the case of the missing Solway. He and Meade plunged into a discussion of the investigation upon which the latter was engaged, and they were still in the midst of it when the inspector was shown in. Even then Perrin did not mention the affair. He had a fund of stories at his disposal, with which he entertained his partner and the inspector. The three of them sat yarning for an hour or more, and it was not until Philpott reluctantly rose to leave them that Perrin came to the point.

"By the way, Philpott," he said. "I picked up a piece of news today that may interest you. You know Sir Ethelred Rushburton, of course? Well, he's got a secretary whose name is

Cuthbert Solway. And I hear on pretty good authority that he's been absent from his usual haunts for a day or two."

The inspector glanced meaningly at him. "And I suppose Rushburton's commissioned you to find him?" he asked.

"Good heavens, no!" exclaimed Perrin innocently. "If he wanted the man found he'd go to you people, not to me. But if you should hear news of Solway, you'd be doing me a good turn to give me the tip."

"You're a deep one, Perrin," replied the inspector. "I wonder what devilment you're up to now? All right, I'll see what can be done. You've got a description, I suppose?"

Perrin produced the photograph. The inspector glanced at it and put it in his pocket. "This is all on the Q.T., I suppose?" he said. "I won't take any steps officially, but I'll just pass the word round. Good night. Sorry I can't stop and help you and Mr. Meade finish that bottle."

Chapter III

Christopher Perrin was in the habit of dividing the cases which were brought to his notice into two classes, those which demanded immediate action, and those which could be allowed to develop of themselves, and merely needed watching.

The case of Cuthbert Solway fell naturally into the second category. Perrin's own opinion was that Solway would turn up in due course, with some plausible explanation to account for his absence. As Meade had so plainly hinted, there was nothing in the affair which would justify any undue activity on the part of Perrins, Investigators. But, all the same, Perrin could not repress the curiosity he felt as to the private affairs of Sir Ethelred Rushburton.

However, that Saturday morning, he found many things which demanded his immediate attention. He was busily engaged upon these, when, at about half-past ten, his telephone buzzed, and he was informed that Inspector Philpott was on the line.

"Hullo, Perrin, is that you?" came the familiar voice. "You'll be glad to hear that I've found out what you asked me last night."

"What! You don't mean to say that you've got news of Solway already?" exclaimed Perrin. "That's quick work! Where is he?"

"Down at Rushburton's place in the country, Oldwick Manor, I only heard the news ten minutes ago."

"I thought he'd turn up all right," said Perrin, not without a note of disappointment in his voice. "I say, I'm awfully obliged to you for letting me know."

He heard the inspector chuckle at the other end of the wire. "Oh yes. He's turned up, but I wouldn't go so far as to say he's all right. In fact, I'm credibly informed that he's as dead as a door-nail."

"What!" Perrin fairly shouted. "Dead! Oh, come on, man, let's have the whole story."

"I don't know it myself, yet," replied the inspector. "All I can tell you is this. The Surrey police have just rung us up to say that Rushburton's secretary has been found dead under peculiar circumstances, and that they would like the assistance of somebody from the Yard. I've been detailed for the job, and I'm just going down there."

"If you'll meet me in quarter of an hour at the Embankment entrance to the Yard, I'll run you down in my car," said Perrin, without a moment's hesitation. "It'll save you quite a lot of valuable time."

Again the inspector chuckled. "I rather expected that you'd suggest something of the kind," he replied. "All right, I'll let you drive me down, on condition that you tell me all you know about this business."

"Right, that's a bargain!" exclaimed Perrin. "In a quarter of an hour then." He rang off, and immediately put a call through to the garage where his car was kept, giving orders that it was to be brought round to Hanover Square at once. Then he issued a series of hurried instructions to his staff. Exactly at the stipulated time he picked up Inspector Philpott outside Scotland Yard, and the two started southwards over Westminster Bridge, Perrin at the wheel of his luxurious motor.

They wasted no time on the journey, Perrin gave the inspector an account of Miss Rushburton's visit to him on the previous day, and then proceeded to enlighten him as to Sir Ethelred and his family. By the time he had answered all the inspector's questions, they were nearing Oldwick Manor.

"I'm jolly grateful to you for all you've told me, Perrin," said the inspector. "It's a great help to know something about the people concerned in the case before one starts. In return, you want to be let into this, I suppose?"

Perrin grinned. "That's about it," he replied.

"All right. I'll give you an opportunity to keep your mouth shut and your ears open. I can't do more than that, but it ought to be enough for a chap like you. Hullo! Is this the place?"

Perrin had slowed up as they reached an important-looking gateway. A policeman appeared as they turned in, and held up his hand for the car to stop. Philpott put his head out of the window. "It's all right, constable, I'm Inspector Philpott, of Scotland Yard. Here's my card. We're just going on up to the house."

The policeman saluted. "Sergeant Burrage told me to look out for you, sir," he replied. "If you'll leave the car here, sir, I'll take you to the place where the body is lying."

"Why! Isn't it at the house, then?" inquired the inspector.

"No, sir, it's in a building in the grounds. The quickest way from here, sir, is to walk across the park."

The inspector got out of the car, and accompanied by Perrin, followed the constable along a gravelled path, from which a view of the house could be obtained. It was a fine, square Georgian structure, and everything about it was in first-class order. So much Perrin and the inspector had time to see, before their guide pointed out a small building in the Italian style a short distance ahead of them.

"That's the place, sir," he said. "You'll find Sergeant Burrage waiting for you, sir. If you don't mind, sir, I'll be getting back to the gate. The sergeant's instructions were that I was to let nobody in without his permission."

"Right! You get back to your post," replied the inspector. "We'll manage to find the sergeant, I dare say."

The constable saluted and turned back. The inspector and Perrin went on towards the building, which seemed to be a sort of garden pavilion. At the sound of their footsteps on the gravel, Sergeant Burrage, a tall, stern-looking man came out. Philpott introduced himself, and at the mention of Scotland Yard the worried expression on the sergeant's face lightened considerably. "I'm very glad you've come, sir," he said. "This is a queer business, and I hardly know what to make of it."

"Well, I'm here to do my best to help you," replied the inspector cheerily. He nodded towards Perrin. "I've brought this gentleman with me, as he has already given me some information about the dead man. You needn't be afraid of saying anything you like in front of him. Now, let's have the story."

"At eight-thirty-seven this morning, sir, I received a telephone message at the police-station from Sir Ethelred himself. He asked me to come here at once, and bring a doctor with me, as a very extraordinary thing had occurred. He asked me to make as little fuss as possible, and said that he would meet me himself at the entrance to the park.

"Naturally, sir, I didn't like to question a gentleman like Sir Ethelred, so I rang up Doctor Martlock, and as soon as he reached the police-station we came to the entrance together. Sir Ethelred was there waiting for us, looking terribly upset. He told us that he had just found his secretary, Mr. Solway, dead in the pavilion. In answer to my questions he told me that Mr. Solway had been away for a few days, and that he had no idea that he had returned until he walked down to the pavilion before breakfast. Then the first thing he saw was Mr. Solway sitting in his chair. He went up to him, and found that he was dead.

"Sir Ethelred took us to the pavilion, and left us there. He said he was going back to the house, and would be there all the morning. Doctor Martlock and I went in, and found everything as Sir Ethelred had described it. The doctor was able to say at once that the poor gentleman had been dead for some hours. He then left me here, to go and make his report to the coroner. I had a look round, then went up to the house and asked the butler to show me where the telephone was. I rang up my superintendent and he said he'd 'phone up the Yard for someone to come down at once. Then I came back here and waited. Nothing whatever has been touched, sir."

"Well done, sergeant," said the inspector approvingly. "You couldn't have done better. Now, perhaps you'll take us inside and show us round."

The sergeant led the way through the door of the pavilion. This opened on to a small anteroom, devoid of furniture except for a large and heavy table on one side. A second door led into a big room, with a row of windows on the south side through which the summer sun streamed brightly. The floor of this room was polished, and it was furnished with several armchairs, and two large writing-tables. In a chair drawn up to one of these sat the figure of a man. He looked as if he had gone to sleep while at work. His face and the upper part of his body rested on a blotting-pad, and his arms were sprawled across the table on either side.

The inspector stood in the doorway, staring speculatively at the body. Then his eyes wandered slowly over the room. The first thing that struck him was the air of tidiness that reigned. Except for a few newspapers and magazines lying on the unoccupied writing-table, nothing was out of place. The floor was of hard wood, which had been polished, though not apparently very recently. A few particles of gravel, brought in presumably by the boots of those who had used the place, lay scattered upon it, but there was nothing in the nature of a footprint.

"You've had no rain here lately, I suppose?" asked the inspector.

"No, sir," replied the sergeant. "There hasn't been so much as a shower all the week."

"Was the doctor able to decide the cause of death before he left?"

"No, sir. There's no sign of a wound, or anything like that. Doctor Martlock said that it would be necessary to hold a post-mortem before he could say what Mr. Solway died of. All that he could say at present was that he must have died some time during last night. He promised to come back here, sir, as soon as he had the coroner's instructions."

The inspector nodded, and walked up to the body. He raised the head slightly, then replaced it in its former position. There could be no doubt about the dead man's identity. He was obviously the original of the photograph which Perrin had given him on the previous evening. Having satisfied himself as to this, the inspector proceeded deftly to go through the dead man's pockets. He found a card-case, with some cards inscribed "Mr. Cuthbert Solway, Oldwick Manor, Surrey," a wallet containing money, some small change, and a bunch of keys.

He made no comment, but placed these articles on the table. Then he began to walk slowly round the room, examining the furniture and the windows. The latter were, without exception, shut and fastened. There was a door at the further end of the room, which was unlocked and opened into a lavatory and cloak-room. Here, hanging on a peg, the inspector found a dark rain-coat and a bowler hat. He took down the hat and looked inside it. It was comparatively new, and bore the initials C.S. on the lining.

The inspector was thus engaged, when the door of the pavilion opened, and an elderly man came in. Philpott, hearing the sound of his entrance, came back into the main room, where the sergeant introduced him to Doctor Martlock. "Well, Doctor, this is a bad business, by the look of it," he said. "What can you tell us about it?"

"I can make no statement until I have had the opportunity for a detailed examination of the deceased," replied the doctor stiffly. "I have reported the matter to the coroner, and informed him that I cannot at present issue a certificate. He has directed me to carry out a post-mortem, and to inform him of the result. I propose to do so in the anteroom of this pavilion, since there is no mortuary in the neighbourhood, unless Sir Ethelred raises any objection."

"Naturally I did not expect a definite statement," replied the inspector soothingly. "But I hoped you might be able to give me a few hints. Did you know the deceased personally?"

"I had seen Mr. Solway several times, but had never spoken to him," said Doctor Martlock. "I was not his medical attendant. I have never attended anyone at Oldwick Manor. I believe that Sir Ethelred and his family are in the habit of consulting a doctor in London when they require medical advice."

Philpott fancied that he detected a note of resentment in the doctor's voice. He would probably not be averse to getting his own back on Rushburton for this neglect, he thought. But his next remark was quite innocent. "The sergeant tells me that you believe Mr. Solway to have died during last night," he said.

"So far as I have been able to ascertain them, the indications seem to point to such a conclusion," replied the doctor guardedly.

"And there's nothing to show what he died of," said the inspector. "You haven't noticed anything unusual about the dead man's appearance, I suppose?"

"He appears to be extremely emaciated, as though he had lacked nourishment. Beyond that, the outward appearances appear to be normal."

It was quite obvious that Doctor Martlock was not going to volunteer information. To Perrin, who had been listening silently, without moving from the doorway, it seemed that he was completely puzzled, and had no intention of giving himself away. And it struck him that the prestige of Sir Ethelred Rushburton, the Champion of English Liberty, weighed oppressively upon both the doctor and the sergeant. They seemed fearful of saying or doing anything that might offend so great a man.

"Well, I don't think that there's anything else I can do here at present," said the inspector brightly. "I think I'll walk up to the house, and have a word with Sir Ethelred. You'll keep an eye on the place, and not let anybody in, won't you, sergeant?"

He beckoned to Perrin, and the two walked up a path which obviously led to the house. "Well, Perrin, what do you make of it so far?" asked the inspector.

"I don't make anything of it, except of course, that there's a queer story somewhere. What I'd really like to know is where Solway was between Monday morning and last night."

"Perhaps we'll find out. Rushburton doesn't know you by sight by any chance, does he?"

Perrin shook his head, and they covered the remainder of the distance to the house in silence. The door was opened by a footman, to whom the inspector gave his card. A few minutes later the man ushered them across the wide and lofty hall and opened a paneled door. They entered to find themselves in the presence of Sir Ethelred Rushburton himself.

Sir Ethelred was standing with his back to the carved stone fireplace, in which in spite of the fact that it was the middle of

June, a massive log was smouldering. He was a man of impos-
ing presence, tall and broad, with a strong determined face.
But Perrin could see at a glance that he was greatly agitated.
The muscles of his face twitched nervously, and there was a
look of profound disquiet, almost of fear in his eyes.

He looked fixedly at the two men as they entered the room,
but waited until the door was closed behind them before he
spoke. And when he did so, it was in the recriminating tone in
which he was wont to overwhelm his opponents in the House.
"I should be glad of an explanation of this visit, inspector," he
said. "I am at a loss to know what business can have brought
an officer from Scotland Yard to see me."

"My visit is in connection with the death of your secretary,
sir," replied Philpott, respectfully but firmly. "The local police
requested the assistance of Scotland Yard in their investigations, and that explains our presence here."

"I never heard of such a thing!" exclaimed Sir Ethelred
angrily. "I should never have informed the local police had I
imagined that they would go to such ridiculous lengths. Scotland Yard indeed! Of what possible concern can poor Solway's
death be to Scotland Yard?"

"Probably none whatever, Sir Ethelred," replied the
inspector soothingly. "I can only repeat that, as the Yard's
representative, I am here to assist the local police. An inquest
may be necessary, and in that case it will be necessary to lay
all available evidence before the coroner."

"Confound you and your inquest!" stormed Sir Ethelred.
He glared at the inspector for a second or two, and then, seem-
ingly by a great effort, he regained control over himself. "Don't
you see what an extremely unpleasant position I am put into
by this unfortunate affair?" he continued more quietly. "It is a
very serious matter for a man in my position to appear in the
witness-box. My political opponents will seize the opportunity of putting a malicious construction upon the matter. The

inquest itself will attract the most undesirable publicity. And now the fact that Scotland Yard has seen fit to interfere will add enormously to the scandal. It's really intolerable."

Perrin, standing in the background and trying to escape the notice of the angry politician, felt his sense of bewilderment increase. Was Sir Ethelred's indignation as genuine as it appeared? He must have known that he would be interrogated as to the finding of the body, and he had had some hours in which to prepare his replies. Was he trying to gain time? Or was he endeavouring to establish an inferiority complex in the mind of the inspector?

"I quite realize how unpleasant this must be for you, Sir Ethelred," said Philpott quietly. "I am sure that you will realize that my only desire is to obtain your statement. I understand from Sergeant Burrage that you were the first to discover the body of Mr. Solway. Would you mind describing the circumstances to me?"

"I have no objection to doing so. As I have already informed the sergeant, I walked across to the pavilion this morning before breakfast. I unlocked the door and walked in. Sitting at the table which he was in the habit of using, was Solway, apparently asleep. I spoke to him, but received no answer. I then laid my hand on his shoulder, and discovered that he was dead."

The inspector nodded. "It must have been a great shock to you, Sir Ethelred," he replied sympathetically. "You mentioned that you unlocked the door of the pavilion. Was it normally kept locked?"

"Certainly. I frequently worked there during the summer with Solway, and nobody but ourselves had access to it."

"Who, besides yourselves, possessed a key, Sir Ethelred?"

"There are only two keys in existence. I have one, Solway had the other."

The inspector produced the bunch of keys which he had found in the dead man's pocket, and handed them to Rushburton. "Would you mind telling me if Mr. Solway's key is on that bunch, sir?" he asked.

Rushburton selected a Yale key and held it up. "Yes, that is it," he replied.

"Thank you, sir. Now, would you mind telling me when you last saw Mr. Solway alive?"

Rushburton's face became livid suddenly. "Damn you!" he exclaimed. "What the devil has that got to do with you?"

CHAPTER IV

INSPECTOR Philpott appeared not to notice Rushburton's emotion. "I am bound to ask that question, sir," he said easily. "You will understand that it is most important in a case like this, to establish the time at which the deceased was last seen alive."

"Then you'll have to ask someone else," snapped Sir Ethelred. "As a matter of fact I hadn't seen Solway since last Monday."

"Indeed! Had he been absent from Oldwick Manor?"

Rushburton frowned, and an angry look came into his eyes. "Yes," he replied curtly. "He was away on some private affairs of his own. I am not aware of their nature."

"Did you expect him back yesterday or today, sir?"

"I expected him to return here when his business was completed," replied Rushburton with an air of finality.

This seemed to satisfy the inspector, and he started off on a fresh tack. "Since Mr. Solway possessed a key of the pavilion, there was, I suppose, nothing unusual in his entering it by himself?" he asked.

"Nothing at all. As I have told you, he and I frequently worked there together. And on several occasions when he has wished to be secure from interruption, he has worked there by himself. The room is equipped for that purpose."

"Would you mind telling me when you were last in the pavilion yourself, sir?"

"I was there yesterday afternoon. Lord Brimstoke came to lunch with me, and after lunch we strolled through the park for some time and then entered the pavilion, where we sat for an hour or so. I can assure you that Solway was not there then."

"Were the windows shut or open when you were in the pavilion yesterday afternoon, sir?"

"They were shut, as they always are, when we went in. I opened the one nearest the door and closed it when we left. The outer door, as you may have noticed, is fitted with a spring and closes and locks automatically."

"Thank you, sir. I do not think I need trouble you with any further questions. But I should be deeply grateful if you could suggest how Mr. Solway came to be found in the pavilion this morning?"

"The matter seems simple enough to me, inspector," replied Sir Ethelred. "Solway must have returned yesterday at some time after Lord Brimstoke and I had left the pavilion. Instead of coming straight up to the house, he went to the pavilion. This might easily happen without his being seen. How he came to meet his death there is, naturally, beyond my powers of conjecture."

At this moment a discreet knock was heard on the door. "Come in!" replied Rushburton impatiently.

A figure clad in black, whom Perrin guessed at once to be Pearson, the butler, appeared. "Well, Pearson, what is it?" asked Sir Ethelred.

"I beg your pardon for interrupting you, sir," replied Pearson deferentially. "But Doctor Martlock asked me to bring a message to you, sir. He wishes to know whether you have any objection to his performing a post-mortem on Mr. Solway in the anteroom of the pavilion, sir."

"Confound it!" exclaimed Rushburton. "Is there to be no end to these ridiculous formalities? Tell him to do what the devil he likes, as long as he doesn't worry me. And, look here, Pearson, I'm not to be disturbed again this morning on any pretext whatever. Do you understand that?"

The butler retired, and the inspector, followed by Perrin, took the opportunity of slipping out after him. They left the house and went into the park. As they walked towards the pavilion, Perrin chuckled audibly.

"I'm glad you're amused," remarked the inspector acidly. "Perhaps you found our interview with Rushburton more amusing than I did."

"It wasn't without its humorous side," replied Perrin. "'Pomposity embarrassed' or 'the great man who didn't want to divulge all he knew.' Not ineffective in his own way, though, is he?"

"I don't know what the devil you're talking about," growled the inspector. "His answers seemed to me straightforward enough, if they were a bit violent. You don't suppose a man like him would conceal the truth, do you?"

"Good heavens, here's another of them falling under the spell!" exclaimed Perrin. "You don't suppose that because, unless Providence intervenes, the man will be Prime Minister some day, that he has all the attributes of an archangel, do you? Conceal the truth! Why, man alive! it's only by the rarest of accidents that a professional politician ever reveals it."

"This has nothing to do with politics," persisted the inspector. "Here you've got a man who's exceptionally well up in the world, and you suggest that he'd stoop to quibbling in a matter that doesn't really concern him."

"I'd very much like to know how nearly it does concern him," replied Perrin. "However, we won't labour that point now. I'm not suggesting that Rushburton murdered his secretary or anything like that, but I did get the impression that he had the devil of a shock when he found Solway dead in that chair this morning."

"Well! isn't it enough to give any man a shock?"

"I don't mean it in that sense. I don't think Rushburton was so much horrified as frightened. Sheer honest physical terror, I mean. I've seen that kind of look in a man's face before."

"But what the devil is he frightened about? You're talking nonsense, Perrin."

"I don't think I am. But I can't tell you what he's frightened of. I wish I could. You rattled him properly when you asked him when he last saw Solway alive, anyone could see that. And I don't for an instant believe his story that Solway had been away on his own private affairs. You take it from me, Philpott, there's more in this than meets the eye."

"You're the sort of chap who's always looking for trouble," replied the inspector. "I don't see much here to get excited about. We know that Solway has been away since last Monday. He comes back some time yesterday evening, one supposes, and goes to the pavilion, just as Rushburton said. There's very little doubt about that, for that was his coat and hat that I found hanging up in the cloak-room. I'll make sure of that, but it's pretty certain already. And then, when he was in the pavilion, he was taken ill suddenly and died. You often hear of men dying suddenly like that."

"Yes, it's not unknown, I'll admit," replied Perrin. "But what made him go into the pavilion before he went to the house and reported his return? And there's another point, Philpott. The only luggage he had with him when he was last seen on Monday was an attaché-case. What's become of that? You didn't find it in the pavilion, did you?"

"No, it's not there. But then anything might have happened to it between Monday and now. I don't see that it's of any importance. If he had been found with his head bashed in, and the case was missing, then we might have found it useful as a clue."

Perrin smiled. "Because he died nicely and tidily, you jump to the conclusion that there's no mystery about his death," he said quietly. "To me, on the other hand, the whole air in these parts simply vibrates with mystery. It may be that you're right, and that there is nothing sinister about Solway's death. But to my mind, the mystery doesn't begin there. It begins with his failure to return here on Monday."

"But surely anybody, even the secretary of a man like Rushburton, can have private affairs, and get leave to attend to them?"

"Of course he can. But just consider what that explanation involves. Rushburton knew nothing about these urgent private affairs on Monday. He expected Solway back, and displayed uneasiness when he did not return. You'll say that he found out where and why Solway had gone later. Possibly in London on Tuesday morning. But if so, why did he make all this mystery about Solway's absence? He jumped down his daughter's throat yesterday when she asked where he was. And I thought he was going to chuck the furniture about just now when you asked him when he last saw him. It's no use, Philpott. I can't bring myself to believe in those private affairs, somehow."

"Well, where the dickens do you suppose he's been all this time?" asked the inspector.

"I can't even conjecture. Somewhere where he didn't get properly fed, according to Doctor Martlock."

"What on earth are you driving at? You're not suggesting that he was locked up somewhere, are you? Fellows like Solway don't get kidnapped and held up to ransom, at least, not in England. And if they did, and managed to escape, they wouldn't return quietly to a place like the pavilion, and say nothing about it."

"It doesn't follow that he was locked up, and it's just his returning quietly to the pavilion that I don't understand. But I have an idea of my own as to what happened to Mr. Solway. It's pure guesswork at present, though."

"Let's hear it, all the same. I've known you put up some pretty useful theories when you've kept your imagination in order."

"All right. In the first place, we know that Solway went up to London on Monday on some errand or errands for his employer. From the fact that Rushburton was anxious for his return, I assume that he expected an account of the results of Solway's day's work. Finally, suppose that these errands were compromising, in the sense that Rushburton's reputation would be injured if their nature leaked out.

"What I believe to have happened is this. Something went wrong when Solway was in London. What it was, I have no idea, but it must have been something that prevented Solway's return, and even made it impossible for him to communicate with Rushburton. Rushburton naturally got into a devil of a stew when his secretary did not turn up. He wasn't a bit happy at the idea that Solway was at large, with important secrets in his possession, and carrying an attaché-case which may have been full of extremely confidential documents. Every man has his price, they say, and Rushburton may have thought that Solway had bolted, and sold his secrets to those who would know how to make use of them.

"Or again, and perhaps this is more likely, he may have guessed what had happened. Perhaps he had a pretty shrewd idea of what had become of Solway. He may have been some-where where Rushburton's secretary shouldn't have been. What I mean is, he may have been with certain people, and that Rushburton was particularly anxious that his association with those people should not be known. A man like Rushbur-ton isn't above hunting with the hounds and running with the hare, you know. That would explain his irritation at any reference to Solway's absence."

"Yes, but if anything like that had happened, Solway wouldn't have gone to the pavilion," objected the inspector. "The first thing he would have done would have been to see Rushburton, and tell him where he had been."

"Exactly. That's what has been puzzling me all along. But how do you know that he went to the pavilion of his own free will?"

The inspector shrugged his shoulders. "I don't," he replied, in a tone of one explaining very simple matters to a small child. "But when I find a man sitting dead in his own chair, with no signs of a struggle about the room, and his coat and hat hanging on a peg near by, I don't fly to the conclusion that he was carried there by force."

"Your instinct is probably correct," replied Perrin. "That is, if you are sure that the man was alive when he entered the pavilion. I'm not."

They were approaching the pavilion by now, and Sergeant Burrage came out to meet them. "Doctor Martlock is just about to begin, sir," he said to the inspector. "I've been helping him to carry the body into the ante-room."

"Then I think we'll leave him to it for the present. I've no desire to watch him. I say, sergeant, is there a decent pub anywhere handy?"

"There's the Leather Bottle about half a mile away. The constable at the gate will show you the way, sir."

The inspector and Perrin strolled off towards the entrance to the park. "I don't know what your tastes are," said the former. "For my part, I'm not fond of assisting at post-mortems. I think it would be a much better plan to sample the bread and cheese at the Leather Bottle and come back when Martlock has finished. Now, what's this you were saying about Solway not being alive when he entered the pavilion?"

"Very well, suppose that the person with whom Solway has been staying these last few days didn't care to give the necessary explanation. It may be that it would be very awkward for everybody, if it came out that Rushburton's secretary had died in that person's house. In that case, the person in question would be glad of an opportunity of disposing of the body in such a way that it would not be traced to him. Mind, I'm not suggesting criminal action or even intent."

Perrin paused, and glanced at his companion inquiringly. But the inspector merely nodded. "Go on," he said.

"Very well, then, put yourself in that person's shoes. You've got Solway's body on your hands, and you want to dispose of it. I'm assuming that he died a natural death, for which you were in no way to blame. The obvious thing would be to deposit the body where one would normally expect Solway to die, that is to say, at Oldwick Manor, where he lived.

"But to carry the body into the house itself would be very difficult, if not absolutely impossible. But the pavilion provides an excellent substitute. It stands some distance away from the house. The key of it is in Solway's pocket. Nobody uses it but Rushburton and Solway, and then only in the daytime. Finally, Solway is in the habit of working there alone. The finding of the body there would cause no surprise as is proved by the explanation Rushburton himself gave just now."

"I'm beginning to see what you are driving at," said the inspector. "Carry on."

"Right, you decide to deposit Solway's body in the pavilion. You put it in a car, and drive it to the entrance we came in by. Did you notice the gateway particularly, by the way?"

"I didn't see anything peculiar about it. There's a stone archway, and a building of some sort beside it. It's not a lodge, for it isn't big enough."

"I had a look inside that building while you were talking to the local cop. It's merely a shed, with a door with no lock to it. And in that shed there's a wheelbarrow and half a dozen besoms. Outside it there's a great pile of leaves. In the autumn, no doubt, the leaves about the place are swept up and stored there for leaf-mould."

"Jolly good stuff for the garden," commented the inspector. "But I don't quite see the significance of these horticultural details."

"Don't you? How are you going to carry the body from the car to the pavilion? You couldn't drive the car along the gravel path without leaving tracks that nobody could possibly miss. You might sling it over your shoulder and carry it, but even in its emaciated condition, as Doctor Martlock calls it, it must weigh about eight stone. That's a hundredweight, and you wouldn't care to carry it far. But what about that amazingly convenient wheelbarrow? That wouldn't leave any tracks with the ground as it is now."

The inspector laughed. "Sure this chap of yours didn't bring the body in a balloon?" he asked mockingly. "Go on, don't mind me."

"I prefer the wheelbarrow. Having arrived at the door of the pavilion, he takes the key out of Solway's pocket and opens it. Then he carries in the body, arranges it artistically as we saw it, and hangs up the hat and coat all tidy. Then he puts the keys back in Solway's pocket, and shuts the door behind him. It locks automatically, remember. He wheels the barrow back to the shed, and drives off home. What about it?"

"Pretty, if not altogether convincing," replied the inspector. "Who do you suggest as the hero of this adventure?"

Perrin shook his head. "Sorry I can't tell you that. But he can't have lived very far off. The cautious Martlock says that Solway died some time during last night. That's vague enough, but let's put it about midnight. Now the disposal of the body probably took place before dawn. Nobody would risk carting a body about in broad daylight. It begins to get light at this time of year about four o'clock, summer time. That leaves four hours in which to get the job done; less, if Solway died after midnight. I should say that our unknown friend lived not far away from London."

"Where, even if he exists, we shall have a devil of a job to find him," laughed Philpott. "Hullo, that looks like the Leather Bottle. I shan't be sorry for some bread and cheese and a pint of beer."

The Leather Bottle proved fully up to expectation. They remained there for the best part of an hour, then walked back towards Oldwick Manor. Just before they reached the entrance, they met Doctor Martlock.

"Well, Doctor, have you made any startling discoveries?" asked the inspector.

"I have come to certain conclusions which I shall report to the coroner," replied Doctor Martlock. "It is for him to decide upon the course to be pursued."

"Of course," said the inspector. "I shouldn't think of interfering with the correct procedure. But I should be very grateful for a hint as to the conclusions you have come to."

Doctor Martlock hesitated. It was evident that he was a stickler for etiquette. But the prestige attaching to Scotland Yard outweighed his scruples. "I have formed the opinion that Mr. Solway died of trypanosomosis," he replied. "I shall suggest to the coroner that as this type of disease is somewhat uncommon, a second opinion, that of a specialist, should be obtained. But, in any case, there can be no doubt that Mr. Solway died a natural death."

Doctor Martlock went on his way. The inspector turned to Perrin with a bewildered look. "What did he say the chap died of?" he asked.

"Trypanosomosis," replied Perrin. "That means parasites in the blood, I believe."

"The name alone is enough to kill anybody," grumbled Philpott. "Anyway, the doctor says it is a natural death. What do we do next?"

"I don't know what you're going to do, but I'm going back to London," replied Perrin. "I think I can guess what will happen next. You might drop in and see me if you want any more help from me. But I don't expect you will. Anyhow, I shall be at home all the week-end."

And with a cheerful nod to the inspector, he got into his car and drove away.

CHAPTER V

IT WAS not until Sunday evening that Perrin heard anything further from Inspector Philpott. He had finished dinner, and was settling himself down comfortably with a book, when the inspector was announced. He dropped wearily into a chair and Perrin hastened to put a drink beside him.

The inspector took a long drink, and set the glass down appreciatively. "That's just what I wanted," he said. "As for that Solway business, it's finished and over. I've just come from Oldwick Manor."

"I don't know that I'm altogether surprised," said Perrin. "I told you when I left you yesterday that I didn't think you'd want any further help from me. What happened, exactly?"

"Martlock got a chap down from London this morning and they messed about with Solway's body for a bit. Then they went off to see the coroner together and he issued a certificate to the effect that Solway had died of this tripe-something-or-other. Rushburton showed me a copy of the certificate, and gave me pretty clearly to understand that any usefulness I might ever have had was at an end. He was quite right, too. Since the coroner has issued his certificate, there'll be no inquest, and the inquiry is at an end."

"So Solway died of trypanosomosis, did he?" said Perrin reflectively. "Of course, there isn't a shadow of doubt about it. Coroners don't grant certificates unless the cause of death is established beyond question. But to my mind, instead of explaining his death, it makes it all the more mysterious. You didn't get the name of the specialist, I suppose? It wasn't Hardcastle, by any chance, was it?"

"No, it wasn't that, it was a very ordinary sort of name. Sir Somebody Something, I believe. I saw him in the distance, a little short fat chap, with glasses."

"Sir Walton Jones, I expect. He's a specialist in parasitic diseases, I believe. Do you know, Philpott, this is one of the queerest affairs I was ever mixed up in, and I've seen some queer things, as you know."

"Well, queer or not, it's all over so far as the Yard is concerned. It's merely a case of a man dying from natural causes."

"Oh, I'm not worrying about his death," said Perrin. "It's what happened before it that interests me."

"Well, you're a private individual," replied the inspector. "There's nothing to prevent you trying to find out if you want to. That's capital whisky you've got there."

Perrin poured him out a second glass, and when he had drunk it the inspector took his departure. He had not been gone long before David Meade came in. "Hullo!" he said. "I just dropped in to see if you had heard any more of your friend Rushburton and his secretary."

"Then you've let yourself in for it," replied Perrin calmly. "I was just longing for someone to discuss that matter with. Philpott has just been here to tell me he has washed his hands of it, so he's no use. Sit down and listen, and don't interrupt me till I'm finished." Meade listened attentively while Perrin recounted the adventures of the previous day, and the conclusions arrived at by the coroner. "So Solway died a natural death from trypanosomosis, and everybody concerned is satisfied," he concluded.

"Well, that's that," observed Meade. "I thought, all the time, that you were looking for a mare's nest."

"My dear fellow, that most emphatically isn't that," replied Perrin warmly. "Granted that the fellow died of trypanosomosis, but can't you see that that leaves everything else unexplained?"

"I dare say it does," said Meade hastily. "I only meant that the matter is at an end as far as the firm of Perrins is concerned. Our client's lost sheep has turned up, in the form of mutton, certainly, but that's not our fault. There's nothing left for us to investigate."

"Nothing left!" exclaimed Perrin. "Still, I know what you mean. There's no point in our carrying the investigations any further, since there's no prospect of earning a fee if we do. Isn't that it?"

Meade laughed. "As usual, partner, you've hit the nail fair and square on the head," he replied.

"I thought so. Well, I don't agree that that's any reason why we should abandon one of the most fascinating cases I ever heard of. It very often pays us to look into things, not because we earn money directly by so doing, but for the sake of acquiring information which may be useful afterwards. And I warn you that I'm going to do my best to solve the mystery that lies behind Solway's death."

"I should be the last to interfere with your amusements," said Meade. "I'll just ask you one question, and then for ever hold my peace. Would you be so enthusiastic about this business if it concerned anybody but Rushburton, of whom, for reasons of your own, you disapprove so strongly?"

Perrin chuckled. "One to you, David, my lad," he replied. "Honestly, I suppose I shouldn't. Now then, having set your mind at rest on that matter, give me the benefit of your able comment. In the first place, doesn't it strike you as odd that a man like Solway should die of that particular complaint?"

"It might, if I knew what it meant," said Meade.

"It means parasites, trypanosomes, in the blood. Now, those jolly little fellows don't, as a rule, effect people living in temperate climates. They cause all sorts of tropical diseases, though, like various intermittent fevers and sleeping sickness. I don't know which of these particular diseases Solway died of, but I have an idea that it was probably some form of sleeping sickness. Now how, in heaven's name, did a man whom we are told never slept a night away from the majestic portals of Oldwick Manor, acquire sleeping sickness, which is unknown outside the tropics?"

Meade shrugged his shoulders. "I can't answer riddles like that," he replied. "I can only suggest that he may have picked it up years ago, before he entered Rushburton's service, and that it has only just come out. Such a thing is possible, I believe."

"I doubt if it would lie dormant all those years. However, that's a matter for expert medical opinion. In any case, I'm pretty sure that it isn't a disease that comes on suddenly, and proves fatal at once. Solway must have felt ill for some little time before he died. If he felt ill, why did he go to the pavilion instead of the house when he came back?"

"He may have meant to stay there for only a few minutes. Look here, isn't it possible that he did feel ill, as early as last week, and went to Doctor Hardcastle to consult him on his own account?"

"Hardly, I think. I've been making inquiries about Doctor Hardcastle, and I find that he's a specialist upon diseases of the stomach. Probably most of his fees are earned by curing people, who do themselves too well, of indigestion. He may have put Solway on a diet, which would account for his emaciated condition. But he wouldn't treat him for sleeping sickness, or whatever it was. He would have sent him to a man like Sir Walton Jones."

"Your theory, from what you told me just now, is that Solway was carried into the pavilion after he was dead, I gather," remarked Meade.

"That's what I propounded to friend Philpott. But this sleeping-sickness diagnosis suggests another possibility. He may not actually have been dead, but in the state of sleep which precedes death from that disease. It comes to the same thing in the end, except that the person who carried him there may not have known that he was going to die so soon."

"Do you think that Rushburton has any suspicions where Solway was from Monday to Friday night?"

"I can only tell you that Rushburton was a very badly scared man when I saw him yesterday morning. I believe that he guessed, if he didn't actually know, where Solway had been, and was terrified that it would come out somehow. If there had been an inquest, inquiries would certainly have been made. It's just his confounded luck that the coroner should grant a certificate like that."

"What, exactly, do you think is at the bottom of it?" asked Meade.

"I think that Rushburton is, or was, engaged in some disreputable business or other, and that Solway was his agent. What the business was, or who the other parties are, I have no idea. But it oughtn't to be impossible to find out. I'm going to do my best to trace Solway's movements after he arrived in London last Monday."

"You'll have a bit of a job, won't you? How are you going to set about it?"

"I shall find out if he really went to see Lord Brimstoke and Doctor Hardcastle and, if he did, what became of him afterwards. And, while I am at it, I may as well see if our friend Sammy can help us. I don't believe that there is any crooked deal in London that Sammy doesn't hear of sooner or later. And then, of course, there are others as well. I shan't take any of the regular staff away from their present jobs. I'll look after this little matter myself. You needn't expect to see me in the office tomorrow. I shall be back here in the evening if you want me for anything."

"Good luck to you!" replied Meade. "If you've made up your mind to it, nothing that I can say will deter you. By Jove, it's getting late! Time I was off home to bed."

About nine o'clock next morning Perrin walked to St. James's Park underground station, and took a train to the Monument. He had ascertained that Lord Brimstoke had an office and a private staff of his own on the premises of the London and Provinces Bank in Lombard Street. He accordingly made his way there and asked to be directed to the inquiry office.

He was shown into a small but luxuriously equipped room, where an immaculately dressed young man rose to greet him. "Good morning," said the young man affably. "Have you an appointment with Lord Brimstoke?"

"Oh, no," replied Perrin. "I have merely called in connection with an inquiry I am making. I expect that you can tell me what I want to know, if you will be so kind. It is in connection with a Mr. Solway, who, I am informed, called here last Monday."

He watched the young man's face narrowly as he spoke. But the name of Solway did not appear to cause him any concern. "Solway?" he replied. "I don't remember the name for the moment. But, if you'll excuse me asking you the question, are you connected in any way with the press? Lord Brimstoke has given instructions that no information is to be given to the press by anybody except his publicity manager."

Perrin smiled. "I assure you that I have no connection with the press whatever," he said. "My business is simple enough. Mr. Solway spent the day in London last Monday, and mislaid an attaché-case which he was carrying. It contained, among other things, a bundle of share certificates, and I am trying to trace them. I was wondering if he left the case here by any chance?"

The young man shook his head. "No case can have been left here," he replied. "I should certainly have been told about it if it had. What is this Mr. Solway like?"

"Medium height, thin, almost bald, and rather sharp-featured. He was wearing a black coat and striped trousers."

"Ah, then I believe I remember him. Last Monday you said? If you will excuse me, I will refer to the appointment book."

He picked up a small leather-bound volume and consulted it. "Yes I thought so," he continued. "Mr. Solway had an appointment with Lord Brimstoke at eleven o'clock last Monday. I remember him perfectly now. He was only here for ten minutes or so. And, now I come to think of it, he was carrying an attaché-case. I remember distinctly that he had it with him when he went out. No, I think you can rest assured that he did not leave it here."

Perrin was profuse in his thanks as he took his leave. The attaché-case had been only a pretext; he had his own ideas as to what had become of that. But he had at least established that the conversation overheard by Pearson was genuine. Solway's movements were established so far. The next thing to do was to verify his visit to Doctor Hardcastle.

He took a taxi to Harley Street, and alighted at the number which he had ascertained to be the doctor's address. There were three or four brass plates on the door, inscribed with the names of the specialists who had consulting rooms in the house. He rang the bell, which was answered by a man-servant with a mournful and pessimistic expression. Upon his mention of the name of Doctor Hardcastle the man took him up in a lift to the second floor, and ushered him into the presence of a severely-dressed middle-aged woman who seemed to Perrin to have receptionist written all over her. She greeted him with a professional smile. "What name, please?" she asked, poising a fountain pen in readiness.

Perrin gave his name, which she wrote down at his dictation. "You haven't been here before, Mr. Perrin, have you?" she said. "I expect you have brought a letter from your own doctor with you. May I see it?"

"I haven't come to consult Doctor Hardcastle professionally," replied Perrin hastily. "I merely want to ask about a gentleman who called here last Monday. It's a question of an attaché-case that has been mislaid."

She frowned at him and shook her head. "I cannot possibly give you any information about any of Mr. Hardcastle's patients without his consent," she said.

"But I'm not asking for information about him," protested Perrin. "I merely wish to discover whether he left an attaché-case behind him when he called here last Monday."

"I'm afraid it amounts to the same thing. However, if you care to sit in the waiting-room for a few minutes, I will ask Mr. Hardcastle as soon as he is free, and see what he says. What was the patient's name?"

Perrin told her, and she showed him into the waiting-room, a gloomy chamber furnished like a dining-room with innumerable magazines laid in tidy heaps upon the central table. Two or three dyspeptic-looking individuals were sitting about in chairs, each isolated from his neighbour.

Perrin took a chair at the table, picked up a magazine and began turning over its pages idly. He had reconciled himself to a long wait, it might be some time before the specialist was disengaged. He was therefore considerably astonished when, after a few minutes, the receptionist reappeared and whispered in his ear. "Mr. Hardcastle will see you for a moment," she said. "Will you come this way?"

He followed her across the passage. They stopped at a door which she tapped softly. Then she opened it. "Mr. Perrin," she said. Mr. Perrin walked in, and found himself in Doctor Hard-castle's consulting-room.

The specialist was seated at a massive oak writing-table and rose as his visitor entered. He was a tall man, with a pronounced stoop, and the ascetic face of a scholar. Perrin found it difficult to judge his age. His face was lined, his hair was iron grey, and his deep-set eyes looked faint and dim behind his powerful spectacles. But there was a remnant of youthfulness about the way he moved, and especially about his voice when he spoke.

He shook hands with Perrin and motioned him to a chair. "Sit down," he said heartily. "It won't hurt my patients to wait a few minutes while I talk to you. I haven't got anybody on my list this morning who is as ill as he thinks he is. You are Mr. Perrin, of Perrins, Investigators, I suppose? If so, I know you very well by reputation."

For a moment Perrin wished he had given the reception-ist some other name. And then he reflected that there could be no possible harm in the specialist knowing who he was. "Yes, I'm the notorious Perrin," he replied, with a smile. "I don't want to waste your time, Doctor. All I want to know is whether a certain Mr. Solway called on you last Monday, and if so, whether he left an attaché-case behind him?"

"It's queer that you should ask me that," said Doctor Hard-castle. "I have had poor Solway on my mind all the morning. Sir Ethelred Rushburton rang me up this morning and told me of his extraordinary death. It was due to trypanosomosis, I am told. Had any less competent an authority than Sir Walton Jones certified to that effect, I should have refused to believe it. He certainly showed no visible symptoms of such a disease when I saw him last week."

Since the specialist knew all about Solway's death it was no good beating about the bush, thought Perrin. "It does seem extraordinary, even to a layman," he replied. "I suppose that there is no possibility of Sir Walton Jones having been mistaken?"

Doctor Hardcastle tapped impressively on the desk with his fingers. "Walton Jones is not the man to make mistakes in his own line," he said. "If he were to tell me, after due examination, that this desk had trypanosomosis, I should believe him. He's one of the most conscientious men I know, and he has devoted his whole life to the study of tropical diseases."

"Is it the sort of disease that a man might have without knowing it?" asked Perrin.

"I cannot say. I have never had a case under my personal observation. Presumably the parasites must have been in his blood when I saw him, and I blame myself for not discovering the fact. Solway had consulted me once or twice. I do not as a rule discuss my patients, but there is no harm in my telling you, in strict confidence, that he complained of intermittent pains in the duodenum. I could find nothing seriously wrong with him, but I recommended him to see me at intervals. He had made an appointment for noon last Monday."

"He kept this appointment?" inquired Perrin.

"Yes, he arrived punctually. I was rather astonished at his appearance. He looked very white and shaken, and told me that he had felt very faint in the taxi coming here. I could discover no definite symptoms to account for this, and I was inclined to put it down to the heat of the day. The internal trouble had cleared up a good deal since he had taken a prescription I had given him, he told me. But he was most emphatically not himself, and I asked him if he would like to wait in one of the rooms here till he felt better. But he said he would rather get home, and that a friend was sending a car here for him."

"By home, he meant Oldwick Manor, I suppose?"

"So I imagine. I made inquiries, and found that a car was actually waiting for him outside. He insisted upon leaving, so I helped him downstairs myself, and I and the man who let you in just now got him into the car and made him comfortable. And that was the last I saw of him."

"I don't want to be indiscreet, Doctor, but I believe that Sir Ethelred Rushburton is one of your patients. Was it his car that called for Mr. Solway?"

"It was not the car he always comes here in, nor was it the chauffeur I knew. In fact, I'm pretty sure that Solway mentioned that his friend was in the motor trade and had showrooms somewhere in the West End. I don't know, of course, how Solway got on after he left here. But I gather from what Sir Ethelred told me on the telephone this morning that he had been anxious about him for the last few days, though he was far from expecting this sudden death."

Perrin made a mental note of this remark. Evidently Rushburton had said nothing to the specialist of Solway's absence from Oldwick Manor during the previous week. One more evidence of his wishing that fact not to be known. "I expect Sir Ethelred is very much upset," he said. "By the way, Doctor, about that attaché-case. Solway didn't leave it here, I suppose?"

"I happen to be able to reassure you on that point," replied Doctor Hardcastle. "I noticed that he had it with him when he came, and I handed it to him in the car myself when he left."

Perrin thanked the doctor, to whom he had taken an instinctive liking, and took his leave of him.

As he walked slowly down Harley Street towards Cavendish Square, he considered this fresh phase of the problem. Who was Solway's friend, and where had he driven to when he left Doctor Hardcastle?

CHAPTER VI

PERRIN lunched at a quiet little restaurant near Oxford Circus, and while he ate a leisurely meal, he reviewed in his mind the information he had acquired during the morning.

Solway had carried out his program; he had called upon both Lord Brimstoke and Doctor Hardcastle. His business with the former had not transpired, nor was it of any particular importance for the moment. It could hardly have been personal; Solway must have been acting as Rushburton's emissary.

On the other hand, this appointment with Doctor Hardcastle had been of a personal nature. It was not the first time he had consulted him, and he had made the appointment himself. So far so good, but what about that feeling of faintness of which he had complained to the specialist? Was it not very possibly the first symptoms of the disease which had killed him some days later? Trypanosomosis was extremely rare in this country. Doctor Hardcastle could be forgiven for not having recognized it. Incidentally, Doctor Hardcastle's faith in the accuracy of Sir Walton Jones' diagnosis was instructive.

Now what about the car that had come to meet Solway? Could it be traced? Perrin thought that it could. Solway had mentioned to the specialist a friend in the motor trade, with showrooms in the West End, who had promised to call for him and drive him home. Very kind and obliging of this friend. But was there any reason, other than sheer kindness of heart, underlying the offer?

Why had the offer been made, and why had Solway accepted it? Solway had only begun to feel indisposed in the taxi, on his way to Doctor Hardcastle. There could be no question of his friend having offered to drive him home because he did not feel equal to the train journey. The arrangements must have been made some time previously. Why? Solway could have returned to Oldwick Manor by train, or he could have arranged to meet Rushburton and driven back with him.

Perhaps the business in which the friend was engaged might suggest the reason. It was at least possible that Rushburton contemplated buying a new car. Solway knew this, and had mentioned it to his friend in the motor trade. The friend had arranged to drive Solway down to Oldwick Manor in a car of which he was the agent, in order to have an opportunity of demonstrating it to Rushburton on his return from London.

This was a very logical deduction. But how was it to be verified? Possibly Rushburton's chauffeur might know something about it. It would be worth while sounding him on the matter. The problem was to discover the friend, and find out where Solway had gone to in the car. Had he actually driven down to Oldwick Manor? It seemed most unlikely that, since he had felt faint and ill, he would have changed his mind and gone anywhere else. If so, what on earth could have become of him when he got there? Could he have hidden in the pavilion from then until his death? Perrin finished his lunch and went to the nearest telephone call box. Here he rang up Oldwick Manor, and as he had reckoned upon, Pearson answered him. "Is that Sir Ethelred's butler?" he asked. "I am speaking for Lord Brimstoke. Can you tell me if Sir Ethelred is in London today?"

"I believe he is, sir," replied Pearson. "He drove up this morning about ten o'clock."

"You don't happen to know where I can catch him, I suppose?"

"I'm afraid I don't, sir. Sir Ethelred didn't tell me where he was going."

"Dear, dear! That's very annoying. Lord Brimstoke is very anxious to convey a message to him. Let me see, now. Do you know where Sir Ethelred usually leaves his car when he comes up to London?"

"Well, sir, if Sir Ethelred has business in the City the chauffeur takes the car to a garage in Dorset Street, off Salisbury Square."

"Thanks very much. I'll see if I can get into touch with the chauffeur. He'll be able to tell me where I can catch Sir Ethelred. Much obliged to you."

Perrin rang off and left the box. As he did so he glanced at his watch. The time was twenty minutes to two, and he nodded contentedly. He knew pretty well where to find the man he wanted to see. He hailed a taxi. "Put me down at the Surrey end of Southwark Bridge," he said.

Having arrived at his destination, he paid off the taxi and walked slowly towards Southwark Street. Having reached that busy thoroughfare, he stopped for a few moments at the corner, ostensibly lighting a cigarette, but actually looking keenly about him. Then he turned to the left and strolled along till he came to a public-house.

Once more he paused. Then he pushed open the door and went in.

The place was crowded with men of the labouring class enjoying their midday glass of beer. Perrin made his way through the throng to the counter, where he ordered a whisky and soda. Having obtained it, he retired to the least crowded corner of the room. A paper lay on one of the beer-stained tables, and he picked it up and began to read it.

He had not turned over many pages before a seedy-looking individual shuffled up to him. He was poorly clad, with at least three days' growth of grizzled stubble on his chin, and an exceedingly dirty envelope in his hand. Perrin took no notice of his approach.

"Beg your pardon, Captain," whined the seedy-looking man, touching his cap. "Could you spare a few coppers to help a poor man what's an old soldier? I've got some lovely postcards I'd like to show you, sir. The Tower of London, The Bank of England, The Mansion House, where the Lord Mayor lives, and anything else you can want."

The man had opened his envelope as he spoke, and was laying the post-cards one by one on the table. "I don't mind having a look at them," replied Perrin idly, as he picked up the post-cards one by one and pretended to examine them. Then, in a lower tone, he continued: "I've got a job for you, Ben. Listen, now. I want you to find Sir Ethelred Rushburton's chauffeur, and get into talk with him. The car is in a garage in Dorset Street, Salisbury Square, I believe. That's all I can tell you, but it ought to be enough for you to go upon. Got that, so far?"

"They're beautiful cards, Captain," replied the man. "You couldn't buy them anywhere for twice the price I'm offering them to you. Yes, sir, I'll find him right enough if he's anywhere about. What do you want to know?"

"Haven't you got a cleaner one of Buckingham Palace than this? I want you to find out if Rushburton has been thinking of buying a new car, and if so, if any agent has been in touch with him. If he has, I want the agent's name and address, that's all. Very well! I'll take these six for a shilling."

"You couldn't get better value nowhere, Captain, and that's the truth. When shall I see you to report, sir?"

"If you can get those other cards I want, I'll be back here at six o'clock this evening." The seedy-looking individual shuffled off. Perrin stayed where he was for several minutes, finishing his drink in leisurely fashion. Then he got up, left the place, and walked to London Bridge tube station, where he took a train to the Bank. Here he changed on to the Central London and travelled as far as Tottenham Court Road, where he alighted.

From the station he walked through Soho Square to the end of Greek Street. A few paces beyond this thoroughfare he slipped through an open doorway by the side of a shop. He climbed the staircase in front of him, and emerged upon a dark and stuffy landing. Two doors confronted him, one marked "Private," the other "Inquiries." He opened the latter and found himself in the presence of a young man. The young man looked up from the typewriter which he was manipulating, and, recognizing Perrin, leapt to his feet. "Why, good afternoon, Mr. Perrin," he said with an effusive smile of welcome. "It's a long time since you've come to see us, yes?"

"I've been meaning to look in for a long time," replied Perrin easily. "Is your father very busy just now?"

"Dad! He's always busy," said the young man, with a confidential wink. "But he's never so busy that he wouldn't see you, Mr. Perrin. If you'll excuse me a moment, I'll slip in and tell him you're here."

The young man disappeared, and Perrin sat down on the only available chair. He was in the office of Marshfield and Son, a firm which enjoyed a wide and not very savoury reputation. Marshfield senior was the individual referred to by Perrin as Sammy in the course of his conversation with Meade the previous evening. He was a remarkably shrewd and observant man, with a keen eye for business, and had begun his career as a money-lender in a small way. But this profession failed to satisfy his ambitions. From usury he had proceeded to still more questionable activities, which involved sailing very close to the wind indeed. On one occasion he had overstepped the mark, and it had been entirely owing to Perrin that he had appeared in the witness-box instead of the dock.

Since then he had never forgotten the debt he owed.

Perrin had more than once found him a valuable source of information. Sammy's knowledge of the shady side of London business life was phenomenal. He never by any chance lent his countenance to vulgar crime, but he was an expert in every form of sharp practice. He had been employed as a go-between in countless deals, the details of which had never seen the light of day. And Perrin knew very well that he was to some extent in the confidence of men whose names were household words in the City, and in even wider fields than that.

Sammy himself came out to greet his benefactor. "Come inside, Mr. Perrin," he exclaimed, with out-stretched hand. "I was only saying the other day what a long time since we had seen you. Now, sit down and make yourself comfortable. I've just been given a box of cigars like you don't very often see nowadays. Just you light one up and try it. You're quite well, and the good lady too, I hope?"

"Fine, thanks," replied Perrin as he took the proffered cigar and settled himself in Sammy's very comfortable armchair. He had some difficulty in repressing a smile at the undercurrent of nervousness in his host's manner. Sammy was never quite sure what Perrin's appearances at his office might herald.

"I thought I'd just drop in for a chat with you while I was passing," continued Perrin, when he had got his cigar properly alight. "Things are fairly slack in my line of business. Did you ever hear of a chap called Solway?"

He had his eyes on Sammy's face as he asked this sudden question. But his brows merely contracted in a slight frown. "Solway, Solway?" he repeated slowly.

"I've heard the name somewhere, just mentioned casually. But I should not know the man if I were to see him."

"You probably won't see him just yet, for he's dead. Died on Friday night. He was Rushburton's confidential secretary."

A light came into Sammy's eyes. "Oh that's it, is it?" he said. "I remember now. I heard his name in connection with Sir Ethelred. But I never actually met him."

"In what connection did you hear his name mentioned?" asked Perrin quickly.

Sammy's crafty eyes narrowed. "Oh, just in the course of conversation with some of my friends," he replied carelessly.

"Do you know Rushburton personally?"

"Sir Ethelred Rushburton is not the sort of man who does business with a humble firm like Marshfield and Son," replied Sammy ingeniously.

"Oh! come off it, Sammy!" exclaimed Perrin. "You know well enough it's no good trying that sort of stunt on me. What's Rushburton up to? He's got something in the fire, I know that well enough."

"What's he up to? Honestly, Mr. Perrin, I don't know. I've been asking myself that very same question for some time past. All I can tell you is that he has been poking quietly round the City recently. And I hear he's very thick with Lord Brimstoke."

"Yes. I know that. What sort of a chap is Brimstoke? From your point of view, I mean."

Sammy shut one eye and opened it very deliberately. "The Chairman of the London and Provinces Bank is a man of the very highest financial integrity," he replied cautiously.

"Of course he is, everybody knows that. But Brimstoke holds several other positions besides the Chairmanship of the Bank, doesn't he?"

"He is a director of several companies of the highest standing," replied Sammy.

"Look here, if you won't answer my question, I'll go straight to Inspector Philpott, and tell him a few things that will make him open his eyes. Now, then, for the last time, what else do you know about Brimstoke?"

Sammy smiled at Perrin's threat. "His Lordship has financed several deals which have come under my personal notice," he replied.

"Meaning, I suppose, they were on the shady side. Good heavens, Sammy, it's like drawing teeth to get information out of you! So Brimstoke isn't above a little dirty work if it promises to show profit, eh? I suspected as much. Now, what's at the bottom of his sudden friendship with Rushburton?"

"I don't know, Mr. Perrin. Sir Ethelred will be a very influential member of the next government, as you know well enough without my telling you. I can quite understand that he would be very useful to his Lordship. Beyond that I can't tell you anything definite. But I have heard one or two things that suggest that his Lordship has been trying to win over Sir Ethelred to his own views lately."

"Now, what exactly do you mean by that, Sammy?" inquired Perrin.

"Well, just this. A good many little scraps of news come to my ears. Putting two and two together, I'm inclined to think that his Lordship has given Sir Ethelred a tip or two. Inside information about the companies in which he is concerned, I mean. At all events, Sir Ethelred has been dealing in shares of these companies on the Stock Exchange, with considerable profit to himself. I happen to know that for a fact."

Perrin nodded. "I'm beginning to see daylight now, Sammy," he said. "In return, Brimstoke expects Rushburton to give him inside information as to the government's intentions when his party comes into power, I suppose. A neat little reciprocal arrangement, in fact. But I should have thought that Rushburton was well enough off already not to be tempted with a bribe like that."

Mr. Marshfield smiled. "Sir Ethelred's wealth is proverbial," he remarked oracularly.

Perrin glanced at him sharply. "Sammy, you have the most tortuous mind of any man I know," he replied. "Why can't you say right out what you mean? What's behind that last remark of yours?"

"Sir Ethelred lives in a style that very few people can afford," said Mr. Marshfield. "He spares no expense, either at Oldwick Manor or Berkeley Square. Not only himself but his family as well, as I am informed, have the most expensive tastes. And the income which he derives from his securities has been falling steadily for some time."

Perrin whistled softly. "By Jove! I never thought of it in that way. One naturally supposes that a man like Rushburton never has to think about money. You mean that he finds it a bit difficult sometimes to make both ends meet?"

"So much so that on more than one occasion he has been selling stock in order to meet current expenses."

Perrin made no reply. This aspect of Rushburton's affairs, it seemed to him, might prove to be the key he sought. Rushburton, he could easily understand, would be very loth to reduce his expenses in any way. He would regard any reduction in his standard of living as bad publicity, as evidence that he was not so prosperous as he liked people to believe. He would jump at the chance of getting in with a man like Brimstoke, who would certainly not grudge expense in the furtherance of his own financial schemes. From the point of view of either of them, the partnership would be eminently desirable. The financial magnate and the prospective Cabinet Minister! What could they not accomplish between them?

Incidentally, the state of Rushburton's financial affairs, as revealed by Sammy, threw light upon the difficulty experienced by his daughter in extracting money from him. Doubtless he had hidden his position from his family as jealously as he had from the rest of the world. Yet Solway must have known all about it. Had it had anything to do with Solway's death, which appeared to Perrin to be more deeply shrouded in mystery with each fresh piece of knowledge he acquired?

He roused himself from his meditations. "Look here, Sammy!" he said. "I told you just now that Rushburton's secretary was dead. He died under rather peculiar circumstances, but I need not go into all that. The point is, that nobody seems to know where he was for the best part of the week before his death. Any suggestions?"

"You say that this Mr. Solway died?" asked Mr. Marshfield, with a peculiar emphasis in his tone.

"Yes, he died all right, and from natural causes. There's no question of his having been murdered, at least in the technical sense, if that's what you're getting at. He was found dead by Rushburton himself at Oldwick Manor."

"And how did the discovery affect Sir Ethelred?" inquired Marshfield.

"I don't know for certain. I wasn't on the spot until a couple of hours or so later. I didn't see his first reaction. But I got the impression that he was a pretty badly frightened man. I'm inclined to think that it wasn't Solway's death that affected him so much as the dread that Solway's movements before his death would be traced. But if Solway had been with Lord Brimstoke, Rushburton would not have tried to conceal the fact. He makes no secret of his friendship with Brimstoke."

Marshfield shook his head. "I'm sorry, but I can't help you there, Mr. Perrin," he said. "I should not be surprised to learn that Sir Ethelred was in touch with other people besides his Lordship, and that it would seriously damage his reputation if the fact leaked out. But I have heard nothing. Still, most things of that kind come to my ears sooner or later. If I learn anything that is likely to be of any use to you, I will not fail to let you know."

Perrin thanked him, and left the discreet little office in Wardour Street. By this time it was getting on for six o'clock, and he made his way back to Southwark Street. He entered the public house as before, and had not been there many minutes before the post-card seller came up to him.

"It's all right, Captain. I've got them for you," he said, touching his greasy cap. "Beauties, they are, just what you was wanting." He produced two or three post-cards and bent down to lay them on the table. "I found him all right," he continued. "Very decent chap, name of Yalding. Bit too talkative, sort of chap that tells you his life's history the first time you meet him. There now, Captain, you can't better them, not wherever you go!"

"They aren't too bad," replied Perrin. "Did you find out if Rushburton was buying a new car?"

"You'll take the lot, won't you, Captain? I've had to go half over London to find them for you. He had mentioned something of the kind to Yalding, but hasn't, so far as Yalding knows, come to any definite decision. No cars have been brought to Oldwick Manor for him to see. No, I couldn't afford to take a penny less, Captain, I don't make nothing on them as it is."

"Well, here's another shilling for you then. Who does Rushburton usually buy his cars from?"

"Crabtree and Watson. Young Crabtree was a friend of his secretary's who died a couple of days ago. Thank'ee kindly, Captain, I knew you wasn't one to pass an old soldier by."

The man shuffled off towards the counter, and a few minutes later Perrin left the place and took a taxi back to his flat. "Not a bad day's work on the whole," he muttered to himself, as he lay back in his seat.

CHAPTER VII

WHEN Perrin reached his office next morning he found Meade waiting for him, with the correspondence which had arrived the previous day. "There's nothing in it that I can't deal with," he said. "If you want to go out on the war-path again there's nothing to prevent you. But you'll have to wait till after ten o'clock. I've made an appointment for you then."

"The devil you have!" exclaimed Perrin. "Who is it?"

Meade grinned. "I wouldn't have made it if I hadn't thought that you would want to see the visitor. It's Miss Rushburton."

"Miss Rushburton, eh?" said Perrin thoughtfully. "What on earth does she want now, I wonder?"

"It may be nothing on earth. She may want you to evoke the shade of the late lamented Solway, for all I know. Anyhow, she rang up yesterday afternoon, and asked if she could see you at once. I told her that you would not be in until today, but that if she came here at ten o'clock I would guarantee that she would catch you. And it's ten to, now."

Meade had barely left Perrin's room when Miss Rushburton was announced. She was evidently in a great state of mind, and hardly waited for the door to be shut before she spoke. "Oh, Mr. Perrin, isn't it dreadful!" she exclaimed. "The old man looked in for a moment at Berkeley Square yesterday, and told us that Solway was dead."

"I knew that, Miss Rushburton," replied Perrin gravely. "I would have informed you myself, but I was sure that your father would break the news to you."

"Yes, yes, of course, but what am I to do? I must have at least two hundred pounds by tomorrow at the latest, and I simply daren't ask the old man. He's terribly upset, as it is, and there would be the most fearful row. You know all about these things, Mr. Perrin. Do tell me what in the world I'm to do."

"I'm afraid that sort of question hardly comes within my scope, Miss Rushburton," replied Perrin. And then suddenly he smiled. "I don't think a young lady in your position would have much difficulty in finding the money," he continued encouragingly. "There are plenty of people who would make no difficulty about lending it to you."

"But I can't go to any of my friends," she almost wailed. "I owe most of them too much already. And I don't know anybody else."

"I think I could introduce you to somebody who would fix the matter up for you, right away," said Perrin.

"Oh, how sweet of you!" she exclaimed fervently. "Who is it? Do let me know, and I'll go there at once."

Perrin wrote an address on a piece of paper and gave it to her. "If you go there and mention my name, I am quite sure that everything will be satisfactorily arranged for you without the slightest difficulty."

She hardly stopped to thank him, and almost ran from the office. When she had gone, Perrin rang up the office of Marshfield and Son. "Sammy," he said, "I'm sending you a client. She's on her way to you now. She's Rushburton's daughter, and wants to borrow money from you. A nod's as good as a wink to a blind horse, eh? So long."

As he rang off Meade entered the room. "Your fair client didn't stop long," he said. "I saw her go through the outer office like a frightened hare. She seemed in a deuce of a hurry! What did she want?"

"She wanted to borrow money," replied Perrin quietly.

"Borrow money!" exclaimed Meade. "Well, that's the limit! What did you say to her?"

"I sent her round to see Sammy. Money-lending is his job, not mine."

"Good Lord, you are a heartless brute! You know perfectly well that once she gets into Sammy's clutches she'll never get out of them. And what the dickens will her father say when he hears of it? He won't thank you."

"I fancy I can dispense with Rushburton's thanks. Look here, I'm going out to make a few inquiries. I shall probably be back again very soon."

Perrin left the office, and walked to the showrooms of Crabtree and Watson, which were within a short distance of Piccadilly Circus. He inquired for the younger Mr. Crabtree, and in a few minutes a pleasant-faced young man appeared. "What can I do for you, Mr. Perrin?" he asked cheerfully.

"I haven't come in to buy a car, but I won't waste more than a few minutes of your time," replied Perrin. "I understand that Sir Ethelred Rushburton is one of your customers, and that his secretary, Mr. Solway, is a personal friend of yours."

Mr. Crabtree smiled. "Well, yes," he replied, "I know Mr. Solway fairly well. But shall we say that he's a business friend of mine rather than a personal one?"

"Has Mr. Solway informed you recently that Sir Ethelred has been thinking of buying a new car?"

"No, he hasn't. But I shouldn't be surprised to hear it. Sir Ethelred usually buys a new car every year, and it is nearly twelve months since we supplied him with the last one he bought. As a matter of fact, I haven't seen or heard of Mr. Solway for some time. I've thought once or twice of dropping him a line, and asking him to lunch with me one day when he's in town."

"I'm afraid that you've missed your opportunity, Mr. Crabtree. Would it surprise you to hear that he died last Friday night?"

"You don't mean it! Solway dead! He looked fit enough when I saw him some weeks back. I suppose that's why I haven't heard anything of him. What did he die of?"

"A very unusual complaint, I believe. His death was quite sudden, for he was in London on Monday of last week. He spoke then about having an appointment with a friend in the motor trade, who was to meet him at his doctor's in Harley Street and drive him back home."

Mr. Crabtree opened his eyes a trifle. "That's queer," he said. "I'm pretty sure that Mr. Solway had no friend in the motor trade except myself. Our firm had an arrangement with him concerning any cars that Sir Ethelred bought from us. I think it most unlikely that he can have had an appointment with anybody else. And he certainly had made no appointment with me. As I say, I have not heard from him for quite a long time."

"You did not send a car and a driver to meet him in Harley Street on Monday last week?" asked Perrin.

Mr. Crabtree shook his head. "Most certainly we did not," he replied.

As Perrin walked back from the showrooms, he tried to find some explanation of what he had just heard. Young Crabtree had spoken the truth, of that he felt convinced. His manner had been entirely free from self-consciousness. His firm had not owned the car in which Solway had driven away from Doctor Hardcastle's.

In that case, Solway had mentioned his friend in the motor trade on purpose to mislead the specialist. He could only have wished to mislead him because the errand upon which he was bound was one which it was necessary to keep secret. And it must have been exceptionally urgent, or he would never have persisted in it in his state of partial collapse.

What had actually happened? Perrin fancied that he could guess. Solway had arranged an appointment, probably on his employer's behalf, with some person or persons who were on no account to appear in the matter. A car had been sent to Harley Street to carry him to that appointment. But, by the time he reached his destination, his indisposition had developed into definite illness. The other parties were in a quandary.

They did not want to reveal that Solway had come to see them, and, presumably, there was some reason which prevented them from communicating with Rushburton.

Their only course was to detain the sick man, hoping for his recovery. But, instead of getting better, he got steadily worse, and had finally died. Then they had taken the course which Perrin had already outlined to Inspector Philpott. They had driven the body down to Oldwick Manor and deposited it in the pavilion. This explanation was the only one which would account for all the circumstances.

As Perrin reached his office, Miss Avery met him. "Inspector Philpott is waiting to see you, Mr. Perrin," she said. "He said it was very urgent, so I told him I thought you would not be long. I've shown him into your room."

"Philpott, eh?" replied Perrin. "All right, I'll go in and see him. I wonder what his trouble is?"

He entered his own private room, and greeted the inspector familiarly. "Hullo, Philpott!" he said. "What's brought you along here like this? Have Perrins got to do your job for you, once again?"

But Philpott's unusually stern expression did not relax. "It's a devilish awkward business, this time," he replied. "And I'm afraid that you're involved. We've just heard that a man's body has been fished out of the river just below Wapping, by the river police. They found nothing whatever on him by which they could identify him but this."

He produced a picture post-card of London Bridge and showed it to Perrin. Then he turned it over. The post-card was dirty and crumpled, showing signs of having recently been soaked in water. But on the back of it could be clearly distinguished, neatly traced in block letters, the words "Perrin's, Investigators."

Perrin stared at them for some time without speaking. He was conscious of a most unpleasant cold thrill creeping up and down his spine. "Was it a case of drowning?" he asked at last, sharply.

"No, it wasn't," replied the inspector. "The man has a knife wound in the back. Stabbed and thrown into the water at once, the doctor says. However, you'll be able to see for yourself. I'm going to take you down there to identify him."

Perrin made no reply. He and the inspector left the office, and hailed a taxi. "East London mortuary," said Philpott, as they entered the vehicle. Neither spoke during the drive. The inspector did not seem inclined for conversation, and Perrin's thoughts were too busy for him to offer any remark. They reached the mortuary and Philpott led the way in. There, on a slab, lay the body of a man whom Perrin recognized at the first glance. He nodded slowly, as though his expectations had been realized. It was Ben, the postcard seller of Southwark Street. Inspector Philpott watched him curiously. "Well, do you know him?" he asked.

"Yes, I know him," replied Perrin quietly. "And so do your people at the Yard, inspector. This is Ben Hammerton, who was sentenced to a term of penal servitude for robbery with violence, some good few years ago."

The inspector took out his notebook and wrote down the name. "Ben Hammerton?" he said. "I seem to remember the name. But what on earth is he doing with a post-card on which the name of your firm is written?"

Perrin shrugged his shoulders. "That I can't say," he replied with a glance in the direction of the mortuary-keeper, who was standing by. "I suppose that you are going to the Yard to look up his record. Your fingerprint department will have his marks, and you can identify him by them without any possibility of mistake."

"Yes, I'm going back there now. I'll ask you to come with me, as I've plenty more questions to ask you."

"I was going to suggest it myself," said Perrin, gazing with genuine sorrow at the dead man's face.

It was not until they were seated together in Philpott's room at the Yard that the inspector began his catechism. "Look here, Perrin, I don't understand this at all," he said. "I don't suspect you of having murdered that poor chap, but things look pretty queer, you'll admit. You recognized him the minute you set eyes on him, yet you don't seem surprised to find him lying there dead—murdered, we can safely say. How's that?"

"I recognized him easily enough, for I was talking to him no longer ago than six o'clock yesterday evening," replied Perrin.

"I wasn't surprised, for I guessed who he must be from the moment you first showed me that post-card."

"We'll soon verify your identification. I've sent for the description and particulars of Ben Hammerton and if they tally with the dead man's appearance, I'll have an expert go down and take his fingerprints. That'll settle it definitely one way or the other. Supposing that you're right, how was it that you were talking to him yesterday evening?"

"That's a long story," replied Perrin. "I'll tell you later, if you really want to know. I think you'll agree, however, that it would be better if nothing were said at the inquest about our conversation. It's not the first time that I've had dealings with poor Ben lately.

"Ben came to me some time ago after his release. He knew me, for I had had a hand in his arrest, as your records will probably show. He told me that he had made up his mind to go straight in future, and asked me if I could put anything in his way. He told me that he was picking up a living selling post-cards and rubbish like that, and doing any odd jobs that came along.

"It struck me at once that Ben could be very useful to me. I've got several acquaintances among the underworld, as you probably guess, but I'm always glad to add to their number. Besides, I knew that before his arrest Ben was in touch with half the crooks in London.

"Finally, I made this arrangement with him. We were never to communicate with one another openly. But he would be selling post-cards every day between twelve and two, and I could find him either in Southwark Street or in a pub which he mentioned. I have met him in that way several times, and asked him to find out things for me. Of course, I have paid him well for every job he has done. And it was in search of certain information that I looked him up yesterday. He got it for me, as he nearly always did. In fact, he turned out to be one of the most useful men of his type that I ever came across."

"If that's the sort of chap he was, it's not difficult to guess why he was done in," remarked the inspector significantly. "Where did he live?"

Perrin shook his head. "I've no idea," he replied. "I don't even know whether he still used the name of Ben Hammerton."

"The next thing is the post-card. What have you got to say about that?"

"There are one or two queer things about the postcard. In the first place, I said just now that part of his livelihood was earned by selling post-cards. He pretended to be selling them to me when we had our chat yesterday. But this isn't the one he showed me. It's a different type of thing altogether, quite a superior quality to the things he carried about. Let me have another look at it, will you?"

The inspector laid the post-card on his desk, and Perrin bent over it. "This was found in his pocket when his body was recovered, I suppose?" he asked.

"Yes, it was the only thing that was found on him at all," replied Philpott.

"And yet the ink on the back has not run at all. The reason is that it is India ink, you can see how black it is. Not the sort of thing that Ben would be likely to use. He didn't write those words on it, I'll stake my reputation on that!"

"Well then, who did, and what the dickens did they do it for?"

"I think I can guess," replied Perrin, with a queer smile. "Anyway, you can take it from me that those words were written in India ink so that they would be legible when the body was found."

"You mean that they were written by the chap who did him in? That's possible, I suppose. Now look here, Perrin, I don't want to interfere with your business. You've done me a good turn more than once, and I'm duly grateful. But you've told me yourself that you employed this man Ben Hammerton to trail crooks for you. It seems to me a pretty sure thing that these same crooks saw through his little game, and decided to put an end to it. And it's probably the one you sent him after yesterday. You'll understand I'm bound to ask you who this was?"

Perrin smiled and shook his head. "No good, I'm afraid," he replied. "I didn't set Ben to trail a crook yesterday. I asked him to find out something for me, and all that he had to do was to get into talk with a man who, as far as I know, is perfectly honest and respectable."

"I know that sort," said the inspector incredulously. "Come on, Perrin, out with it, who was it?"

"Sir Ethelred Rushburton's chauffeur," replied Perrin calmly. "I don't really think he can have murdered Ben, do you?"

"Hell!" exclaimed the inspector. "Why couldn't you have said so at first? You haven't still got your finger in that pie, have you? What the devil did you want to find out from Rushburton's chauffeur?"

"Whether or not his employer thought of buying a new car. No, poor old Ben was not murdered because he asked that perfectly innocent question. And now you'll understand why I suggested just now that my conversation with Ben was better not divulged at the inquest. Rushburton wouldn't care to have his name dragged into an affair like that."

"He'll only have you to thank if it is," grumbled the inspector. "I'll have to make inquiries about that chauffeur, of course, though it doesn't seem likely that he's the man we want. The doctor says that Ben Hammerton, if it is him, must have been killed about ten o'clock last night, and Rushburton's chauffeur should have been safely at Oldwick Manor by then. What's the fellow's name?"

"Yalding, I believe," replied Perrin. "Or at least that's what Ben told me."

"Right, I'll send a chap down to find out what Yalding was up to yesterday evening. Now, when did you last see Ben alive?"

"I saw him twice yesterday. Once for a few minutes just before half-past two, when I asked him to go and see Yalding for me, and the second time just after six, when he gave me the information he had obtained. Both interviews took place in the North Star public-house in Southwark Street."

"How did he know where to find Yalding? Was he a friend of his?"

"No, he had never seen him before. I told him where Yalding was to be found, at a garage in Dorset Street."

"Where did you leave Ben?"

"At the North Star. It was his regular port of call and the people there are sure to know him. You may be able to find out from them something about his movements after I left him."

"It's worth trying. I'll go round there myself when I've got this matter of identity finally settled. As I said at first, this is a queer business, and I don't know that what you've told me makes it any clearer. That post-card seems to me to show that Ben was killed because he was in your employ. Who knew that besides Ben and yourself?"

"The only person to whom I have ever mentioned it is Meade. Who may have been in Ben's confidence I can't say."

"He may have talked a bit too freely when he had had a drink or two," suggested the inspector. "I agree with you that this matter of Yalding isn't likely to have had anything to do with it. I shan't say anything about that, if I can help it. But what the devil possessed you to go making inquiries like that? What's it to you whether Rushburton means to buy a new car or not?"

"It doesn't concern me directly," replied Perrin. "But I hoped it might throw some light upon Solway's movements."

The inspector made a gesture of impatience. "What an extraordinary chap you are, Perrin," he exclaimed. "That business is over and done with. What's the good of going all over it again? Rushburton probably knows a good deal more than he's told us, I'll admit that. But you won't find out what it is by interrogating his chauffeur. You take my tip and let it drop. You'll only stir up trouble, and all for no good, as far as I can see."

Perrin laughed. "A man must have his hobbies," he replied. "Is my cross-examination over, Philpott?"

"Yes. I don't think there's anything more I want to ask you now," replied the inspector. "I'll probably look in and see you tomorrow morning."

Perrin left the Yard, and took a taxi back to his office. As soon as he was alone, his face took on a strange, almost fierce expression, like that of a man who accepts a challenge to the death.

CHAPTER VIII

PERRIN had no doubt as to the real significance of the murder of Ben Hammerton. A single glance at the post-card found on his body had told him that, as clearly it had been intended to. Ben had been murdered as a warning to Perrin of what his own fate would be if he continued to concern himself in other people's business.

It followed from this that those who resented his interference were the persons concerned in Solway's movements before his death. But as to who those persons were, the murder of Ben gave no clue. All that could be deduced from it was that Perrin had been followed to the North Star, and had there been seen in conversation with Ben. Either this conversation had been overheard, or Ben had been tracked to Dorset Street, where his interview with Yalding had been witnessed. This in itself would be sufficient evidence that Perrin was still on the scent of this mystery which those concerned, were determined should not be revealed.

Perrin, following his usual custom, put himself in the place of these people. Had he been one of their number, he would have been anxious as to what might follow the discovery of Solway's body. He would have taken up some convenient post of observation in the neighbourhood of Oldwick Manor, and watched events. He would have learned of Rushburton's message to the local police. He would have seen the arrival of the inspector from Scotland Yard, accompanied by his friend. And, under the circumstances, he would have taken the trouble to learn the identity of that friend, if indeed, it did not happen to be already known to him.

If the unknown had acted thus, Perrin's interest in the case would have become known from the outset. It was not impossible to imagine that it had become known the day before. The persons concerned might have been aware of Miss Rushburton's visit to the office in Hanover Square, and of its object. Perrin might have been under observation ever since that Friday afternoon.

The fact that an inquest had been dispensed with would have satisfied the unknown that the police would take no further interest in the matter. But would the private investigator let it drop so easily? Perrin decided that had he been concerned, he would certainly have kept an eye upon him. His proceedings on Monday, his obvious following up of Solway's movements, shown by his visits to Lord Brimstoke's office and to Doctor Hardcastle, would prove that he was still on the scent. From that moment he would be carefully watched.

It was not a pleasant thought that that watch had probably never for an instant been relaxed, and was even now being maintained. From his own experience, Perrin knew how easy it was to dog anybody's steps in London. He did not even trouble

to look out of the window. He credited his opponents with sufficient ability to keep their eye on him without the use of any
such clumsy expedients as men loafing around his doorway.

Under ordinary circumstances Perrin might have abandoned an investigation which, after all, he had undertaken
out of mere curiosity. His aversion to Rushburton was not so
great as to induce him to spend time and money in the vague
hope that he might discover something to his discredit. But
the murder of Ben Hammerton acted upon him like a direct
challenge. If his adversaries were prepared to go to the length
of murder, their secret must be more than an ordinary one.
Besides, Ben was in a sense his employee. It was up to him to
revenge him.

Thus Perrin reasoned with himself, seeking some justifi-
cation for the course which he would pursue in any case. He
would devote all his energies to bringing to justice the men
responsible for Ben's murder.

The difficulty was that he had no clue whatever to their
identity. That Rushburton himself had had him watched, and
had taken this means of warning him, he did not for a moment
believe. Rushburton, however unscrupulous he might be politically, was not the sort of man to incite people to murder. All
other considerations apart, the game would not be worth the
candle. Besides, Perrin could not get away from the idea that
Rushburton himself was in the power of some stronger agency.
The obvious terror he had displayed at any mention of Solway's
absence seemed to indicate that. It was this stronger power
that must be Perrin's task to unveil.

He found it difficult to visualize the nature of this power.
It must consist, he supposed, of some man, or group of men,
call them a syndicate, who were working for some definite
end, whatever it might be. A man of Rushburton's political
eminence was necessary to their plans and by some means
they had got him into their power. Perrin's conversation with

Sammy might suggest that these conditions applied to Lord Brimstoke and his group.

Yet Perrin felt convinced that he must look further afield than this. It was quite conceivable, as Sammy had suggested, that Lord Brimstoke should contemplate making use of Rushburton in the future. Influence with a prospective Cabinet Minister would be a very valuable asset to a financier. But that Lord Brimstoke had been the instigator in the concealment of Solway seemed absurd. What possible advantage could he derive from such an action? And again, it was hardly conceivable that he had connived at the murder of Ben.

No, the only possible theory, and that was fantastic enough, was that some mysterious syndicate existed, with whom Rushburton had relations, and who were determined that the mystery of Solway's disappearance should not be revealed. But how to obtain any clue to its activities, or to the identity of the men who composed it? Even if Rushburton possessed this knowledge, there was no possible means of extracting it from him. So far, the only clue was the car in which Solway had left Harley Street, and Perrin's inquiries in that direction had failed. But it would be worth while persevering. It was dimly possible that Doctor Hardcastle had noticed something about the car by which it could be recognized. Or, if not Doctor Hardcastle himself, perhaps the misanthropic-looking man who had assisted Solway into it.

But this brought Perrin up against the problem created by the fact that he was himself being shadowed. It would be merely playing into his opponents' hands to take any further steps while that surveillance continued. The best way to terminate it would be to appear to take to heart the warning conveyed by Ben's murder. He decided that for the next week at least he would make no further inquiries. Let it appear that he had lost interest in the matter.

In accordance with this decision, he remained in his office for the rest of the day and went home as usual in the evening. In spite of the utmost watchfulness on his part, he could discover no sign of his being followed. Nor when he returned to the office on Wednesday morning was he any more successful. But he did not delude himself into believing that the surveillance was at an end. That he had seen nothing merely proved that his adversaries were men who knew their job.

Towards noon that day Inspector Philpott called. "You were right about that poor chap," he said, as soon as the two were seated in Perrin's room. "His description agreed with that of Ben Hammerton, so I had his fingerprints taken. They corresponded exactly to those in our records. So the question of identity is settled."

"I never had any doubts about it," replied Perrin. "You've got no clue to his murderer, I suppose?"

"No, nor likely to have. We don't even know where he was killed. I went to see the people at that pub you mentioned. They know him well enough there, but only as Ben. Apparently nobody knew him by his surname. They also told me that he lived in a room by himself somewhere round about the Surrey Docks. Pretty vague, but M Division are looking round that neighbourhood for me."

"Did anybody see him after I left him on Monday evening?"

"Yes, the barman at the North Star saw him. He doesn't remember noticing him at the time you mentioned, six o'clock or thereabouts. But he saw him talking to a gentleman, presumably you, soon after two and he saw him come into the pub about nine o'clock."

"He must have gone out after I left him, and come back again. I wonder where he went to?"

"I don't suppose we shall ever know that. He left the North Star again just before closing-time, having had a few drinks. The barman didn't see him speak to anybody before he left.

It's reasonable to suppose that he meant to go home. But I don't for a moment suppose that he ever got there. Somebody followed him, or else waylaid him. There are plenty of nice secluded spots round about the Surrey Docks where it would be easy enough to knife a man, especially if he was a bit fuddled and hadn't all his wits about him. And the river's conveniently close for getting rid of the body."

"It'll be a verdict of murder by some person or persons unknown, I suppose?" remarked Perrin.

"Yes, and that's where it'll end. It's almost impossible to get any further in a case like this. The inquest's tomorrow, but you won't have to attend. You weren't the last person to see Ben alive, and there's no use dragging that post-card into it. It doesn't get us any further. So you can consider yourself lucky."

Perrin smiled. "I rather thought you'd see it in that light," he replied. "Yalding can have had nothing to do with this. You're satisfied about that, I suppose?"

"Oh yes, I had Yalding's movements checked up. He drove Rushburton back to Oldwick Manor, arriving there about half-past five. Then he changed out of his livery, washed the car, and had his tea. About eight o'clock he turned up at the local pub, the place we had bread and cheese at that day, and stayed there till half-past nine. Then he went home to bed, and didn't get up till six o'clock yesterday morning. There's no doubt about all that. Yalding's not the man."

"Nor was it any of the crooks I've employed him to keep his eye on from time to time, I'm pretty sure of that. I know most of them pretty well, and they aren't the type to stick a knife into a man. Too much afraid of their own skins, for one thing."

"Well, then, who did do it?" asked the inspector. "You've got an idea at the back of your mind, I do believe."

"It's not an idea, it's merely a suspicion. It's my opinion that the murderer was employed by someone else. If I could tell you who that someone else was, it might explain a lot of things. But I shouldn't wonder, from what you tell me, if the fellow who actually did the job had studied knife-play as an art."

"You may be right. The doctor said it was a particularly skilful blow. But that doesn't help us much. They are common enough in that part, you know that as well as I do. As for the murderer being hired for the job, I don't know. It's just as likely that Ben got mixed up in some scrap or other."

"Yes, I suppose that's possible," replied Perrin without much conviction. He was about to continue when he was interrupted by the buzzing of the telephone. He reached out his hand for the instrument and listened. "Scotland Yard is on the line asking for Inspector Philpott," came the voice of Miss Avery.

"All right, put them through," replied Perrin. He handed the instrument to the inspector. "Your people at the Yard are asking for you," he said.

Philpott took it from him. "Inspector Philpott speaking," he said. "What do you want? I beg your pardon, sir, I didn't know it was you." An expression of profound astonishment spread over his face as he listened. "Very good, sir, I'll take a taxi and get down there at once."

He put down the instrument, picked up his cap and hurried out of the office. "Got to meet the chief at the House of Commons," he called over his shoulder as he went.

This time Perrin had sufficient curiosity to look out of the window. He saw the inspector rush out of the building and hail a passing taxi. He said something to the driver and the man set off at breakneck speed down George Street.

"Well! I wonder what the dickens is up now?" Perrin muttered to himself. Something unusual must have happened for the assistant commissioner to summon one of his subordinates to such an urgent rendezvous as the House. It was no concern of his, reflected Perrin.

He had his own affairs to think about. And yet it was curious. The House of Commons! Could Rushburton be involved in whatever it was that had happened?

Now that he came to think of it, what he knew of Rushburton's movements showed that he had been far from regular in his attendance at the House lately. When he was not engaged in those mysterious visits of his to the City, he seemed to have spent most of his time at Oldwick Manor. He could very rarely have occupied his seat on the front bench of the Opposition.

Not that there was anything very surprising in this. During the past week or so there had been no very controversial measures before the House, and his attendance would not have been necessary. The Opposition appeared lately to have adopted a Fabian policy. They were biding their time, and meanwhile conducting a vigorous campaign in preparation for what was coming. It was an open secret that their massed attack upon the government was reserved for the second reading of the War Debts Bill, which was to be introduced the following week.

That the government must stand or fall by this bill was common knowledge. Opinion in the country was fairly evenly divided upon the wisdom of the proposed measures. It was rumoured that within the cabinet itself there had been differences of opinion, and that agreement had only been reached by the personal efforts of Mr. Wedderley, the Prime Minister. Wedderley was a man of commanding personality, and more than once during the past few months his exertions alone had saved the government from defeat.

It was by no means certain that even Wedderley could secure a majority for the War Debts Bill. On the whole the opinion of those who had their fingers on the political pulse was, that he would manage to scrape through and so save the government once again. If his influence were to be removed, or if in spite of his utmost efforts he failed to secure the passage of the bill, the government would have no option but to resign.

In that case the Opposition would come into power and would probably have no difficulty in securing a majority in the country.

Perrin glanced at his watch. It was barely twelve o'clock. Whether or not Rushburton meant to attend the House that day he would certainly not be there yet. Philpott's sudden summons could not concern him. It was annoying that the inspector had been called away like that. There were several questions Perrin would have liked to ask him. If the murderer of Ben Hammerton could be run to earth, a clue might be obtained leading to the mysterious syndicate in which Perrin was so deeply interested.

There was nothing more to be done in that direction for the moment. Perrin turned his attention to the correspondence which Miss Avery had laid on his table. But he found it impossible to concentrate his attention upon it. The murder of Ben Hammerton, the grim warning which he was certain it conveyed, the thought that at that very moment there were unseen eyes waiting to watch his every movement, drove consideration of everything else out of his mind. After some time he thrust the correspondence aside with an impatient gesture. He rose from his chair and went to the window, where he stood gazing speculatively out upon Hanover Square.

He had not been there long when a newspaper boy came racing in from the direction of Regent Street. He carried a bill, which from Perrin's position he could not read. Nor could he distinguish the raucous words which the boy was shouting. He opened the window and leaned out. Then, as the boy approached, he caught something about "'Orrible disaster" and "'Ouse of Commons."

"Hullo!" he muttered. "Now we shall learn what took Philpott off in such a hurry." He opened the door of his room and called to Miss Avery to send someone down to buy a paper.

While he waited for the messenger's return, he felt an inexplicable thrill of foreboding. Whatever it was that had happened, he had a presentiment that in some way he was himself concerned. He snatched at the newspaper when it came, and opened it with trembling hands. The head-lines stared him in the face. "Terrible disaster at the House of Commons. The Prime Minister killed in his room."

Perrin's first thought betrayed the groove in which his mind ran. Then Rushburton would be a Cabinet Minister before long! He stared at the head-lines as though fascinated. Wedderley was dead. Without his persuasive presence the government would never secure the passage of the War Debts Bill. The Opposition would come into power, and in the front rank of the Opposition stood the menacing figure of Rushburton, Ethelred the Ready, the Champion of English Liberty. A bitter smile twisted Perrin's lips. If only the people whom Rushburton imposed upon so successfully had an inkling of what he suspected!

He turned once more to the paper, which was a special edition rapidly rushed out. Only a few hastily gathered particulars were available. The Prime Minister had an appointment to receive a deputation at the House of Commons at eleven that morning. He had left Number Ten, Downing Street, and had driven in his car to the House, where he arrived shortly after half-past ten. He had gone straight to his room, where his private secretary, Mr. Charles Durrant, was awaiting him. He had not been there more than a few minutes when a sharp report was heard. Attendants rushed to the room, to find the Prime Minister lying dead beside his desk, and Mr. Durrant unconscious a short distance away. It was surmised that an explosion of some kind had occurred, but there was no smell of smoke in the room, and practically no sign of disorder, except that the objects normally standing on the Prime Minister's desk were scattered on the floor.

An explosion of some kind! What could have produced such an explosion? Not gas, certainly. Its presence would have been detected long before any explosion could have occurred. A bomb conveyed there in some way by an anarchist or a lunatic? Apart from the impossibility of such a thing having reached the Prime Minister's room, the conditions, if they were correctly described, precluded the idea. A bomb, whatever explosive it had been charged with, would have produced fumes of some kind, and would almost certainly have wrecked the room.

Perrin crumpled up the paper and threw it down impatiently. The particulars it gave were too vague to make it possible to form any theory. What had Wedderley died of, shock or wounds? Had the report heard been that of a fire-arm? If so, it must have been fired by the Prime Minister himself or his secretary. But, if a shot had been fired, how was it that Durrant had been found unconscious? For only one report was mentioned.

Never for a moment did Perrin contemplate the idea that the tragedy had been due to an accident. He knew instinctively that the Prime Minister had been murdered. And his mind, preoccupied as it was with the unaccountable death of Solway and the murder of Ben Hammerton, sprang at once to the conclusion that those who had been responsible for these two sinister incidents had contrived also the death of the Prime Minister.

For a few seconds he paced up and down the room. His thoughts worked swiftly. Then, utterly forgetful of the watch that he guessed was being kept upon him, intent only upon this new mystery which called to him irresistibly, he put on his hat and dashed from the room. A taxi had just set down its passengers a couple of doors away. He dived into it without ceremony. "House of Commons!" he called out to the astonished taxi man. "And drive like the devil!"

Chapter IX

The taxi-driver got no further than the end of Parliament Street. A cordon of police surrounded the Houses of Parliament, and strong posts were established at every avenue of approach. The news had evidently spread, for the whole space between the Houses of Parliament and the Abbey was blocked by a crowd of anxious spectators.

They were docile and orderly, as a London crowd almost always is, and they endured patiently the efforts of a handful of perspiring constables to keep open passages for traffic among them.

Perrin took in the situation at a glance. He paid off the taxi, and began to insinuate his way through the crowd towards the western side of Bridge Street. It took him many minutes to accomplish the journey, but at last he found himself standing opposite the closed gates. He knew that it was useless to expect to get any further unaided, but he scanned the faces of the police guarding the gate, hoping that he might recognize among them some officer of Scotland Yard whom he knew. In this he was disappointed, but his luck did not desert him. He had not occupied his post of vantage for long when he caught sight of Inspector Philpott hurrying across New Palace Yard towards him.

The men on guard unlocked the gate for him and as they did so Perrin stepped forward and touched him on the shoulder. The inspector restrained those who would have pushed back this audacious individual. "Hullo, Perrin!" he exclaimed. "I thought you'd turn up on the spot pretty soon. So much the better, we shall want all the brains we can lay hands on to solve this business. Since you're here you'd better come with me."

With a pair of burly policemen acting as a snowplough they made their way through the crowd. Not until they were outside Westminster Hospital, where the spectators were less densely packed, did Perrin find an opportunity for speech. "Where are we going to?" he asked.

The inspector nodded towards the building in front of them. "In there," he replied. "Durrant was carried off to hospital directly it had happened, and I've got the job of hearing what he's got to say about it. Come on, we'll find out if he's conscious yet."

They entered the hospital and, in reply to their inquiries, learned that Durrant had just come round. He did not appear to be injured in any way but was suffering from the effects of shock. In a few minutes, if the doctor permitted, they might see him.

Meanwhile they were shown to a waiting-room, and left alone. The inspector mopped his brow. He looked utterly bewildered and Perrin thought it best not to interrogate him too directly. "I may be of some use to you, Philpott, after all," he said quietly, "I know Durrant slightly. We were at school together, and we've met at intervals since."

"All right, you can introduce me to him," replied the inspector. "I tell you, Perrin, my head's in a whirl. What does it all mean?"

"I only know what the papers have got, and that's not much," replied Perrin.

"Well, I'll tell you what I know, which I don't suppose is much more. When I left your office, I got to the House and found most of our fellows there already, with the chief at their head. We were taken to the Prime Minister's room, and there we saw the most extraordinary sight. The Prime Minister was lying huddled up on the floor. He was quite dead, and there was a pool of blood round his head. The doctor told us that this was caused from the bleeding from the nose and mouth, and that there was no external injury, except his left hand was badly lacerated."

"Half a minute," interrupted Perrin. "Was there any sign of singeing about his hair or clothes?"

"Not the slightest. We looked for that, of course. Then an attendant who was there was questioned. He said that he was passing along the corridor outside the room, when he heard a sharp report. He described it as being not so loud as the crack of a rifle, but if possible sharper. He could tell that it came from the Prime Minister's room, so he knocked on the door. Getting no answer, though he knew that both the Prime Minister and Durrant were in there, he opened the door and looked in.

"We asked him how he knew they were there. He said that he had taken some papers in to Durrant about two minutes before he heard the report. The Prime Minister and Durrant were alone in the room then. He had remained in the corridor after he came out and he was certain that nobody could have entered or left the room without his seeing them. There seems no doubt that his statement is correct in every particular.

"He gave the alarm at once, and the corridor was soon full of people. The police on duty would allow nobody to enter the room except a doctor. He is an M.P. and happened to be on the terrace at the time. The first of our people got there a few minutes after it happened, and took charge at once. The next thing we did was to search the room. We were pretty thorough, as you may imagine, but we found absolutely nothing that would give us any clue to the affair."

"It's the state of the room that seems to me to be most important," said Perrin. "The papers talk about an explosion, I suppose, because the attendant mentioned a report. But surely you would have found some traces of that."

"That's what nobody can make out. The doctor said that both the Prime Minister and Durrant's condition suggested that they had been subjected to a violent shock. But there was no sign of any sort of explosion. We could smell no smoke, or anything like that, and the attendant, who was on the spot almost immediately, swears that he didn't either. Besides, an explosion would have blown the windows out and chucked everything about the room. The only trace of anything having happened was that the Prime Minister's desk had been swept clear. An inkpot, a blotting-pad, pens, pencils, and things like that lay scattered about the floor. Durrant was found lying on the floor about five yards from the Prime Minister."

At that moment a nurse came in to tell them that Durrant was now in a fit state to be questioned. She led them to a private ward where they found Durrant, clean-shaven and with an intellectual face, lying in bed, very white and shaken. He looked up as they entered the room, and recognizing Perrin, raised his head from the pillow.

"Hullo, I didn't expect to see you here," he said, with a faint smile. Then he beckoned him to the bedside. "Look here, old chap, tell me what happened," he said in a low voice. "The people here won't say anything. Is Wedderley all right?"

Perrin hesitated. He had not anticipated this question. But Durrant put out his hand and gripped him almost fiercely by the arm. "Tell me," he exclaimed. "Is he badly hurt?"

Perrin nodded solemnly, and Durrant read the answer in his eyes. His grip relaxed, and he let his head fall back on the pillow. A tear welled from his eyes and trickled slowly down his cheek. "I always looked upon him as my friend rather than my chief," he muttered brokenly. "What was it? Who killed him?"

"It's because you can help us to answer that question that we have come to see you," replied Perrin quietly. "Do you feel fit enough to talk to Inspector Philpott here, who is an old friend of mine?"

"Yes, I'm fit enough. I'd do anything to avenge Wedderley. But there's nothing I can tell you. I was walking across the room when suddenly I was knocked out, and I don't remember anything more. When I came to, I found myself here."

Inspector Philpott had come forward. "Perhaps you can tell us what happened up to then in your own words, Mr. Durrant," he said.

"I can do that, but nothing whatever happened outside the ordinary routine. I reached Number Ten at nine o'clock this morning, or perhaps a few minutes before, as I always do, and went into Wedderley's study. He came in a few minutes later and we went over his appointments for today. There were only two for this morning, as it happened."

"One moment, Mr. Durrant," put in the inspector. "Did you notice anything unusual in Mr. Wedderley's appearance or manner?"

"Nothing whatever. He had been rather worried at times lately, he had this War Debts Bill on his mind, and the difficulties connected with it depressed him sometimes. But this morning he was in his usual health, and in better spirits than I have seen him for some days. He told me that, judging by the papers which he had glanced at during breakfast, there was a growing tendency to support the bill."

The inspector nodded. "Thank you, Mr. Durrant," he said. "You were speaking of Mr. Wedderley's appointments when I interrupted you, I think?"

"I was. As I said, he had only two for this morning. The first was with Lord Brimstoke at a quarter to ten. The second was to receive a deputation from the United Artists' Association at eleven."

At the mention of Lord Brimstoke's name Perrin felt a thrill of excitement. He could not forbear a glance at Philpott, who acknowledged it with a slight motion of his head. "Excuse me, Mr. Durrant," he said. "You will realize that every detail of this morning's happenings is of importance. Can you tell me when these appointments were arranged?"

"The United Artists' deputation was arranged a week or more ago. They were to have been introduced by a personal friend of Wedderley's. They wanted legislation introduced to prevent the exhibition of foreign pictures in this country. The interview with Lord Brimstoke was only arranged yesterday. Lord Brimstoke rang up, and asked if he could have a few minutes' conversation with the Prime Minister. In view of the War Debts Bill Wedderley was always anxious to keep in the closest possible touch with leading bankers. They are naturally much interested in the Bill, and Wedderley was always glad of the chance of an informal talk with any of them. He likes to hear their views.

"Knowing this I told Wedderley of Lord Brimstoke's message. He seemed pleased that Lord Brimstoke had asked to see him. He believed that he was opposed to certain provisions of the Bill and seemed glad of the opportunity of a chat with him. He told me to send a message to Lord Brimstoke that if he could come to Number Ten this morning, at a quarter to ten, he would have half an hour or so to spare. I sent this message and got a reply that Lord Brimstoke was very grateful for the appointment which he would certainly keep."

"And did he in fact keep it?" asked the inspector.

"He did, I believe; I was not present at the interview. Soon after half-past nine I left Number Ten and walked to the House, where I went straight to the Prime Minister's room. I had to get a few notes ready for Wedderley's use when he received the deputation, which he was to do at the House. I also had to look over the draft answers to the questions on the notice paper for this afternoon."

"Now, Mr. Durrant, I want you to think very carefully," said the inspector in impressive tones. "You were familiar, of course, with everything in the Prime Minister's room. Did you notice this morning anything, however slight, out of the ordinary? Was there any object there which you had not previously seen or was any object usually there missing? Or was anything displaced from its usual position?"

"I saw nothing in the slightest degree abnormal," replied Durrant positively. "You will understand that I did not make a detailed examination of the room. There was no reason for me to do so. But I sat for a few minutes at Wedderley's desk arranging his papers ready for him. If there had been anything unusual there I should certainly have noticed it. Then I went to my own desk at the further end of the room. Here again there was nothing out of place or missing."

"Did you leave the room again, once you had entered it?"

"I did not. I sat there working until Wedderley arrived, between half-past ten and a quarter to eleven."

"Were you alone all that time?"

"I was, except for two occasions when a messenger came in with papers for me. The first occasion was soon after I got there, the second was just after Wedderley came in."

"The messenger was the attendant you were accustomed to see, I suppose?"

"Certainly. His post is in the corridor. Papers are brought to him from the other parts of the building, and he brings them into the room. He is a thoroughly trustworthy man, and has carried out these particular duties for many years."

"He brought nothing into the room but papers?" suggested the inspector.

"Nothing whatever, he merely stayed in the room long enough to give me the papers and take away some others in their place."

"I see. And now, Mr. Durrant, we come to the most important period of all. What time was it exactly when the Prime Minister joined you?"

"I could not say within a few minutes. I believe that it was about five and twenty minutes to eleven. He came straight into the room and sat down at his desk. He had nothing whatever in his hands when he came in. He leaned back in his chair, with his arms folded in front of him, a favourite attitude of his, and spoke to me about his interview with Lord Brimstoke. He told me that he found him much more favourably inclined to the bill than he had supposed. His visit had been for the purpose of drawing Wedderley's attention to one or two clauses in the bill which in Brimstoke's opinion would affect the banks adversely. Wedderley told me that, apart from these comparatively minor details, which could easily be adjusted, his attitude was on the whole favourable to the bill.

"Wedderley was rather surprised that this should be the case, as, indeed, I was myself. We had supposed that Brimstoke's political opinions, if he had any very pronounced opinions, were those of the Opposition. Wedderley was naturally very pleased to think that we had been mistaken. He said that it would be a great advantage to us to have the bankers on our side. He also remarked that Lord Brimstoke was a man of great financial insight.

"This conversation lasted, I suppose, for three or four minutes, during which Wedderley did not change his position. The papers which I had arranged were lying on the desk before him, and beside them was a pad of blank paper, which he always liked to have at hand. I was sitting at my own desk, completing the notes concerning the deputation which he was to receive at eleven o'clock. Is this quite clear?"

"Absolutely, Mr. Durrant," replied the inspector. "I have seen the room and its arrangements, and I quite understand from your description how you were both engaged."

"As Wedderley finished telling me about the interview with Lord Brimstoke, the attendant came in. He walked straight to my desk and handed me a file of papers. In return I gave him the file containing this afternoon's question papers, which I had looked through for distribution to the departments concerned. He left the room, after being in it, I suppose, less than a minute,

"Now I come to the inexplicable incident itself. As soon as the attendant had left the room, Wedderley leaned towards his

desk, and drew the pad of blank paper towards him. He said
something about jotting down one or two points in Lord Brimstoke's conversation while they were still fresh in his memory.

"In order that you should understand fully the details of the
next few seconds, I must explain one of Wedderley's peculiarities. He nearly always jotted down the points of an important
conversation, and gave them to me to put in a private file which
I kept for the purpose. Sometimes he would dictate to me a
precis of the conversation, but as a general rule he made the
notes with his own hand.

"For this purpose he invariably used a pencil. But pencils
were another of his peculiarities. He never would use a silver
pencil-case, but always a wooden pencil, which he liked to be
of a certain softness. Never, by any chance, though, could he
keep such a pencil. What he did with them has always been
a mystery to me. As soon as he had finished with a pencil, he
put it in his pocket, from which it always seemed to disappear
within the next few minutes. I had long ago given up keeping
pencils on his desk. They used to disappear as fast as I put
them there. Latterly, I have always kept a supply of pencils
ready sharpened in a drawer in my own desk, and handed him
one whenever he wanted it.

"As soon as he'd put the pad ready for his use, he began
to feel in his pockets for a pencil. This was a favourite trick of
his, I must have seen him do it a thousand times. He would
do it when he was not about to write. I have even seen him in
the midst of delivering a speech of the first importance, feeling
surreptitiously in his pockets for a pencil which his subcon-
scious mind must have remembered putting there. Sometimes,
but rarely, a pencil was forthcoming. Far more often than not,
his search proved unavailing.

"As soon as I saw him fumbling in his pockets this morning,
I knew what he wanted. I opened the drawer in my desk and
took out a pencil. But while I was doing so, a look of humorous

triumph came into his face. 'It's all right, Durrant,' he said. 'I've got one this time. I knew I had, for Brimstoke left one on my table, and I remember putting it into my pocket after he had gone.' These were the last words he spoke to me.

"By then I had got up and taken a step across the room towards his desk, the pencil I had selected for him in my hand. I saw him produce another pencil from his pocket. It was the stub of an ordinary wooden pencil, about three inches long. Wedderley looked at it critically, and I remained where I was standing, in case he decided that it did not suit him. But he seemed to approve of it, though apparently the point was not sharp enough. He picked up a penknife which always lay on his desk, and began to sharpen it."

Durrant paused, and a puzzled expression came over his face. "I can't tell you any more," he said. "Suddenly I felt a violent blow, not in any particular spot, but as though I had been struck all over. I remember a sensation of falling backwards through space, but that is all."

Perrin listened to this account with rapt attention. He could see every incident as Durrant related it, the Prime Minister sitting at his desk, sharpening his pencil, and his secretary watching him. So much was ordinary, even commonplace. But what could have been the cause of that mysterious and violent shock, which had stunned Durrant and killed the Prime Minister?

Inspector Philpott listened too, but his mind was fixed on more practical details. "You say that you had the sensation of a sudden blow, Mr. Durrant," he said. "Did you form any impression of the direction in which the blow came?"

Durrant shook his head. "I can only say that it seemed to come from all directions at once."

"How far from the Prime Minister's desk were you standing when this happened?"

"Within a foot or two. Near enough to be able to hand him the pencil which I had in my hand if I saw that he wanted it."

"Did you notice the pencil which the Prime Minister had taken from his pocket? If so, could you describe it?"

"I looked at it, because I could usually tell at a glance whether any particular pencil would suit the Prime Minister or not. This one was the remains of a red hexagonal pencil, and of a superior make, probably a Royal Sovereign. I saw the Prime Minister examine it, and he must have satisfied himself that it was of the grade of hardness known as B. or he would not have attempted to use it."

"Just one more question, Mr. Durrant. Have you formed any theory of the cause of this blow or shock that you describe?"

"Why, no, I haven't," replied Durrant with some surprise. "I was going to ask you that, for surely you must have discovered it?"

"I assure you, Mr. Durrant, that up to the present we have discovered nothing which would account for anything of the kind," replied the inspector. "I am very grateful for all you have told me, and I hope that you will soon be fully recovered. Now we had better leave you to get some rest."

He turned away, and Perrin approached the bed. "I hope you'll get along all right," he said cheerfully. "Oh, by the way, the Prime Minister wasn't left-handed, was he?"

"Why, no, certainly not, he was more right-handed, so to speak, than the majority of people. He broke his left wrist some years ago and it was stiff and slightly troublesome ever afterwards."

"Well, so long! I'll drop in and see you again some time, if you'll let me." And with that Perrin followed the inspector out of the room.

Chapter X

By the time that Perrin and the inspector left the hospital the crowd had, to a certain extent, dispersed, and they had little difficulty in making their way along the pavement. The inspector was the first to speak. "I don't know that we're much forrarder," he said. "Beyond the fact that Mr. Durrant felt a blow or shock we haven't learned much. That shock caused the report heard by the attendant, and killed the Prime Minister, no doubt. But where the devil did the shock come from?"

"I don't know yet," replied Perrin absently. His mind had jumped that step, and was occupied with speculation as to the motive which might have inspired anyone to murder the Prime Minister. That it was a case of murder he felt certain, though he was as far as Philpott from understanding how the murder could have been perpetrated.

The two walked side by side for some yards in silence. And then suddenly Perrin awoke to the facts of the moment. "Where are we going?" he asked.

"I'm going back to the House," replied the inspector. "I expect my chief is still there, waiting for my report. You'd better come with me. The House won't sit this afternoon for a certainty, and you may get a chance of seeing the Prime Minister's room. I don't suppose anyone will object, if I take you in."

This supposition proved correct. Perrin was allowed to follow the inspector into the carefully guarded precincts without question, and they reached the Prime Minister's room together. Here the assistant commissioner was waiting Philpott's return. He already knew Perrin, at least by reputation, and seemed glad to see him.

"Well, Mr. Perrin," he said after the inspector had introduced them, "if you can help us to get to the bottom of this business, you're welcome to try. Now then, Philpott, let's hear what Mr. Durrant had to say to you."

Perrin took advantage of this to examine the Prime Minister's room. Nothing had been touched except that the articles scattered about the floor had been replaced on the Prime Minister's desk. It was to these that he turned his attention, after he had surveyed the room thoroughly.

There was the pad of blank paper which Durrant had mentioned, and a file of papers, no doubt the ones which his secretary had placed on the Prime Minister's desk. The inkstand, a massive concern with three wells and a tray for pens, had been picked up. The stain on the carpet showed where it had fallen. Three pens, with nibs of various thicknesses, lay in the tray. The blotting-pad lay beside the inkstand and on it was the penknife.

Perrin first turned his attention to the blotting-pad. The blotting-paper was white and new, and had not been used. Except for a few spots of ink upon the top piece, which had clearly been splashed there when the objects had been thrown from the table, the blotting-paper was perfectly clean. The desk itself was covered with leather, and this, though old and worn, and spotted with occasional ink spots, most of which were of ancient date, appeared at first to be undamaged. It was not until Perrin passed his hand over it that he discovered that in one place, to the right of the desk, the leather had been cut as with a sharp knife. Beneath this cut the wood was broken and splintered, as though it had been struck a violent blow.

The next thing that engaged Perrin's attention was the penknife. It had a black tapering ebony handle and a fixed blade. The blade appeared to be reasonably sharp, but in the centre it was badly notched. A triangular piece had been broken clean out of it, and the edges of the notch were still bright, showing that the damage was recent.

Of the pencil which Durrant had mentioned as being in the Prime Minister's hand there was no trace. It was not on the desk with the rest of the things which had been found on the floor. A pencil lay on the blotting-pad, but this was certainly not the one. It was yellow in colour and brand-new, with the point freshly sharpened. This, Perrin thought, must be the one that Durrant had been holding. He opened the drawers of the secretary's desk one by one, and found a box of exactly similar pencils. That seemed to settle the matter.

What had become of the short red pencil? That it had not been in the room when the detectives arrived on the scene was pretty certain. They had searched the room thoroughly, and an object, the size of a pencil, was not likely to have escaped their notice. It would not have attracted any particular attention, perhaps, but it would have been replaced on the desk with the other things picked up from the floor. What had become of it?

At this stage in Perrin's investigations Philpott came to the end of his report to the assistant commissioner. "You'd better see if you can verify that account," said the latter. "I'm going back to my office now. Report to me at once if you find anything fresh."

As soon as he had gone, the inspector turned to Perrin. "Well! Have you found anything?" he asked.

"I don't know yet," replied Perrin. "I suppose that chap we saw in the corridor as we came in is the attendant. You might ask him to come in for a minute, will you?"

The man came in, and Perrin showed him the damaged spot on the desk. "How long has that been done?" he asked.

"I've never noticed it before, sir," replied the man. "I'm certain it wasn't done when I tidied up the room this morning. I should have noticed it if it had been, for I always rub the desk over with a duster every morning when I put fresh blotting-paper in the pad."

"Very well! Now look at this penknife. You see that it has a notch out of the blade. Was that there when you tidied up the room this morning?"

"I'm sure it wasn't, sir. Besides, if the Prime Minister had seen it, he would have sent me for a new knife. He was very particular that the knife on the desk should be kept sharp, as he always liked to sharpen his pencils himself. I've heard him say, sir, that nobody seemed able to sharpen a pencil properly but himself."

Perrin nodded. "By the way, talking of pencils," he said casually. "You didn't happen to pick up one when you first came into the room after hearing the report, did you?"

"No, I certainly did not, sir. I ran out again at once to give the alarm."

Perrin dismissed the man with a nod, and turned to the inspector. "There's the notch in the knife and the damage to the desk, if you can make anything of them," he said. "And it's a queer thing, but that pencil which Durrant says the Prime Minister found in his pocket, seems to be missing."

The inspector frowned and shook his head. "I don't see anything there that's likely to help us," he replied.

"Don't you? Well, to be quite candid, nor do I. This affair is brimful of contradictions. It's easy enough to form a theory if one takes only some of the facts into consideration. But the theory becomes impossible if one considers them all."

"Well, you're ahead of me," said the inspector. "I can't think of a reasonable theory which will explain any of the facts. You aren't going to suggest that some Guy Fawkes had hid an infernal machine in the room, are you? All that's been gone into already the chief told me just now, and everybody is convinced that it's impossible."

"I know it's impossible, and that's just what worries me. I could produce plenty of reasons against it and I'm going to do so in a minute. But I'll tell you what I thought of, until I saw that it wouldn't do. Suppose the shock was in fact an explosion, and that it was caused by the Prime Minister sharpening his pencil?"

The inspector shrugged his shoulders wearily.

"I'll suppose anything you like," he replied. "I suppose you've some explanation of how the act of sharpening a pencil could kill one man and knock another out?"

"I want you to think where that pencil came from," said Perrin in a low voice. "What if it wasn't a pencil at all, but a stick of explosive with some kind of detonating composition at the end, which would explode when scratched by the knife, on the principle of a match-head?"

The inspector looked at him as though he had taken leave of his senses. "What on earth are you talking about?" he exclaimed. "You don't mean that seriously, do you?"

"I mean it seriously enough. Unfortunately the thing's impossible. But it would account for so many things. It could be done all right, that's not the difficulty. A stick of gelignite, or some similar explosive, could be cut and painted to look just like a pencil. And a little fulminate of mercury, which would go off by the friction of a knife, would explode it. Look at that desk, too! You notice that the waste-paper basket stands to the right side of it, don't you? Wedderley wants to sharpen the pencil. What does he do? He was a right-handed man, so he takes the pencil in his left hand and the knife in his right. He then turns round in his chair so that the pencil is over the waste-paper basket. He wouldn't want the shavings to fall on his desk.

"The first touch of the knife sets off the fulminate and the explosion occurs, producing the shock which Durrant describes. It kills the Prime Minister and it has some secondary effects. It hurls the things off the desk for one thing. It notches the knife, and tears it out of the Prime Minister's right hand. The knife strikes the desk with great force, and lacerates his left hand on the way. It would probably hit the desk on the right side where you see the mark. Every trace of the so-called pencil disappears, of course."

"By Jove! Perrin. When you put it like that it sounds as though there might be something in it!" exclaimed the inspector.

"I know it does," replied Perrin regretfully. "It's a beautiful theory, but unfortunately it won't work. Having put it up let's proceed to knock it down again. In the first place the Prime Minister was, according to Durrant, a specialist in pencils, so to speak. He would only use them if they were of a certain degree of hardness. Durrant tells us that he examined this one carefully before he tried to use it. I doubt if it would be possible to disguise any form of explosive as a pencil sufficiently thoroughly to pass examination by a man who was perfectly familiar with pencils. In fact, it seems difficult to believe that this particular pencil was anything but just an ordinary pencil.

"Having got so far, let's consider the next point. I don't know whether you are familiar with the action of explosives. I am. What happens when a substance explodes is this. It instantaneously changes its chemical composition, with the production of a large volume of gas and of considerable heat.

"Now, what would have happened, if a piece of gelignite, for example, had exploded in the Prime Minister's hand? It would almost certainly have blown his hand off, for one thing. His clothes would have been torn and they and his hair would have been singed by the heat generated by the explosion. The desk would probably have been turned over, or at all events, very seriously damaged. The papers and the pad on his desk would have been torn to ribbons. In fact, the room would have been completely wrecked, and the windows would have been blown out.

"Instead of that, what do we find? No damage anywhere, except to the desk itself, and that very slight, and to the two men, one sitting at the desk, the other standing close by. In fact, the effects of this completely inexplicable shock are localized to a very small area indeed. It's a matter for experts, of course, but I'm willing to bet that not one of them would entertain for a moment the idea that these effects and these alone, could be produced by any possible explosion."

"All it amounts to is that you come to what everybody else says," remarked the inspector despondently. "There's a man killed from shock, the sound of a report, and yet there can't have been an explosion."

"I know, that's the puzzle we've got to solve," replied Perrin. "It isn't the report that worries me so much. A report can be produced by other means than an explosion. For instance, the crack of a whip can sound almost exactly like a pistol shot. It doesn't even follow that the report heard by the messenger was caused by the shock which killed the Prime Minister."

"No, I suppose not. I'm beginning to wonder if we aren't taking too much for granted, Perrin. There were two people, and two people only, in the room when the Prime Minister was killed. That means that nobody can confirm the surviv-or's evidence."

"You mean that Durrant may have killed him, and contrived that he should be knocked out himself so as to divert suspicion? It's possible; that sort of thing has been done before. But even if Durrant is responsible, we're still as far as ever from discovering the method he employed."

"I don't want you to think I've got anything definite against Mr. Durrant," said the inspector hastily. "Especially since he is a friend of yours. But I can't help wondering if the details of what he told us are correct. After being knocked out like that, his memory might well be a bit treacherous. That incident of the pencil, for instance. If I understand properly what you've just said, the disappearance of the pencil would be accounted for, if it wasn't a pencil at all, but a stick of explosive. But since it can't have been a stick of explosive, its disappearance isn't accounted for. That sounds a bit involved, but I think you know what I mean."

"Yes, I know what you mean. We've got to form some other theory to account for the fact that we haven't found the pencil."

"Exactly. We're both satisfied, I take it, that the pencil isn't in the room now?"

"Not visibly in the room, certainly. But we mustn't lose sight of the possibility that the shock, whatever it was, played some queer trick with it. It might have thrown it into some place that hasn't been examined yet. It might, for instance, have got up the Prime Minister's sleeve."

"I hadn't thought of that," confessed the inspector. "I'm very much obliged to you for the suggestion. If that pencil ever existed, I'll have it found before very long. Not that it's of any importance of itself. Since it can't have been explosive, it can't have had anything to do with the Prime Minister's death. But it's valuable as a test of Mr. Durrant's evidence. If it can't be found, Mr. Durrant must have been mistaken about what the Prime Minister was doing, exactly, when the shock occurred."

"And that's the most important point of the lot," remarked Perrin. "However, let's see if we can deduce anything definite from what we really do know. The Prime Minister and Durrant were alone in here together. One was killed and the other rendered unconscious, by a shock of some kind. What sort of a shock was it, and how was it caused? An explosion properly defined is out of the question, for the reasons we have already discussed. What remains? By Jove! I wonder?"

Perrin stopped suddenly and looked upwards towards the ceiling with a speculative expression. The inspector watched him keenly. He had an irritating feeling that the affair was altogether beyond him, and he looked to Perrin to find the clue that would bring it within the limits of his comprehension. "Well?" he said encouragingly.

"I don't know," replied Perrin slowly. "There may be nothing in it. Have you ever come across a case of a man being struck by lightning?"

The inspector shook his head. "I can't say that I have," he replied.

"Nor have I, but I have read of several cases. It often happens that no signs of injury can be found on the body; no burns or markings of any kind. But the passage of the current can often be traced by other indications."

"I dare say," replied the inspector dryly. "But you're not going to suggest that the Prime Minister was struck by lightning, are you? That's more fantastic than your suggestion of the explosive pencil. For one thing, there hasn't been even a threat of a thunderstorm."

"The flash of lightning may have been produced artificially," said Perrin. "A powerful electrical discharge would produce the same effects. As I was going to tell you, there are usually other indications. For instance, metallic objects worn or held by the person struck are sometimes broken, fused or magnetized. You don't happen to have a needle about you by any chance, do you?"

"A needle?" replied the inspector. "I'm afraid I haven't. Mrs. Philpott sews my buttons on for me. I may have a pin, though."

"That's no good. A steel pen nib will do. I wonder if there's one on the desk? Yes, there is. Now watch."

Perrin extracted the nib from one of the penholders, and laid it on the desk. Then he picked up the penknife and pushed it gently towards the nib. As he did so, the nib quivered and finally sprang to the knife, by which Perrin was able to lift it from the desk. "How's that?" he asked in a tone of satisfaction.

"It seems as though the knife had become magnetized, certainly," replied the inspector.

"And Durrant says that the Prime Minister was holding it. Now that in itself is no proof of anything. But I believe that an electrical discharge similar to lightning would account for the shock and for the state of the knife, which is notched and magnetized, as you have seen for yourself."

"But how could such an electrical discharge have been produced?" asked the inspector.

"That I can't tell you. Once again it's a matter for the experts. But there are two means by which electricity is brought into this room. One way is by the electric-light fittings. There are no table lamps, I see, but there are no less than six pendants. The second way is by the telephone, which is on Durrant's desk, not the Prime Minister's."

"Do you mean that they would both have got a shock from one or other of these?"

"A shock from the lighting circuit might have killed the Prime Minister and stunned Durrant," replied Perrin. "But I don't think it would have produced the effects we've seen on the knife. That is, if only the ordinary voltage were present. But cases have been known of electric light and telephone wires coming in contact with the mains carrying much higher voltages. I don't quite see how this could have happened in a place like the House of Commons, but it might be worth while to have an expert examination made."

"I'll have that done, certainly," said the inspector with alacrity. "I'm not much of an electrician, I'm afraid. Can you suggest how such a discharge could have taken place?"

Perrin shook his head. "I'm afraid I can't," he replied. "I never came across such a thing myself. But, if you notice, there's a pendant right above the place where the Prime Minister was sitting. I'd get your expert to have a look at that, first, if I were you." The inspector nodded, but his expression was still puzzled. "Suppose we do find that the Prime Minister was killed by some sort of electric shock," he said. "Could such a thing be caused deliberately or would it be purely accidental?"

Perrin smiled. "Your expert may be able to throw some light on that point," he replied. "I'm hardly competent to express an opinion. I only suggest the theory as one which is at least possible."

"I'm awfully grateful to you, Perrin. I'll get an electrical expert sent along at once. Have you any other suggestions to make?"

"It seems to me that I've made enough to go on with for the present. It's no good speculating until we've got all the facts. The post-mortem may reveal the cause of death, for instance. I take it that since you've taken me into your confidence so far, you'll let me know how things go on?"

"Rather. If you like, I'll get the chief to authorize you to take part in the investigation. He'd do that willingly enough, I'm sure."

But Perrin shook his head. "Thanks," he replied. "But I'd rather not. For one thing, I don't suppose the Home Office would pay my fee. And, for another, I've plenty of other things to occupy my time. I'm quite ready to discuss any point with you, unofficially of course. You've only got to let me know when you want to see me."

"All right, if you'd rather have it that way," said the inspector regretfully. "I'll let you know as soon as I've any further news."

"Then I'll get back to my office. You'd better see me off the premises, or I shall be arrested as a suspicious person."

The inspector did so, and Perrin walked swiftly back to Hanover Square.

CHAPTER XI

PERRIN, on reaching his office, was relieved to find that David Meade was out, engaged upon some investigation of his own. The senior partner was in no mood to be questioned. He felt the urgent need of sitting down quietly by himself to consider the startling event by which he had just been confronted.

So startling was it, and so utterly inexplicable, that ordinary logical reasoning seemed powerless to deal with it. That the Prime Minister should be overtaken by sudden death in his own room in the House of Commons, was in itself remarkable enough. That the cause of this death should baffle the combined forces of Scotland Yard was almost sufficient to suggest a miracle. Yet Perrin, at the bottom of his heart, was quite satisfied that no miracle had taken place.

Perhaps because his mind was already preoccupied with the affairs of Sir Ethelred Rushburton he found it impossible to exclude the eminent politician from his thoughts. He, at least, would hardly feel a genuine share in the general regret. The death of the Prime Minister would be to him no more than the event which must crown his ambitions.

Any casual newspaper reader could foretell what would happen. Deprived of Wedderley's guiding hand, the government would fall asunder, and would certainly fail to secure the passage of the War Debts Bill. The Opposition would come into power, and Rushburton would become a member of the cabinet; probably, as had frequently been rumoured, as Home Secretary. And as he contemplated this practical certainty the full significance of the office dawned upon Perrin for the first time. Once at the head of the Home Office, Rushburton would be in a position to control the activities of Scotland Yard.

Perrin leaned back in his chair and smiled. How tactful of the police it had been not to be unduly inquisitive in the matter of Solway's death! To annoy the man who would one day be in a position of authority over them by inconvenient inquiries about his secretary would have been the height of indiscretion. Especially when an acknowledged expert was ready to certify the cause of death. No wonder Inspector Philpott, and apparently his superiors, had so quickly lost interest.

But all this had nothing to do with the death of the Prime Minister, or so, at least, Perrin assured himself. It was ridiculous to suppose that Rushburton had had any part in contriving that mysterious tragedy. And yet Rushburton's name had an uncanny way of cropping up throughout the events of the last few days. Solway, whose movements before his death were still unexplained, had been Rushburton's secretary. Perrin felt convinced that Ben Hammerton had been murdered as a warning to himself against undue inquisitiveness. Yet he had merely been entrusted with the comparatively innocent task of engaging Yalding in conversation. It might be quite a coincidence that Yalding happened to be Rushburton's chauffeur.

Finally there was the reception of Lord Brimstoke by the Prime Minister, the last official action of his life. The interview had been arranged informally at less than twenty-four hours' notice. There might be nothing in this, Durrant had said that the Prime Minister was always glad to hear the opinions of leading bankers on the bill. But the Prime Minister had been surprised, pleasantly surprised, certainly, but still surprised, at Lord Brimstoke's attitude. And then there was that curious, though perhaps trifling incident, of the pencil left behind by Lord Brimstoke and picked up by the Prime Minister. It was already known that relations of some kind existed between Lord Brimstoke and Rushburton.

Having once allowed his thoughts to wander in that direction, Perrin abandoned himself to their guidance. The mystery surrounding Solway's disappearance and the murder of Ben Hammer ton had already suggested to him the existence of some syndicate, working behind the scenes. This syndicate had appeared to have some definite object in view. Although this object might not in itself be criminal, the syndicate had no compunction in resorting to criminal methods in order to further it.

So much was at least fairly logical deduction. But when it came to speculating upon what the object might be, imagination alone could be employed. Was it possible that the scheme of the syndicate involved the cooperation of Lord Brimstoke as a financial, and of Rushburton as a political partner? If so, did these two give this assistance to the syndicate willingly or had they somehow fallen into its power? Rushburton's evident terror when Solway disappeared rather suggested the latter.

Lastly, Rushburton, however eminent, could be of little influence while his party remained in opposition. He could only be really effective as a member of the cabinet. Had the death of the Prime Minister been contrived so as to hasten his achievement of that position? Wasn't it, in fact, the last act in the syndicate's campaign of preparation? In that case, was the ultimate object to control the country financially and politically? If so, the mere sweeping aside of such insignificant obstacles as Ben Hammerton, or even Perrin himself, for that matter, would be a matter that would cause the syndicate no compunction.

And yet, the prospect of personal danger did not trouble Perrin overmuch. If his reasoning, however fantastic it might be, was correct, the aim of the syndicate had been practically achieved with the death of the Prime Minister. They were now safe from interference, for political events would follow one another without any interposition on their part. The only risk they ran was that responsibility for that event might be traced to them. But they would have foreseen that that could not be the task of a private investigator.

Scotland Yard would employ every effort to solve the mystery, no doubt. That was a risk that they must run. But unless the Yard succeeded fairly rapidly Rushburton would shortly be in a position to discourage any inconvenient activities on the Yard's part.

On the whole Perrin thought that the immediate danger to himself, had it ever existed, was over. The syndicate would now have other things to think about and might well dismiss him as not worthy of further attention. Especially if he ostentatiously took no active part in the present investigation. And that, as he had informed Inspector Philpott, was his intention.

Conjectures such as these, which, it must be confessed, were of no great practical value, occupied Perrin's time this Wednesday afternoon. His physical inactivity was in sharp contrast to the energy displayed by Inspector Philpott. As soon as Perrin had left him, he had got in touch with the assistant commissioner, and had repeated to him as much as he thought fit of Perrin's conversation. As a result he had obtained a free hand to take any steps necessary to follow up the hints he had obtained.

At his request an electrical expert was sent to him. The expert listened to his request and smiled in a superior manner. "I'll certainly go over the wiring for you," he said. "It'll be a long job, I warn you. And I'm pretty sure that no electrical discharge such as you speak of can have taken place. There is one way in which the effects you describe could have happened. If Mr. Wedderley had touched a conductor carrying a high-tension voltage with one hand, and at the same time touched his secretary with the other, he might have been killed and his secretary knocked down. I don't for a moment think that the ordinary lighting voltage would have done it. But I'll see if there's any possibility of a higher voltage having found its way into the room. That's what you want me to do, I take it?"

Philpott having seen the expert start upon his work left him to his own devices. The body of the Prime Minister had been taken to another room in the House, where the post-mortem was to take place, and thither the inspector made his way. The body had already been undressed, but the inspector on inquiry learned that no pencil had been found. He then went over the clothes very carefully for himself, but his minute search failed to bring to light the missing pencil.

It is not too much to say that this confirmed the inspector's suspicions. He had a great respect for Perrin's powers of deduction, and was always prepared to consider any theory that he might care to propound. But his own mind worked on simpler lines, and clung instinctively to the obvious.

Ever since his visit to Westminster Hospital, a feeling of skepticism had been growing upon him. The case presented itself to him in this way. Two men had been alone in a room together, and one of them had been killed. Was it unreasonable to suppose that the other must know something of the circumstances? Yet Durrant had professed utter ignorance. Everything in the room had been perfectly normal until he experienced the shock that had rendered him unconscious.

A very easy line of defence to take, after all. But suppose everything had not been normal during those few minutes between the Prime Minister's entrance and his death? Suppose that something out of the ordinary had taken place, which Durrant was anxious to conceal. He had described the dead man as sitting in his chair sharpening a pencil when the shock occurred. If this was the truth, what had become of the pencil?

It was a small point, but a suggestive one. If Durrant had lied in the matter of this detail, how far was the rest of his statement to be accepted? The inspector decided that it was his duty to verify it, step by step.

He left the House of Commons and went to Number Ten Downing Street. Here he learned that Durrant had arrived shortly before nine, and left again at twenty minutes to ten. A few minutes later, at approximately quarter to ten, Lord Brimstoke had arrived in his car, and had been shown into the Prime Minister's study. He left at twenty minutes past ten, and at half-past the Prime Minister had entered his own car, which was waiting for him, and had been driven to the House of Commons.

This confirmed Durrant's statement, so far. But, as the inspector reflected, he would not be likely to misrepresent facts which could easily be verified. After a few questions as to the Prime Minister's appearance when he left Downing Street, which he was assured had been perfectly normal, Philpott took a taxi and drove to Lord Brimstoke's offices in Lombard Street.

He was received by the same urbane young gentleman who had interviewed Perrin. He shook his head doubtfully at the inspector's request to see his chief. "Lord Brimstoke has been very greatly upset by this terrible tragedy at the House," he said. "He has given orders that he is not to be disturbed on any account."

"I can quite understand that, especially as his Lordship was one of the last people to see the Prime Minister alive," replied Philpott sympathetically. "But since I am the representative of Scotland Yard, perhaps he would make an exception in my favour?"

"Well, I'll tell him that you're here," said the other, "but you must not be surprised if he asks you to come again tomorrow."

The young man left the room, and returned again in a remarkably short space of time. "Lord Brimstoke will see you," he said curtly. "Will you come with me, please?"

The inspector followed him at once. His guide led him to a door, which he opened, and Philpott walked in. He heard the young man announce him, and then the door was shut, leaving him in semi-darkness.

It was a second or two before he could distinguish his surroundings. Then he discovered that he was in a luxuriously furnished room. The curtains were partially drawn across the windows, excluding most of the light. For a moment he thought he was alone until he became aware of a figure seated in a heavy armchair, and almost hidden by a massive table.

Philpott had never before set eyes on Lord Brimstoke, and the great financier's appearance was something of a surprise to him. He was small and slightly built, almost insignificant at first glance. But when he caught sight of his face, the inspector forgot the undersized body. It was one of the most powerful faces he had ever seen, with strong clear-cut features, and eyes that seemed to glower at him from under heavy brows.

There was something feline in their expression, the eyes of a cat that watches the bird before she springs.

The inspector felt distinctly uncomfortable. Lord Brimstoke sat perfectly motionless, saying nothing, but fixing him with those piercing eyes. Had he known it, the inspector was not the first to experience this unpleasant sensation. There were very few people who felt thoroughly at ease in Lord Brimstoke's presence.

At last, the inspector felt constrained to break the silence. "It's very kind of you to see me—" he began and then he hesitated. Did his title involve an obligation upon lesser people to address him as "My Lord?" Somehow Philpott fancied that it didn't. He concluded his sentence with the non-committal "sir."

"What do you want with me?" asked Lord Brimstoke shortly. His voice was harsh and sounded irritable.

"I should like to ask you certain particulars about your interview with the Prime Minister this morning, sir," replied Philpott.

"Naturally. I suppose that is part of the police routine," said Lord Brimstoke, with a touch of disdain. "Well?"

"May I ask if you noticed anything unusual in Mr. Wedderley's appearance or manner when you were with him, sir?"

"That is a ridiculous question," replied Lord Brimstoke quietly, but in a contemptuous tone. "I am not acquainted with Mr. Wedderley's usual appearance or manner. This was, I believe, the third occasion on which I have spoken to him."

"I beg your pardon, sir, I worded my question wrongly. I should have asked whether you noticed anything that would have struck you as unusual in anyone else?"

"You mean, I suppose, did I see anything to lead me to suppose that he would die within the next few minutes? If so, my reply is that I certainly did not."

Philpott, standing awkwardly in that shaded room, felt an increasing sense of inferiority. Lord Brimstoke was clearly too big a man to be interviewed by a mere inspector of police. He heartily wished he had never undertaken the job. But now he had no option but to continue with it.

He resolved to start on a new tack. "Your conversation with the Prime Minister was in the nature of an official interview, sir?" he ventured.

Rather to his surprise, Lord Brimstoke proved rather more expansive than hitherto. "Certainly," he replied. "I had obtained possession of some statistics, which I believed would be of interest to the government at the present juncture. Since I was already slightly acquainted with the Prime Minister, I applied for an opportunity of discussing these statistics with him. As a result, I was accorded an interview this morning, as you appear to be aware."

"Thank you very much, sir," said Philpott. "Could you give me an outline of what took place at the interview?"

"I will do so if you wish it, though I fail to see what bearing it has upon the death of the Prime Minister, which is, I suppose, the subject of your investigation. After a short preliminary conversation, I took two typed copies of the statistics from my pocket. One I handed to the Prime Minister, the other I retained myself. I then went through them, explaining each item as I came to it, and answering such points as the Prime Minister raised. During this time we were both seated at the table in his study.

"When I had completed my explanation, the Prime Minister asked me if he might keep the copy I had given him. I readily agreed and he put the papers in one of the drawers of his desk. The other copy I retained myself. The Prime Minister and I then spent a few minutes in discussing the attitude of financial circles towards the War Debts Bill. I was able to convince him that, so far as my own interests were concerned, we looked upon it favourably. I then took my leave of him and returned here. My only knowledge of what occurred subsequently is derived from the inadequate reports contained in the news-papers. I shall be glad to know exactly what happened at the House of Commons, inspector."

There was a note of authority in this last sentence which Philpott could not resist. "I'm afraid, sir, that nobody knows exactly what did happen," he replied. "I have interviewed Mr. Durrant, who was present, and he could throw no light upon the matter at all. The only thing that we can say definitely is that some sort of shock occurred, which killed the Prime Minister and rendered Mr. Durrant unconscious."

"When you say shock, do you imply the shock of an explosion?" asked Lord Brimstoke.

"Hardly that, sir. In fact, it seems to be definitely established that no explosion took place. We have reason to believe that the shock may possibly have been of an electrical nature."

"I gather that the cause of this most extraordinary shock has not been satisfactorily explained," remarked Lord Brimstoke. "There can be little doubt, however, that the highly trained officers of Scotland Yard will eventually solve the mystery, if indeed any mystery is involved. I claim for myself no skill in detection, but as a man of the world I should suggest that Mr. Durrant be further interrogated. Now, inspector, my time is valuable. Have you any further questions to put to me?"

"Only one, sir. Do you happen to remember if you left a pencil behind in the Prime Minister's study at Downing Street?"

"A pencil!" exclaimed Lord Brimstoke. Philpott gathered from his tone that he was irritated by such a trifling question. "It's quite possible. I remember using a pencil to underline certain figures on the copy of the statistics which I gave to the Prime Minister. What became of that pencil I cannot say. Nor do I recall where I got it from. I may have picked it up from the table, or the Prime Minister may have handed it to me."

"Is it possible that you found it in your pocket, sir?"

"I suppose everything is possible," replied Lord Brimstoke acidly. "Is this matter of the pencil of any particular importance?"

"Only to this extent, sir, Mr. Durrant told me that when the Prime Minister reached his room in the House of Commons, he produced a pencil which he said he had picked up in his study after you had left him. Mr. Durrant described it as a piece of an ordinary lead pencil, painted red."

"Scotland Yard can scarcely be accused of neglect of detail," remarked Lord Brimstoke contemptuously. "I am not prepared to state definitely that the pencil I used in the course of our interview was painted red. I did not examine it with any particular attention. But in that case it is highly improbable that I took it there. The pencils supplied to me are, I have observed, of a different colour."

He touched a bell on his table and in a second or two the young man from the inquiry office appeared.

"Bring me a pencil!" said Lord Brimstoke curtly.

The young man vanished silently, to return an instant later with a pencil which he presented to his employer. But Lord Brimstoke waved it aside. "Give it to the inspector," he said. Then, addressing Philpott: "That concludes our interview, I think. My clerk will show you out."

And before Philpott had time to say another word he found himself in the passage outside.

Chapter XII

It was nine o'clock that evening before Inspector Philpott reached Perrin's flat in Victoria Street. Tired out though he was, he felt that he could not rest until he had found a gleam of light somewhere. And the only chance of that seemed now to lie with this shrewd friend of his.

Perrin welcomed him warmly, and in spite of his protestations, insisted on taking him into the dining-room and setting a cold joint of beef before him.

"I'll bet you have had nothing to eat since breakfast," he said. "I hadn't myself till just now. And it's no good to try to think on an empty stomach, whatever people may say. You can tell me your adventures between mouthfuls."

"Well, I am a bit peckish, I don't mind admitting," replied the inspector. "And cold beef and pickles is one of my weaknesses. Thanks very much. But there's precious little to tell you, except that everything I've tried has come to a dead end."

"Things often seem like that till one sees the way round the corner," said Perrin cheerfully. "Let's hear the worst, and then put our heads together over it. Have you heard the result of the post-mortem yet?"

"Yes, I heard that just before I came along here. I don't understand all the medical terms, but what it amounts to is this. There are no signs of injury, except the laceration of the left hand. Nor was the Prime Minister suffering from any disease which could have killed him suddenly. There is no doubt that he died as the result of a severe shock to the whole system. The appearances, it was explained to me, were very similar to those of a man killed by a shell bursting close to him, yet without any fragment of it touching him."

"It almost sounds as if there might be something in my theory of an electrical discharge," remarked Perrin. "Did you act upon that suggestion at all?"

"I did, but I'm afraid it won't do. I asked the doctors if the post-mortem suggested anything of the kind, and they said no. It seems that there are usually certain peculiarities to be found in the body of a man killed by electricity. His blood is unusually fluid, for one thing. But none of these peculiarities were found."

"That's not altogether conclusive, is it? I imagine that these peculiarities are not always visible after death."

"It isn't conclusive by itself. But I put an electrical expert on the job, and I got his report before I saw the doctors. He tells me that it is quite impossible for a high-tension current to have found its way into the room. And he also said that it was equally impossible for anyone to get a shock from any of the electrical fittings."

"Well, that seems to dispose of that theory," said Perrin regretfully. "We shall have to cast about for another. Unless you've picked an idea for yourself, that is?"

The inspector shook his head. "If the facts are as we have been told, I have no ideas at all," he replied meaningly.

"That the facts are not as we have been told is possible. Has anything fresh occurred to make you doubt Durrant's story?"

"Mr. Durrant's story is confirmed except at its most interesting point, the short period when he and the Prime Minister were alone together at the House of Commons. I've been to see Lord Brimstoke."

Perrin's eyes lighted up, but he managed to conceal his interest from the inspector. "Have you?" he replied carelessly. "It was probably a very wise step on your part. What did you make of him?"

The inspector frowned. "It's the first time I've interviewed a big man like him, with the exception of Rushburton the other day, and I don't want to repeat the experience. I don't mean big in the physical sense, he's an undersized little blighter. But he's no end of a big pot, and he makes you feel it as soon as you see him. He was polite enough, in that he answered my questions and didn't tell me to go to the devil. But he's got a nasty sarcastic way about him and he treats people as though they were dirt beneath his feet."

Perrin smiled. "Not altogether a flattering portrait," he said. "I'd like to hear what you asked him and what his answers were."

The inspector gave a detailed account of his interview with the banker. "What he said about his visit to the Prime Minister was pretty much the same as what Mr. Durrant told us," he continued. "That was what I expected. It's that business about the pencil that set me thinking."

"You said that he made his secretary, or clerk, or whatever he calls him, give you one of the pencils used in his office. Can I see it?"

The inspector's hand dived into his pocket, and he produced a pencil, which he handed to Perrin. "This isn't the sort of thing that Durrant described," said the latter, as he turned it over in his fingers. "In fact, it differs in every possible way. For one thing it is green instead of red, and round instead of hexagonal. It has never been used, by the look of it, and it has been sharpened with a pencil-sharpener, not a knife. There's something stamped on it, too. 'The All British Pencil Company, Ltd. Extra Quality. H.' Durrant said that the Prime Minister wouldn't use a pencil unless it was a B."

"I know, I've had a look at the thing myself. Now this is the way I look at it. Lord Brimstoke sent his clerk for a pencil, without specifying any particular kind, and this is what he brought. It's pretty safe to infer, therefore, that this is the sort of pencil Lord Brimstoke is in the habit of using. If he had left a pencil behind in the Prime Minister's study it would have been one of these."

Perrin nodded. "So one would imagine," he remarked.

"Now, Lord Brimstoke says that he used a pencil during his interview to mark the Prime Minister's copy of the statistics. But he cannot say where that pencil came from. He mentioned three possibilities, that he brought it with him, that he picked it up off the table, or that the Prime Minister handed it to him.

"If Durrant's description of the pencil is correct, it's pretty certain that he didn't bring it with him. If it was already lying on the table, or if the Prime Minister handed it to him, it seems odd that the Prime Minister should have remarked to Mr. Durrant that Lord Brimstoke had left a pencil behind him, doesn't it?"

"Oh, I don't know," replied Perrin. "Frankly, I don't think the point is of any great importance. The Prime Minister may have thought that Lord Brimstoke brought it and left it behind him, although, in fact, it was in the room before he came in. A pencil isn't an object of any remarkable interest, after all."

"This one is," said the inspector grimly. "Where has it got to, that's what I want to know. If it was ever in the Prime Minister's room, what's become of it now?"

"Why should Durrant have mentioned it, if, in fact, it never existed?" retorted Perrin.

"That's another thing I want to know. Why should he have told us that the Prime Minister was sharpening a pencil when the shock occurred? Because, if he hadn't supplied us with every detail, we should have asked him for it. In the same way, he was ready with a reason for his being found beside the Prime Minister, and not at his own desk."

"You think that his statement of what happened during those few minutes is incorrect?"

"I think that his statement is correct, up to the point when the attendant entered the room for the second time. But I believe that he deliberately misled us as to what happened between then and the Prime Minister's death."

"Even if that is the case, I don't see that it helps us much," said Perrin thoughtfully.

"It helps us to this extent. Accepting Mr. Durrant's statement as it stands, the whole thing is inexplicable. The shock must have taken place without the intervention of any human agency. But if Mr. Durrant was standing beside his desk, he could have caused the shock by some means which we have not yet discovered. And the Prime Minister's hand may have been wounded in trying to ward off whatever it was that caused the shock."

"That brings you no nearer to an explanation of the Prime Minister's death. I'm not trying to defend Durrant, I've got as open a mind on the matter as you have. But if Durrant had possessed any apparatus by which such a shock could have been caused, that apparatus would have been found."

"Traces of it may be found yet," replied the inspector. "Nobody has been through Mr. Durrant's pockets as far as I know. That's a job for me first thing in the morning. How long has he been the Prime Minister's private secretary?"

"I couldn't tell you for certain. Ever since the present government came into office, I believe, and that's three years ago. I can't somehow imagine him having any motive for wanting to kill the Prime Minister."

"You never know. There have been attempts to assassinate Prime Ministers before, I believe."

"Before you take that line, you've got to prove that Wedderley was assassinated, as you put it. Look here, Philpott, I'll be perfectly frank with you. I don't believe that the Prime Minister's death was accidental, though heaven knows, I can't produce any facts in support of that belief. But I don't think that Durrant killed him, and I should be surprised to find that he knew anything more about the facts than what he told us."

The inspector looked at him sharply. "If the Prime Minister was murdered, and Mr. Durrant didn't do it, who else could have?" he asked. "You must remember that they were alone in the room together."

"I have not the faintest idea how the murder, if it was one, was committed," replied Perrin. "I am looking at it from the point of view of motive."

"That's just it. Look here, Perrin, you know more about these political chaps than I do. Was Mr. Wedderley a man who had many enemies?"

"I should say that few men in his position can escape having enemies. But Wedderley was extremely popular, even with his political opponents. I should imagine that he had not a personal enemy in the world. If he was murdered, the motive must be looked for in the consequences that must follow his death."

The inspector looked slightly puzzled. "The government's bound to fall, they say," he replied. "But this isn't a Central American republic, you know. Politicians don't go in for murdering one another here. They fight with words, not weapons."

Perrin laughed. "And they don't seem to do one another much harm. No, I'm not suggesting that Wedderley was the victim of an opposition conspiracy. But, you know, there might be people—however, that's all conjecture."

The inspector looked disappointed. He had hoped to get a lead from Perrin, but it seemed that the private investigator was as much at a loss as Scotland Yard itself.

"Much obliged to you for that meal," he said. "I realize now how badly I wanted it. I'm just going to look in at the Yard, to see if there's anything fresh, then I'm going home to bed."

Perrin sat up for a long time after the inspector left him. A thousand absurd fancies coursed through his brain, but by midnight he was bound to confess that he was as far from any explanation of the Prime Minister's death as he had ever been. He was certain in his own mind that he had been murdered. But how, and by whom?

One thing was certain. He would not allow the matter to occupy his mind to the exclusion of everything else. Next morning he plunged desperately into the routine work of his office, astonishing Miss Avery by his sudden interest in trifling matters which normally the staff attended to, as a matter of course. But it seemed as though fate would not allow him to remain aloof from the mystery which was almost the sole topic of discussion throughout the country. He had only just returned from a hurried lunch when he was informed that he was wanted on the telephone. As soon as he picked up the instrument he recognized the voice of Durrant.

"Is that you, Perrin? May I come round and see you? I know how busy you must be, but I should be most awfully grateful if you could spare me a few minutes."

"Come round by all means," replied Perrin heartily.

"But are you fit enough to leave hospital? I could run round and see you if you'd rather."

"You are a brick, Perrin," said Durrant gratefully. "I came out of hospital this morning, I couldn't stand lying in bed and doing nothing. I'm at Number Ten now, and I'll be with you as soon as a taxi can bring me."

Durrant was as good as his word. Within ten minutes he was seated in Perrin's room, looking very drawn and shaken but with perfect command over himself. He plunged into the business which had brought him without wasting time.

"As I told you over the 'phone just now, I left hospital this morning. They weren't overanxious to let me go, but I told them that it would do me no good to stay there and worry. I went straight to Downing Street and there I saw Mr. Nottingfield, the Minister for Foreign Affairs, who, as no doubt you've seen in the papers, is taking over the Prime Minister's duties for the present.

"Nottingfield was very nice to me and asked me if I felt fit enough to carry on with my usual duties. He said that he would like to have me on the spot, as I could tell him exactly what Wedderley had been doing. I agreed at once, and I have spent all the morning in the study at Number Ten, looking over Wedderley's papers and sorting them out. Half an hour ago Nottingfield said that I had better knock off for the day and go home. But I couldn't do that till I had seen you."

"I take that as a compliment," replied Perrin cheerfully. "Tell me exactly what I can do for you. My time is entirely at your disposal."

"I don't know how to thank you. What I wanted to tell you was this. Inspector Philpott came to Number Ten this morning to see me."

"Did he?" said Perrin easily. "That's only natural. Your evidence is of the greatest importance, and dozens of questions are bound to crop up which you will be able to answer. Philpott's an excellent fellow, with considerably more than the average share of common sense."

"I dare say. But, all the same, there was something odd about his manner. It may have been my imagination, but I got the impression that he was trying to catch me out. He asked me immeasurable questions about the pencil Wedderley was sharpening when it happened. It seems that it hasn't been found. You might think my nerves are still on edge. Perhaps they are. I've never had anything to do with the Scotland Yard people before. It may be their usual manner, but it seemed to me that Inspector Philpott suspected me of something."

Perrin's laugh was a trifle forced. "I shouldn't let that worry me," he replied, as lightly as he could. "Detectives are always apt to seem suspicious. They can't help it, they're so used to interrogating criminals."

"But it does worry me, and that's what I've come to you for. I know well enough that I was alone with Wedderley when he died, and that there is nobody who can confirm the statement I made to you and Inspector Philpott yesterday. I want you to help me prove it. Will you undertake an independent investigation into Wedderley's death on my behalf?"

Perrin hesitated for a moment. He saw at once the advantages and the disadvantages which were involved in his acceptance of this request. The thought that he would have a rational excuse for indulging his own inclinations decided him. "Yes, I'll take the job on for you," he said quietly.

"I knew you would," exclaimed Durrant. "Now look here, this is a matter of business between us. Don't spare any expense, and make your fee what you like. I'm pretty well off, and I'd spend every penny I've got to get to the bottom of this terrible business. And I need hardly say that I'll do everything I possibly can to help you."

Perrin inclined his head gravely. "You give me an entirely free hand, I take it. If I am to have any chance of success, I must ask you a few questions. Forget that we have known one another for so many years, and look upon me purely as an inquisitor. In the first place, do you wish to amend, or to add anything to the statement you made yesterday?"

Durrant shook his head. "That statement contained everything I know. I have thought of nothing else, as you may well imagine, and no single detail occurs to me that was not included."

"Very well. We will begin with the point which seems to puzzle Inspector Philpott, the pencil which the Prime Minister was sharpening. What opportunity had you for examining it?"

"Short of actually holding it in my hand, I had every opportunity. I was standing by Wedderley's desk as he held it, and knowing his peculiarities in the way of pencils, I looked at it pretty closely. As I told you before, it was red, hexagonal, and three or four inches long."

"And you are absolutely certain that the Prime Minister mentioned that Lord Brimstoke left it behind?"

"Absolutely certain. He said that he had picked it up from the table in his study after Lord Brimstoke had gone."

"Is there no possibility that he was mistaken? Could the pencil not have been on the table before Lord Brimstoke arrived?"

"I should say that was utterly impossible. There has never been a pencil of that sort in the study at Number Ten ever since Wedderley has been there. There was certainly not one in the room when I left to go to the House."

"There are, however, other possibilities. Someone may have brought it in after you left and before Lord Brimstoke came. Will you inquire for me if anyone did enter the room during that period? Again, there's another thing. You told me that the Prime Minister had a trick of picking up stray pencils and putting them in his pocket. May he not have found this one in his pocket after you had gone out?"

Durrant shook his head. "No, I am sure he did not," he replied. "I'll tell you why. When he first came into the study yesterday morning, he went through all his pockets looking for a pencil. As I told you, it's a sort of nervous trick he had. He did it regularly every morning, and sometimes he found one or two. But yesterday morning he had not got one, and I gave him one from my desk. It was of the same kind as I kept for him in his room at the House."

"Have you any idea of what has become of that particular pencil?"

"Yes, I found it lying on the table in the study at Number Ten this morning. Nothing there had been touched since yesterday."

"It's queer where the red pencil can have got to," said Perrin thoughtfully. "It must have hidden itself somewhere in the room at the House, where nobody can find it. However, it's only a detail after all. Let's get on with something else. Do you know Sir Ethelred Rushburton personally?"

Perrin's question was asked in a purely casual tone. But Durrant flushed suddenly, and to Perrin's observant eye looked distinctly embarrassed. "Why, whatever makes you ask that?" he replied with unfeigned astonishment.

Chapter XIII

"Why, idle curiosity as much as anything," said Perrin, without appearing to notice anything unusual in the other's manner. "He'll be a big man in the next government, by all accounts."

"There's no doubt about that," replied Durrant. "He's an able enough man in his own way. I've met him once or twice, but I can't say I know him well. I meet his son Osmond fairly frequently, though."

"Is that so? I have some slight acquaintance with Osmond too. And I met his sister for the first time a day or two ago."

"What! Millicent! did you?" exclaimed Durrant. "I know her quite well. That is to say, we meet pretty often at dances, and that sort of thing. She's not a bit like her father, you know."

The confusion in Durrant's manner did not escape Perrin. "So I should imagine," he replied carelessly. "Yes, Miss Rushburton has been to this office twice, lately. She's one of my clients, as I dare say you know."

"One of your clients?" repeated Durrant, with a hint of suspicion in his tone. "No, I certainly did not know it. She has never mentioned a word of anything of the kind to me."

"Oh, it was the merest trifle that she came to consult me about. Her brother sent her along, as a matter of fact. It was in connection with Rushburton's secretary, who died last week. Solway his name was. Did you ever come across him?"

"I can't say that I ever actually saw him. I've heard Millicent mention him, often enough. She was quite fond of him, I believe, at all events she seemed very much cut up by his death."

"I gather that Solway was by way of being a family friend. But I expect Miss Rushburton will soon get over it. Have you seen her lately?"

"I saw her on Tuesday evening, and she seemed in better spirits than she has been for some days." Perrin repressed a smile. On Tuesday evening Millicent Rushburton would have seen Sammy. Her more cheerful demeanour was no doubt due to the fact that she had come to some satisfactory arrangement with him. But of this Perrin said nothing.

"I'm sorry you don't know Rushburton well," he remarked casually. "I'm interested in the man, and I thought you might be able to give me a personal impression of him. However, we're getting away from the business that brought you here. There's another thing I want you to do for me when you get back to Number Ten. Naturally, I don't want to appear there in person."

"Of course, I'll do anything you ask me."

"Well, it appears that in the course of the interview which Lord Brimstoke had with the Prime Minister yesterday morning he gave him a copy of certain statistics. Have you come across that copy by any chance?"

Durrant glanced at Perrin in astonishment. "How in the world did you know that?" he asked. "Yes, I have come across a couple of sheets with some typewritten notes and figures on them. They were in a drawer in Wedderley's desk. I guessed that Lord Brimstoke must have brought them, because the paper bears the heading of the London and Provinces Bank."

"It's my business to keep my eyes open," replied Perrin. "Is there anything very confidential in the figures?"

"I can't say that I looked into them very carefully. Judging from the casual glance I gave them, I should say not."

"In that case, would it be possible to bring them here? I should very much like the opportunity of inspecting them."

"I don't see that there would be any harm in it. You don't want to make any use of the statistics, I suppose?"

"Oh, dear no, it's the paper they're typed on rather than the figures which interests me. I'd like to see them tomorrow if you can manage it. And I'd like you to look round the study as carefully as you can, and see if you can find any other stray pencils lying about."

Durrant promised to obey Perrin's instructions to the letter and shortly afterwards went home to a much-needed rest. Perrin, left alone, had leisure to consider the magnitude of the undertaking he had let himself in for. He had pledged himself to an investigation into the death of the Prime Minister, a problem which had hitherto baffled the vast resources of Scotland Yard. Hardly an encouraging prospect for a private investigator with no machinery at his disposal but his own wits.

But Perrin was not easily daunted. Instead of dwelling upon the difficulties of the problem his mind was already considering the best way of tackling it. He came to the conclusion at once that it would be useless to follow in the steps of the Yard. For one thing, Philpott would keep him informed of any fresh discoveries that he and his colleagues might make, and for another, he would merely be covering the same ground. No, the only hope of success lay in taking an entirely different line.

He rapidly made up his mind what this line should be. In spite of his failure to find an iota of evidence in support of it, he clung to his theory of the existence of some mysterious syndicate. The only clue that held out the slightest hope of leading to this syndicate was the disappearance of Solway. Although a logical mind might find not the slightest connection between the movements of Rushburton's secretary and the death of the Prime Minister, Perrin decided to concentrate upon the former.

It was while he was making inquiries in this direction that Ben Hammerton had been murdered. That seemed to suggest that in that direction lay a secret which the syndicate was determined should not be revealed. If he persisted, Perrin realized that he might incur considerable personal danger, unless he was correct in his assumption that now its end was achieved, the syndicate would relax its vigilance. But in any case he would go cautiously. Perhaps he had been unduly rash in openly calling at Lord Brimstoke's offices, which would undoubtedly be watched by the syndicate's agents.

If he meant to get on to the track of Solway he must start from the moment when he left Doctor Hardcastle's house in Harley Street. He had been too hasty in assuming that the car which was waiting for him had been sent by Crabtree and Watson. Solway had certainly told the specialist that a friend of his in the motor trade would send a car for him. But he may have said that on purpose to mislead the doctor. If he had business with the syndicate, he would be careful not to drop any hint as to the owner of the car or its destination.

Would it be possible to find the car and its driver? Rather like hunting for a needle in a haystack, but still there was a chance. It was just possible that Doctor Hardcastle, or the pessimistic-looking man-servant, might be able to give a rough description of both car and driver. This would be valuable in itself. And Perrin felt that he could go a step further. If his theory that Solway was dead before he reached the pavilion at Oldwick Manor was correct, his body had probably been conveyed thither in the same car. During the journey it might have been seen by somebody who would recognize the description.

The first thing, obviously, was to get into touch with Doctor Hardcastle. Perrin put a call through to his number and recognized the voice of the receptionist at the other end. "Mr. Perrin speaking," he said. "You will remember that Doctor Hardcastle was good enough to grant me an interview on Monday. I wonder if I could see him again some time at his convenience?"

"I will ask Mr. Hardcastle as soon as he is disengaged," came the business-like reply. "If you will give me your telephone number, I will call you up later."

Perrin complied with her request. Twenty minutes or so later, the telephone rang and Perrin, picking up the instrument, heard the voice of the doctor himself. "Is that you, Mr.

Perrin? My receptionist tells me that you want to see me. I have no appointments after six, and if you care to come along then I shall be delighted to see you."

Perrin expressed his gratitude, and at the appointed time presented himself at the house in Harley Street. He hoped for an opportunity of having a few words with the man-servant, but to his disappointment the door was opened by a stranger. The pessimist had disappeared, and his place had been taken by a supercilious-looking individual, who looked him up and down and conveyed him upstairs in the lift without a word.

The thought passed through Perrin's mind that specialists were usually unfortunate in their choice of servitors. Surely patients would prefer to be greeted by somebody who had at least the appearance of being friendly and sympathetic. It would create a more favourable impression from the start. By the way, he must remember that specialists preferred the prefix of "Mr." rather than "Doctor."

This time he was not kept waiting, but was ushered straight into the consulting-room. Mr. Hardcastle rose and shook hands. "I'm very glad to see you again, Mr. Perrin," he said cordially. "You haven't come as a patient, I hope? You've no idea what a relief to me it is to talk to someone who has some other topic than the dreadful things that are happening in his inside."

"No, I haven't come as a patient," replied Perrin, "I'm on the same errand as I was the other day. Between ourselves, Doctor, I'm very anxious, on behalf of one of my clients, to trace Mr. Solway's movements after he left here last Monday week."

"He was hardly in a condition to undertake anything very energetic when I last saw him. In fact, he assured me that he was going straight back to Oldwick Manor."

"Well, you must be used to confidences, Doctor. It isn't generally known, but Mr. Solway was not seen at Oldwick

Manor between the morning of that Monday and Saturday morning when his body was found in the pavilion."

Mr. Hardcastle stared at Perrin incredulously. "What an extraordinary thing!" he exclaimed. "Sir Ethelred mentioned nothing of that when he rang up and told me of Mr. Solway's death! I can quite understand that he has commissioned you to find out what happened to him during that period. In my opinion, he could not have put the matter in more capable hands."

If the specialist chose to assume that Rushburton was his client, so much the better, thought Perrin. "It's very kind of you to say that," he replied. "I shall do my best, of course. Naturally I can only start from the time when he left here on the Monday. So far I have failed to trace the car into which you helped him. I have reason to believe that he deliberately misled you when he said that it had been sent for him by a friend of his in the motor trade."

"Possibly, I had observed before that Mr. Solway was of a secretive nature, shall we say? He may have had reasons of his own for concealing his destination from me. For one thing, I should have protested very strongly had I guessed that he was going anywhere but straight home. In the condition he was then, he was not in a fit state to undertake any exertion."

"Exactly. I was wondering whether you noticed the car sufficiently to be able to give me any description of it."

Mr. Hardcastle frowned. "I am very sorry, Mr. Perrin," he replied contritely. "I am afraid that I am not a very observant person, except where my patients and my own experiments are concerned. And most unfortunately the man who assisted him into the car has left us. His wife was taken very ill on the afternoon of the day you were here last and he had to go off at a moment's notice. He might have observed the car more closely than I did."

"Perhaps you can give me some idea what the car and the driver looked like. Was the car closed or open, for instance?"

"It was a closed car, I remember that distinctly. Quite a large one, I think. And I believe that it was painted some light colour. The driver was in livery, I'm sure of that. I remember when we got Mr. Solway to the door, asking him if that was the car. He replied, 'Yes, that's the one.' The chauffeur knew all about him, for he drove off without waiting for instructions. Naturally I supposed that he was going straight back to Oldwick Manor."

"Thank you, Doctor," replied Perrin. "I'll do my best to have the car traced. It's no good asking you for the number, of course. Nobody notices a car's number unless there's some peculiarity about it."

Mr. Hardcastle smiled. "I certainly did not notice the number," he said. "And I haven't the slightest idea how you will set about looking for a car on such slender data. But I suppose you have methods that the ordinary person would not think of."

The specialist paused, and Perrin could see the remains of his smile flickering over the strong scholarly face. "If you will pardon my presumption," he continued. "There's one thing that puzzles me very greatly."

"What is that?" asked Perrin, who found his original liking for the man increasing.

"Just this, that you should employ your time on such a relatively unimportant matter at this juncture. I should have thought that the country would have snapped up a brain like yours at once. After all, the nation is confronted with what appears at present to be an inexplicable mystery."

"You refer to yesterday's tragedy at the House of Commons? The country has brains enough at its disposal without consulting the private investigator. If the mystery is capable of solution you may trust Scotland Yard to solve it."

The specialist leaned back in his chair. "I wonder if you mean exactly what your words imply?" he said speculatively.

"Do you know, Mr. Perrin, I, too, indulge in the endeavour to solve problems. Not quite in your sense, of course. But you must not suppose that my life is bounded by the internal organs of my patients. In my leisure moments I am a student of physics. By the way, what a remarkable language ours is! I dare say that many people believe that physics is the science of dispensing physic."

Perrin laughed. "Very likely they do," he replied. "I can only claim some knowledge of the rudiments of the science myself. I am woefully ignorant of such things as the conception of space, time, the quantum theory, and so forth."

"And yet a man of your perception and reasoning powers would find the subject extraordinarily fascinating. What I was going to say is that in the course of my studies I have found that every problem is, strictly speaking, capable of solution. One's powers may not be adequate to the task, but that does not alter the fact. And it appears to me from what I have read in the papers, that Scotland Yard has not the mental ability to solve the problem of what occurred at the House of Commons yesterday morning. But perhaps I am detaining you, Mr. Perrin?"

"Not a bit!" exclaimed Perrin. "Naturally, I am greatly interested in the problem. In confidence, I may tell you that I had an opportunity of examining the Prime Minister's room yesterday."

"Indeed?" said the specialist, and Perrin fancied that he detected a note of envy in his voice. "You are indeed fortunate. Do you know, I fancied that you would have a finger in the pie somewhere. I must confess that the affair interests me enormously, chiefly from the scientific aspect. I have not your inside information, of course. But I gather from what I read that Mr. Wedderley died as the result of some shock. Although what he describes as a report was heard by an attendant in the corridor outside the room, the cause of that report or the shock has not yet been discovered."

Perrin nodded. "That's it exactly, Doctor," he replied. "Even with my inside knowledge, as you call it, I can add nothing essential. The difficulties of the police are greatly increased by the fact that Mr. Durrant, the Prime Minister's secretary, who was the only other occupant of the room, was rendered unconscious presumably by the shock that killed Mr. Wedderley."

"So I understand," remarked the specialist. "It is only natural that my interest should be centred in the medical evidence and that, I imagine, will not be made public until after the inquest which, according to the papers, is to be held tomorrow morning."

"From what I hear, there will be nothing very sensational in it. A post-mortem has already been held, and I am told that nothing was discovered beyond the usual appearances accompanying death from shock. That is with the exception that Mr. Wedderley's left hand was lacerated. For my own part I attribute that to the fact that, according to Mr. Durrant, the Prime Minister was holding a penknife at the moment when the shock took place."

"A penknife?" exclaimed the specialist. "Your assumption is probably right, Mr. Perrin. No doubt Mr. Wedderley made some convulsive movement resulting in his hand being cut. That is merely incidental. It indicates, however, that the report or the shock was entirely unexpected."

"Yes, that is so," replied Perrin. "I hadn't thought of it in that light, exactly."

Mr. Hardcastle made a deprecating gesture. "It's only an idea," he said. "As I have already remarked, the injury to the hand is purely incidental. Now, from the medical point of view, what did Mr. Wedderley die of? The technical answer is syncope as opposed to asphyxia or coma. Syncope in this case means failure of the heart's action, due to shock. It is comparatively common for certain persons to have unsuspected disease of the heart, which renders them liable to sudden death from syncope. But from what you tell me, the post-mortem revealed nothing of the kind in the case of Mr. Wedderley."

"I have heard no suggestion of it," replied Perrin. "Then assuming that Mr. Wedderley's heart was perfectly healthy we must seek some other explanation. It seems to be assumed that some actual physical shock, producing the effects of a blow, must have occurred. But cases, admittedly very rare, are recorded in the medical textbooks of perfectly healthy persons dying suddenly as the result of some sudden and severe mental shock, unaccompanied by any form of violence. That this might have occurred in Wedderley's case does not seem to have been considered."

"I certainly had not considered it," said Perrin. "My mind has been prepossessed by two facts, the report heard by the attendant and the fact that Mr. Durrant was thrown to the floor and stunned. He describes his sensations as that of receiving a blow all over."

The specialist smiled. "Surely there is room for some confusion of thought here?" he said. "Mr. Durrant may have been subjected to some physical shock, but it does not follow that this shock was the cause of Mr. Wedderley's death. Let me make my meaning somewhat clearer. Suppose that Mr. Durrant received the full force of this physical shock, I am not going to conjecture the nature of this shock or its cause. He is flung to the floor, to all appearances dead. I maintain that it is possible that the mental shock of witnessing such a wholly unexpected and terrifying event caused the syncope from which the Prime Minister died."

"Well, Doctor, that's an entirely fresh point of view, so far as I am concerned," said Perrin thoughtfully.

"I should not like you to regard it as more than a suggestion," replied the specialist. "I merely state that, from a medical point of view, such a sequence of events is possible. Whether or not this theory contributes towards the solution of the problem, I cannot, of course, say. But I have led you a long way from the subject that you came to discuss with me, Mr. Perrin."

"Don't apologize for that, Doctor. I've found our conversation deeply interesting. By Jove, I had no idea it was so late. I'm afraid I've wasted a lot of your valuable time."

"Not a bit of it!" exclaimed the specialist cordially. "I hope we may meet again. And, I say it with all diffidence, if ever any medical advice would assist you in your investigation, my stock of information is unreservedly at your disposal."

Perrin thanked Mr. Hardcastle warmly. He left the house, meditating upon the possible new light which the specialist had thrown upon the case.

Chapter XIV

But, however interesting his conversation with Mr. Hardcastle had been, Perrin remembered that he had not been very successful in the primary object of his visit. A large roomy car painted some light colour, and driven by a chauffeur in livery. Not very much to base a search upon.

Still, it was something. The car had stood for some minutes in Harley Street on the Monday of Solway's visit to the specialist. It might be possible to get into touch with someone who had noticed it. And there was another way in which it might be traced. If it belonged to the imaginary syndicate, as seemed at least possible, the members of the syndicate would use it to get about in. If, for instance, they had business with Lord Brimstoke or Sir Ethelred Rushburton, they might use this car.

Rather a slender chance, perhaps, but still one worth gambling on. Under ordinary circumstances Perrin would have set his own staff to work to watch and make inquiries.

But the warning conveyed by the murder of Ben Hammerton had not gone unheeded. Perrin had no intention of exposing any unsuspecting person to the vengeance of the gang. He resolved to take Inspector Philpott into his confidence and persuade him to undertake the search for the car.

On Friday morning a messenger brought him a note from Durrant, who explained that he was unable to come himself as he had to attend the inquest on Mr. Wedderley. He had ascertained from the staff at Number Ten that nobody had entered the Prime Minister's study on Wednesday between the time he left and the time Lord Brimstoke arrived. He also enclosed the sheets of paper with the typewritten notes which he assumed to have been brought by Lord Brimstoke.

Perrin examined the latter with interest. There were two sheets of paper headed "The London and Provinces Bank, Head Office, Lombard Street, E.C.3," and these were covered with a series of notes and tabulated figures, apparently dealing with international purchases of gold. Perrin was by no means an expert in such matters, but he made out that the tendency of the statistics was to show the advantage England would derive under the provisions of the War Debt Bill.

Lord Brimstoke's visit to the Prime Minister seemed thus to be adequately explained. The statistics were in the form of a summary, and would be unintelligible without some accompanying explanation. This explanation Lord Brimstoke had undoubtedly given verbally. And, as he proceeded, he had underlined certain sentences and figures in pencil. This confirmed the account which Lord Brimstoke had given to Inspector Philpott.

Perrin examined the pencil-marks very carefully through a lens, and as he did so he frowned. He sat for a moment considering the papers in front of him, and then rang up a friend of his, who was an artist and worked extensively in pencil. He was lucky enough to catch the artist at his studio in Chelsea, and he asked him if he could spare the time to come round for a few minutes. The artist consented and shortly afterwards appeared at the office.

"Hullo, Perrin!" he said. "What's up now? Am I suspected of being implicated in some crime? My conscience is pretty clear, considering. You just caught me at the right moment. I've got an appointment with an art dealer in Regent Street this morning, and I've looked in here on my way."

"I'm very much obliged to you," replied Perrin. "I didn't ask you here as a suspect. I want your expert advice. In return I'll stand you dinner at the Café Royal any night you like to fix. I wish you'd have a look at these pencil-marks."

He handed over the two sheets of paper, and the artist glanced at them idly. "They seem to me very ordinary," he said. "What about them? They don't show any great sign of artistic promise, if that's what's in your mind. Golly! look at these figures! Is there so much money in the world? I wish a bit of it came my way."

"Never mind the figures. Try to concentrate your mind upon the pencil-marks. What sort of a pencil were they made with?"

"An ordinary common or garden pencil, such as may be purchased at any stationer's for twopence. That is, if you happen to have twopence on you, or can persuade the man to give you tick. What's the great idea?"

"The great idea is this. I want you to tell me what was the degree of hardness of the pencil with which these marks were made."

The artist examined the sheets of paper more carefully. "'H,'" he replied, "or maybe 'HH.' It depends upon the make of pencil. A foreign 'H' is usually harder than an English one. Lend me your lens a moment. Yes, 'H,' I should think. Anyway, it was a pretty hard sort of pencil."

"I thought so," remarked Perrin. "You're quite sure that it couldn't have been a softer pencil, a 'B' for instance?"

"That's a childish question for a man of your intelligence, Perrin. A 'B' used in the ordinary way, makes a black wide mark. An 'H' makes a greyer, narrower mark. And this pencil was used with a pretty firm hand. You can see how the paper is indented; the marks show right through to the back. If a 'B' had been used with that pressure, the marks would have been much broader, and quite black instead of grey as these are."

"Thanks, that's just what I wanted to know. I won't keep you from your art dealer any longer. Ring me up some time and we'll fix up that dinner."

When the artist had gone, Perrin drew a scribbling-pad towards him and began to make notes. He headed a sheet of paper "Pencils" and under this heading wrote as follows:

1. The kind habitually used by Wedderley, and kept by Durrant at Number Ten and the House. These are grade B, are hexagonal in shape, and painted yellow. No maker's name, but stamped S.O. (Stationery Office).

2. The kind used by Lord Brimstoke at his office in Lombard Street. These are grade H, are round in shape and painted green. Maker's name, The All British Pencil Company, Ltd.

3. The pencil said by Durrant to have been sharpened by the Prime Minister in his room at the House. This is described as being hexagonal in shape and painted red. The Prime Minister is said to have examined it carefully, and to have been satisfied. Since he is said to have refused to use a pencil unless it was of grade B, it may be presumed that this pencil was of that grade.

At this point Perrin laid down his pen and stared thoughtfully at what he had written. The statistics sent to him by Durrant were undoubtedly those brought by Lord Brimstoke. They corresponded with the account given by him to Inspector Philpott, and the heading on the paper was conclusive. They had been underlined by a pencil of grade H. Where had that pencil come from?

According to Durrant's evidence, no pencils of that grade were to be found in the study at Number Ten. On the other hand, the pencils used in Lord Brimstoke's office were of grade H. It seemed certain therefore that Lord Brimstoke must have brought with him the pencil with which he underlined the statistics.

There was nothing improbable in that. But it rendered the origin of pencil Number 3, the one mentioned by Durrant, still more obscure. If Lord Brimstoke had left his pencil behind him, it could not have been this one. And yet, according to Durrant, the Prime Minister had distinctly stated that he had found Number 3 on the table after Lord Brimstoke's departure.

And Durrant had stuck to his statement. He had maintained that it was impossible that the Prime Minister should have picked it up previously, and had it in his pocket for some time. And again, if the origin of the pencil was involved in contradictions, its disappearance was no less puzzling. What could have become of it?

Perrin was not concerned with the pencil itself. But as Inspector Philpott had suggested, the circumstances connected with it pointed to a flaw in Durrant's statement. Logical argument suggested very strongly that the pencil could never have existed. Therefore the Prime Minister could not have been sharpening it when the shock occurred. If he had not been sharpening a pencil at that moment, what had he been doing? And why had Durrant so persistently misrepresented his action?

Perrin's mind went back to his conversation with Mr. Hardcastle on the previous evening. He congratulated himself that he had gone to see the specialist. The views of a medical man of his standing on the possible causes of the Prime Minister's death were worthy of the deepest attention. It was in many ways an attractive theory of his, that Mr. Wedderley might have died as the result of a mental, as opposed to a physical shock. Was it possible to reconstruct the scene in the Prime Minister's room at the House with this theory as a basis?

The attempt might be made. Perrin closed his eyes and every detail of the room came back to him. He imagined Mr. Wedderley sitting in his chair, and Durrant standing beside him. That was the setting of the stage. But what was the cue? What events had produced the shock from which Wedderley had died?

For a long time Perrin's imagination conjured up one impossible picture after another. And then at last a theory which seemed within the bounds of possibility began to take shape. Suppose that Durrant had been stricken suddenly with a fit, or a stroke, or whatever the correct medical term might be?

The picture grew clearer in Perrin's mind. He saw Durrant standing there, and Mr. Wedderley, his thoughts upon his recent interview with Lord Brimstoke, within arm's length of him. Suddenly Durrant utters a queer choking sound, and sways forward. He spreads out his arms across the desk to save himself as he feels himself falling, but his muscles have lost their power. He crashes to the ground, sweeping everything on the desk to the floor with him in his collapse.

Such an unexpected and terrifying event would be enough to startle anybody. Occurring in the sacred calm of the Prime Minister's room the effect it would have produced must have been intensified. Mr. Wedderley's nerves could not have been at their best. For weeks he had borne single-handed the task of keeping the government united, and the anxieties connected with the War Debts Bill had fallen on his shoulders alone.

Mr. Hardcastle had given his authority to the statement that death could be caused, though admittedly rarely, by mental shock alone. Would not the spectacle of his secretary collapsing, apparently lifeless, in such dramatic circumstances be a sufficiently powerful mental shock? Undoubtedly it would.

The more Perrin thought about it, the more clearly he saw how this theory could be reconciled with the facts. Durrant's description of his sensations was quite compatible with a sudden seizure. The "report" heard by the attendant might have been the crash of the heavy inkpot as it fell to the floor. Noises heard through a stout oaken door were notoriously deceptive. The fact that only the objects on the desk were disturbed would be accounted for.

There only remained the damage to the desk, and that confounded pencil.

Even supposing that these inconsistencies could be explained, Perrin was not satisfied with the theory, plausible though it seemed. It led to the conclusion that Mr. Wedderley's death had been accidental, and in spite of the absence of any evidence to the contrary, Perrin felt utterly unable to accept this as a fact. He felt convinced that some mysterious agency had contrived his death and the theory of a seizure on Durrant's part would not fit in with this theory. It was incredible that anyone could have contrived that Durrant should have a seizure at this particular time and place. Nor could Durrant have simulated a seizure and his subsequent unconsciousness.

And yet, if the Prime Minister's death had been due to foul play, it seemed extraordinary, as Inspector Philpott had long ago pointed out, that Durrant should have failed to perceive any evidence of it. Perrin found it difficult to believe him guilty of complicity. Not only on account of his friendship for him, but because he failed to imagine what possible benefit he could derive from it. Now, however, a possible, though a far-fetched motive suggested itself. It had been perfectly plain to Perrin, from Durrant's manner when he mentioned Miss Rushburton, that he was in love with her.

Rushburton, Lord Brimstoke, the syndicate that owned the car in which Solway had been spirited away!

These elusive figures moved in a whirling witch-dance in Perrin's brain. That they were in some way concerned with the tragedy in the Prime Minister's room he felt convinced. But what had Solway's disappearance, and his death from such a strange and unusual disease, got to do with it?

Perrin realized that his thoughts were revolving in a circle, from which they refused to be straightened out. He rose abruptly from his chair and went out to lunch.

He had not returned very long when Durrant was announced. He looked worried and ill at ease, and Perrin could see at a glance that the situation was telling upon him. Was it that he had something on his conscience, or was it merely the knowledge that his statement was regarded with suspicion by the authorities? Perrin motioned him to a chair.

"You look pretty well done up," he said, sympathetically. "Wait a minute and I'll prescribe for you." He went to a cupboard in the corner of the room, and took from it a bottle of brandy. It was not the first time that he had found it useful; more than once his clients had been on the verge of hysteria before they summoned up the courage to come and consult him. He poured out a generous peg and handed it to Durrant. "Drink that up," he said commandingly. "It'll do you good."

Durrant drained the glass, and set it down. "Thanks awfully, Perrin. I was feeling pretty rotten," he said.

"You must take care of yourself, you know, or you'll be having a breakdown," said Perrin. "Have you ever suffered from fainting fits or anything like that?"

Durrant shook his head. "Not I," he replied. "I'm as strong as a horse, as a rule. But that ghastly business has shaken me up pretty badly, and I've just been through a most unpleasant ordeal. That's what I came to tell you about. I've just got back from the inquest."

"I heard that it was to be held this morning," said Perrin. "It must have been pretty beastly. What was the verdict?"

"The coroner adjourned the inquiry for further evidence. The truth was that he wasn't satisfied with what I could tell him. He seemed to think that I must know more about it than I said. I couldn't tell him more than I told you and Inspector Philpott. That's all I know, Perrin, I swear it is."

Perrin nodded. It seemed to him that his client's sincerity was beyond a doubt. And yet he could realize vividly that in the unsympathetic atmosphere of the coroner's court his statement must have sounded very thin.

"There was a whole lot of medical evidence first," continued Durrant. "Very involved and full of technical terms. But the gist of it was that Wedderley died from shock, the cause of which could not be ascertained. Then came the attendant, the Scotland Yard people who were the first on the scene, and finally myself. The coroner cross-questioned me on every detail, but I couldn't tell him more than I knew. I'm not a superstitious chap, but I believe that there was something supernatural in what happened. I feel that if you don't find the answer to this ghastly riddle, I shall go mad."

There was such evident earnestness in his client's manner that Perrin saw it would be worse than useless to discuss the matter any further with him just then. "Look here," he said, "I'm going to call a taxi. You're going straight home in it and you're going to send for your doctor as soon as you get there. He'll give you a sleeping draught, I expect, and you'll feel much better tomorrow. Come along, I'm not going to listen to another word now."

He went down to the entrance and saw Durrant into his taxi. The vehicle had hardly driven off when the familiar form of Inspector Philpott loomed into sight.

"Hullo, Perrin, had a visitor?" he asked with a grin.

"You come upstairs to the office," replied Perrin. "You don't suppose that I'm going to discuss my business on the public pavement, do you?"

"I'll trouble you to tell me where Durrant's bound for," said the inspector with a touch of his official manner.

"He's off home," replied Perrin curtly. "I can give you the address, if you want it."

"Thanks, I've found that out myself." He beckoned to a plain-clothes man, who was apparently deeply interested in the architecture of the houses near by, and said a few words to him in a low voice. "Now I'm ready to come up to your office, Perrin," he continued.

Perrin led the way to his private room, and pointed to the chair which Durrant had just vacated. "Now then, out with it, Philpott," he said. "What's the meaning of all this tomfoolery?"

"You know as well as I do," replied the inspector. "Or if you don't, you will as soon as you read the reports of the inquest. Durrant's evidence was no more satisfactory than the yarn that he told us. Even the coroner wasn't satisfied, and he adjourned for further evidence. The chief and I had a talk about it afterwards and he gave orders that Durrant was to be watched. And the next thing I hear is that he came straight here to see you."

"Once more the Yard regards me as an associate of criminals," said Perrin brightly. "Oh, don't apologize, I don't mind in the least. I wish for some reasons that you'd have me shadowed. It might lead to rather interesting developments. Don't you think you could manage it?"

"Oh, don't talk nonsense!" exclaimed the inspector irritably. "I'm asking you what Durrant came here to talk about?"

"I'm quite serious about having myself shadowed. As for Durrant, he came here to tell me what happened at the inquest. He is as well aware as anybody else that his evidence was not considered satisfactory."

"I'm glad of that," remarked the inspector grimly. "It may induce him to think of something else. Dash it all, man, look at it sensibly. He must have some idea what happened!"

"And since he says he hasn't, you jump to the conclusion that he had a hand in whatever it was himself. That's your affair, not mine. I can only assure you that Durrant has told me nothing fresh. Now let's put Durrant out of our minds for the moment. I want you to do something for me. I won't say that it has any direct bearing upon what happened at the House, but it may be remotely connected with it. I want to find the driver of a car, and ask him a question."

"I don't mind having an inquiry put round for you. What are the particulars?"

"Good man!" exclaimed Perrin. "You're not so harsh and unrelenting as you try to appear, you know. The car is described to me as a roomy one, painted some light colour. The driver is a liveried chauffeur. The car is known to have been standing outside Number Five-hundred Harley Street on Monday, the third. It probably drove down to Oldwick Manor on the night of the seventh. And, lastly, there is a possibility that it occasionally visits Lord Brimstoke's offices in Lombard Street."

"You are a persistent devil!" exclaimed the inspector. "I'd forgotten all about that Solway business. All right, I'll send round word that a look out is to be kept for this car. It seems to me that the only chance of hearing anything of it is if it calls at Brimstoke's place. If anybody sees anything of it, I'll let you know."

"Perhaps you would go one further than that. You might tell the driver that there is a reward waiting for him if he will communicate with me here. Do you think you could manage that?"

"I dare say that it could be done, unofficially, of course. But if I do this for you, it's up to you to tell me what's in your mind."

Perrin hesitated. He knew that the inspector would deride his theory of the existence of a mysterious syndicate. "I can't explain at length," he said. "But it is just possible that the owner of this car knows something that may help us to explain the

Prime Minister's death. It's only the remotest possible chance, but in my opinion it's worth following up."

"It seems to me that your time would be better spent in trying to get out of Durrant what he knows. However, I'll do what you want, always on the understanding that if you learn anything you'll let me know at once."

"That's understood, of course. By the way, one more question while you're here. Has anything more been found out about the murder of Ben Hammerton?"

"Not much. We've got a chap on the job who specializes in these dockland affairs. He's not particularly hopeful of finding out anything. He doesn't believe it was a deliberate murder. Ben doesn't seem to have been carrying anything valuable about with him, and there's no evidence that he had got up against one of the regular gangs."

"I wonder how he accounts for the post-card found in his pocket?" remarked Perrin idly.

"I don't think that worries him much. Ben knew who you were, and he may have written your name himself on one of his own post-cards. There is just one thing fresh. Ben was seen, after he had left the North Star, in company with a man with a broad-brimmed hat and cloak, like some of those fellows wear. This was in Jamaica Road, leading towards the Surrey Docks. The most likely thing is that the two had some stunt on together, that they quarrelled and that Ben got knifed and thrown into the river."

"A very comforting theory, but I'm not sure that I altogether agree with it," replied Perrin. "However, I won't interfere. I'm not going to wander round Jamaica Road looking for fellows in cloaks. Poor old Ben! It's on my conscience that I ever sent him to make that inquiry for me."

"I shouldn't let that keep you awake," said the inspector. "I don't believe for a moment that it had anything to do with his death. Well, I must get on with my job. I can't stop yarning here to you all day. So long! I'll see what can be done about this car of yours."

CHAPTER XV

DESPITE Perrin's habitual optimism, he felt that for once he was up against something beyond his powers. The tragedy at the House of Commons was wrapped in such complete mystery that it seemed impossible it could ever be explained. If the death of the Prime Minister had indeed been contrived, those responsible had acted with such extraordinary skill that it was doubtful if their secret could ever be discovered.

Again, looking at the matter from a detached point of view, the conjecture that these same people were responsible for the events preceding Solway's death seemed almost fantastic. Still, it was in the nature of a forlorn hope. Perrin, rack his brains as he might, could think of no other line of approach. But the only clue to Solway's movements was a vague description which might apply to hundreds of cars, and a purely conjectural hypothesis as to where this car might again be seen.

What had been Solway's intention when he came to London on Monday the third. He and Rushburton had discussed his proposed visits to Lord Brimstoke and Mr. Hardcastle in the presence of Pearson, the butler of Oldwick Manor. But it seemed certain that he had a third appointment of so secret a nature that it had been concealed from everyone. Rushburton himself might or might not have been in the secret.

This appointment was to follow Solway's visit to the specialist. He had arranged for a car to meet him in Harley Street and to take him to the rendezvous. He had deliberately misled Mr. Hardcastle both as to the origin of the car and its destination. This, in itself, was evidence of his anxiety not to give any clue as to his intentions. Further, in spite of his condition, bordering upon collapse, he had insisted upon proceeding to the rendez-vous. Surely, then, it must have been of vital importance.

The door of Perrin's room opened and David Meade looked in. "Hullo!" he said. "Are you free for a few minutes?"

"As free as I am ever likely to be," replied Perrin. "What is it, anything of importance?"

It turned out that Meade's business, though of some urgency, did not occupy much time. When it was disposed of Meade started towards the door, but his partner called him back. "Sit down there," he said. "I must talk to someone, if it's only to get my thoughts into proper shape, and you'll do as well as anybody else. No, I didn't ask you to speak. Just listen."

Meade obeyed and Perrin described to him the circumstances surrounding the case and the theory he had formed of some criminal syndicate. "It's preposterous, of course," he continued. "What's more, it's verging on the impossible, for as far as I can see, nobody can have deliberately murdered Wedderley, unless it's Durrant, and that I'm loath to believe. Besides, even if he is guilty, how did he do it?"

Meade shook his head. "I don't know how he did it," he replied. "But I've just been reading the report of the inquest. There's a special edition of the evening paper just out. And it looks very much to me as though Durrant was hiding something."

"That conclusion is hardly original," snapped Perrin. "I may tell you that Philpott arrived at it a couple of days ago. Sorry, I didn't mean to be offensive, but this business is getting on my nerves. Can't you make any useful suggestion?"

Meade considered the matter deeply for several seconds. "Bar waiting for news of that car, I don't see what you can do," he replied.

"You're not much help," replied Perrin. "Whether that's the case or not, I can't sit here doing nothing. I'm going out.

I shall be in the office at the usual time tomorrow morning if you want me."

Perrin reached the pavement without knowing where he intended to go. Anything was better than sitting indoors brooding over a problem that held no hope of solution. But, as he hesitated, wondering in which direction to turn, an idea struck him. He turned towards Regent Street, crossed that thoroughfare and plunged into the maze which lies to the eastward of it. He came out eventually in Greek Street and mounted the stairs which led to the offices of Marshfield and Son.

Sammy greeted him warmly. "Why, Mr. Perrin, it is good to see you here again," he exclaimed. "You'll have a cigar, of course. Now make yourself comfortable, that's right."

Perrin lighted the proffered cigar. "Well, Sammy, and what did you make of that charming client I sent you the other day?" he asked.

Sammy winked portentously. "Nice girl, eh?" he replied. "My son Victor outside there hasn't thought of anything else since she came here. A regular peach, Mr. Perrin. She's one of Sir Ethelred's assets, no doubt about that."

"I rather gathered that she was a bit of a liability," suggested Perrin.

Sammy waved the implication aside with a sweeping gesture. "No, no, asset, Mr. Perrin," he insisted. "If you had a nice piece of property, now, you wouldn't mind spending a bit of money on it from time to time to keep it looking attractive, would you? Especially if by so doing, you knew you'd find a purchaser at your own price, would you?"

"You're incorrigible, Sammy! And has Rushburton got a purchaser in his mind's eye?"

"Lord Brimstoke's eldest son came of age a few weeks ago," replied Sammy cryptically.

"My hat!" exclaimed Perrin. "Have I been on the wrong tack all this time? Is it a projected marriage and not some sort of financial understanding that accounts for the friendship between Brimstoke and Rushburton?"

"Well, a marriage is a financial arrangement, isn't it?" protested Sammy. "But I think there's more than that in it. There's a rumour going about that his Lordship is forming a syndicate to acquire the rights in some invention or other. The invention, they say, is to be offered to the government, at a price. It would be very useful to his Lordship to have a friend in the Cabinet, wouldn't it? And now that the Prime Minister's dead, it won't be long before Sir Ethelred will be a very influential member of the government."

"Here, wait a bit, Sammy!" exclaimed Perrin. "Let's have a bit more detail. What is this invention?"

Sammy spread out his hands in a gesture of ignorance. "How should I know, Mr. Perrin?" he replied. "His Lordship wouldn't talk about it until everything is settled, would he? I don't suppose he cares what the invention is, so long as he can make money out of it. He's only concerned in buying the rights cheap and selling them dear. But you may depend upon it that if he's interested in it, it's a good thing. From the financial point of view, I mean."

"I see the game," said Perrin thoughtfully. "Look here, Sammy, what political party does Lord Brimstoke belong to?"

"The party that's most likely to serve his own interest," replied Sammy promptly. "Since he seems to have sought Sir Ethelred's friendship, I suppose that at present he belongs to the party that's now in Opposition."

"That's just what I supposed. But lately I've been wondering. You've seen in the papers, of course, that Lord Brimstoke had an interview with Wedderley at Number Ten on Wednesday morning. Now I have it on very good authority that during that interview he assured Wedderley of his approval of the War Debts Bill."

This time Sammy showed signs of genuine astonishment. "He approved of the bill!" he exclaimed. "Are you sure of that, Mr. Perrin?"

"I've long ago given up being sure of anything, even if I've got the evidence of my own senses for it. But that is what I believe."

"Well, that's a most extraordinary thing! It's common talk in the City that the bill, if it becomes law, will hit the banks that have commitments in certain quarters abroad. And it is believed that the London and Provinces is very heavily committed. From all I hear, that is certainly true."

"Wedderley was surprised himself, I hear. I can only suppose that Lord Brimstoke was trying to make a friend in the present government, in case the bill should pass, which it certainly won't now. All that's very interesting, Sammy. But you haven't told me how you got on with Miss Rushburton? You managed to accommodate her, I suppose? That's the word, isn't it?"

"We came to an arrangement which both considered satisfactory," replied Sammy virtuously. "I am very much obliged to you for sending her to me, Mr. Perrin. Such clients are always welcome. She could offer no security, of course. Sir Ethelred is my security."

"You mean that he'll pay you anything you like to ask, rather than risk a scandal? You're a thorough-paced rascal, Sammy."

"Then why did you send Miss Rushburton to me, if you think that?" retorted Mr. Marshfield.

"Because I think we understand one another," replied Perrin. "You did not grant Miss Rushburton's request without making some inquiries, I suppose?"

"I didn't imagine that you sent her to me out of pure affection, Mr. Perrin," said Sammy, with a cunning smile. "I asked her every question I could think of, and I fancy I pumped her fairly dry."

"I hope you were satisfied. Did you learn anything of any particular interest?"

"Not about Sir Ethelred. I'm pretty sure that she neither knows nor cares anything about his affairs. She looks on him merely as a well from which to draw supplies, and a well that isn't deep enough to suit her tastes. She seems to be a very expensive young lady. And from what she told me, she's been borrowing money from her friends. One man in particular, but she didn't tell me his name."

"Not that son of Lord Brimstoke's whom you mentioned just now, eh?"

"No. I hinted at that and she shied off at once. Sir Ethelred is likely to be disappointed there, if he isn't careful. She's mortally afraid of anyone finding out that there's anything between her and this man. I expect that she's afraid that supplies would be cut off altogether if it came out."

"I believe I've an idea who the man is. You're probably right. He's not nearly big enough game for Rushburton. Well, Sammy, you've given me a very good cigar and a very pleasant chat. Keep your eyes and ears open, and I'll come round and see you again soon."

Perrin spent the rest of the afternoon and evening visiting certain discreet public-houses in out-of-the-way parts of London. Here he met many acquaintances of his, most of whom earned a very precarious livelihood by hanging round the public parking places on the chance of picking up a few stray coppers. But none of them could give him any information about the car he sought. Closed cars, painted in various light colours, seemed plentiful enough, but none of them appeared to tally with the car which had carried Solway from Harley Street.

He continued his inquiries throughout the week-end, still without success. By Monday he had come to the conclusion that the car rarely visited London, or that its appearance had been completely changed since Mr. Hardcastle had seen it. His only remaining hope, and that a faint one, was that Inspector Philpott's instructions to the police would produce some result. But his luck had not, apparently, deserted him.

Just before lunch on Monday he was informed by Miss Avery that a chauffeur in livery was asking to see him. "He tells me that his name is Quentin," she said. "And he says that he's come about a reward that you have offered."

"That's right, Miss Avery," replied Perrin, concealing his exultation as best he could. "Bring him in, will you?"

Quentin appeared, smart, well groomed and with the bearing of a well-mannered servant. He stood at attention, waiting for Perrin to address him.

"Sit down, Quentin," said Perrin. "What brings you here?"

"Well, sir, I hardly know. I had just put my car in the parking place in St. James's Square when a ragged-looking chap comes up and says that a gentleman has been making inquiries about me. I asked him who it was, and he said it was Mr. Perrin. He told me where your office was, sir, and asked me to go along and see you. I thought he was getting at me, sir, but he said there was a reward out, and offered to come along with me. So as I had nothing to do for an hour or two I thought I'd come along on the chance."

"I'm very glad you did. There is a reward offered. What does the car you drive look like?"

"She's a twenty-five horse Rambler, sir, painted light grey. As nice and comfortable a car as you could meet."

"Who does the car belong to?"

"Belong to, sir? Why she belongs to me! I've got a little place out Barnet way, and I keep the car for hire work. Five shillings an hour and go anywhere. That's how I do business. There's lots of gentlemen in the neighbourhood that won't have anybody else, sir."

"That shows that you give them good service. Now, Quentin, what I want to know is this: were you in Harley Street some time between twelve and one on Monday the third, just a fortnight ago?"

"Let me see, sir," replied Quentin. "I'm out most days and it's a bit hard to remember any particular journey. Yes, I've got it, sir. That must have been the day that I had a 'phone message to fetch a gentleman from the doctor's house there."

"I expect that is the journey I mean. Do you remember the gentleman's name?"

"I never heard it, sir, but I remember him well enough. He was a little short chap, rather sharp-featured. It was like this, you see, sir. I had a call early that morning asking me if I was free in the middle of the day. As it happened I was, and I said so. Then the gentleman at the telephone said that I was to go to a number in Harley Street. I forget the number, but it was about half-way up on the left-hand side. I was to be there at half-past twelve and pick up a gentleman, whom I was to drive to a house between Ware and Buntingford."

"You don't know where the call came from, I suppose?"

"I can't say that I do, sir. I didn't recognize the voice, but I expected that the gentleman was one of those I had driven before. Well, sir, I went to Harley Street and waited, and I hadn't been there long when the door opened. There was this little gentleman I spoke of, sir, and he looked pretty seedy. There were two others with him; one I took to be a doctor, and the other his butler, or something of that kind. They helped him into the car, and the doctor asked him if he was sure he was all right, or something like that. I didn't hear what the gentleman said, but the doctor went on to tell him that the best thing he could do was to go to bed as soon as he got home. Then they shut the door of the car, and I drove off."

Perrin nodded. There was no doubt that he had run the car to earth. Quentin's story was an almost exact repetition of Mr. Hardcastle's.

"I didn't have to ask which way I had to go, for I knew that already," continued Quentin. "The gentleman was sitting in the back of the car, and I glanced round at him now and then. He sat very still at first, and I didn't altogether like the look of him. However, by the time I got clear of the traffic, he began to pick up a bit. After a while I asked him, respectful-like, if he was feeling a bit better. As soon as he answered, I recognized the voice that I'd heard on the telephone. 'Don't you worry about me, driver,' he said, short-like. 'Just you drive on through Ware, and I'll show you the way to go after that.' I stopped the car and was going to get down to open the gate when the gentleman stopped me. 'You can't get any further,' he said, 'the gate's locked. If you put me down here, I can walk up to the house.' He asked me how much it was, and I said twenty-five shillings. I reckoned the job would take me five hours, door to door. He gave me thirty shillings, a pound note and ten-shilling note, and told me to keep the change for myself. Then he got out of the car, and I noticed that he seemed to be all right, for he walked quite steadily. There were two gates, if you understand me, sir, a big wide one, and a little narrow one at the side for foot passengers. The little one must have been unlocked, for the gentleman opened it and walked up the drive. That's the last I saw of him, sir. I turned the car round and drove home."

"The gentleman didn't ask you to wait for him?" asked Perrin.

"Why no, sir. I didn't expect him to after what I had heard the doctor say. I reckoned that now he'd got home he'd go to bed."

"You haven't heard anything of him since? He hasn't rung up and asked you to drive him anywhere?"

"No, sir. I've never heard of him before or since. The way I looked at it was this. He's probably got a car of his own. He drove up to London in it that morning, and left it somewhere to have something done to it. So he got me to drive him home.

That sort of job often comes my way. I expect one of his friends had told him about me."

"I dare say that you are right, Quentin. What time was it when you got the telephone message?"

"I couldn't say for certain, sir. But I remember I'd just finished my breakfast. It must have been round about eight o'clock."

"Do you know the name of the house you drove him to?"

Quentin shook his head. "I don't, sir," he replied. "I don't remember that I've ever been along that road before. I didn't even catch a glimpse of it, you couldn't see more than a few yards up the drive for the trees. But I could find it again right enough."

"That's just what I was going to ask you. It's this way, Quentin. I'm particularly anxious to meet the gentleman you picked up in Harley Street. I believe that he can give me some information that would be very valuable to me. I'll give you ten pounds, and your charge, if you'll drive me out to that house near Ware."

Quentin grinned. "I'll do it for less than that, and willingly, sir," he replied. "When would it suit you to go, sir? I've just driven a gentleman in from Barnet and I've got to pick him up in Pall Mall at two o'clock, and take him back again. Then I've got a funeral and after that some station work. But I'd put all that off if you wanted to go this afternoon, sir."

"I'm glad to hear that you're so busy. I'm not particularly keen to go this afternoon. I'm more likely to find the gentleman at home in the evening."

"Well, sir, if you like to go this evening that would suit me. I shall be finished by six o'clock, or say half-past at the latest. I could pick you up anywhere in London at eight o'clock, sir."

Perrin thought for a moment. There was just a possibility that he was still being watched, and it would not do for him to be seen entering this particular car. "Very well, then," he said.

"Meet me at the bottom of Lower Regent Street at eight o'clock. And, since you know nothing about me, here's five pounds on account. That's all right, man, shove it in your pocket. Now before you go, there are a couple more questions I should like to ask you. Have you ever driven anybody to the London and Provinces Bank in Lombard Street?"

Quentin frowned, in an effort of memory. "I don't remember that I have, sir," he replied. "I often drive gentlemen from out my way to the City, but I don't remember that particular address."

"Then I suppose that Lord Brimstoke is not one of your customers?" asked Perrin casually.

Quentin looked impressed, but shook his head. "I don't know that I have ever driven a lord, sir," he replied. "Many a time I've sat beside baronets and that, and very nice gentlemen they've been. But never what you might call a real proper lord. Mostly the nobility keeps their own cars, sir."

"Those that can afford it, I expect. I wonder if Sir Ethelred Rushburton is among the baronets you've driven? I expect not, for I know he has a car and chauffeur of his own. But you may have driven to his place in Surrey, Oldwick Manor?"

"No, sir. I've never had that pleasure. I've seen Sir Ethelred's name in the paper often enough, but I've never seen him, nor driven anybody down to his place." After some further conversation, Quentin took himself off, leaving Perrin in such a state of delight that he could cheerfully have danced round the room.

CHAPTER XVI

IT WAS not until he had been out to lunch that Perrin sat down to consider Quentin's story in detail. And it soon became apparent to him that Solway's actions that Monday had been even more mysterious than had at first appeared.

To begin with, the telephone message ordering the car. Quentin had said that he recognized the voice as Solway's as soon as he heard the latter speak. He had received it about eight in the morning. Solway, according to the statements that Perrin had already heard, was then at Oldwick Manor. Quentin had said that Solway was a total stranger to him. So how did Solway know of his existence? Presumably because Quentin had been recommended to him. But not apparently, either by Rushburton or Lord Brimstoke.

Then Solway had deliberately misled Mr. Hardcastle as to his destination. He had told him that he was going home, which the specialist naturally interpreted to mean Oldwick Manor. But if he had wished to conceal his destination why had he driven there openly in a hired car? Surely he could have arranged some more discreet means of transport. Or was it that his journey had to be concealed only from those who knew him personally? Reasoning on these lines, it seemed possible that he had undertaken it unknown to his employer. But in that case would he have risked telephoning for the car from Oldwick Manor?

Another curious thing was that he should have dismissed the car on his arrival. It seemed clearly established that Rushburton expected him back that evening. How did Solway propose to get back to Oldwick Manor?

He expected the person or persons whom he visited to drive him back from London or to the nearest station. Very well then, why had he not arranged to go there in the same way? Perhaps because he wished to arrive unexpectedly.

But the most interesting problem was, what had happened to Solway after he had disappeared up the drive out of Quentin's sight? Incidentally, it was clear that he had been to the house before. He knew the way to it, since he had directed Quentin, and he knew that the gate was locked. He had evidently recovered from his indisposition, but since he had died a few days later, this can only have been a temporary recovery. He must have had a relapse soon after he reached the house, and been incapable of returning unaided.

Perrin reflected that it all dovetailed in with the theory he had already formed. The visit was a secret one, and neither Solway nor the occupants of the house wished it to be known. If it was unknown to Rushburton, they naturally would not communicate with him. Solway would remain for the rest of the day in the hope that he could recover sufficiently to be able to return home. But instead of recovering, he became rapidly worse. A sufferer from sleeping-sickness, Perrin imagined, would be in a state of stupor most of the time, and would therefore be entirely passive. And then by Friday night the occupants of the house decided what to do with him. They would convey him to the pavilion at Oldwick Manor while he was in a somnolent condition. They might or might not have realized that he was at the point of death.

Heartless, no doubt. But then Perrin already suspected that the occupants of the house were not only heartless, but desperate men. He felt sure that behind that locked gate was to be found the headquarters of the mysterious syndicate of which he had already suspected the existence. And before the night was out he hoped to verify that beyond a doubt. He did not conceal from himself that it would be a dangerous undertaking. And for that reason he resolved to carry it out alone.

With reasonable care, he ought to be able to reconnoiter the place without running much risk of detection. It would be practically dark by the time he got there, and the trees of which Quentin had spoken would afford excellent cover. He intended nothing more than a reconnaissance. His idea was merely to collect sufficient evidence to convince Inspector Philpott. It would then rest with the police to take such steps as they thought proper.

But he had found himself in a tight corner too often to neglect precaution. He took an automatic pistol from a drawer in his desk and put it in his pocket. Then he wrote a note, which he addressed to the inspector. This he took into Meade's room. "I'm going on a little expedition of my own this evening," he said. "Not far, only just out beyond Ware. But if I'm not in the office first thing tomorrow morning, and you've no message from me, get hold of Philpott and give him that note. Don't accept any message from me that doesn't contain the word horoscope."

Meade looked at his partner anxiously. "Hadn't I better come with you?" he asked. "It's easy enough to see that you're going to take on something risky. Last time you did that you only escaped with your life by a miracle."

Perrin laughed. "I can't take you," he said. "It's a one-man job. And there's no danger. Besides, once bitten twice shy, you know. I shan't let myself be caught out again. But I may find it convenient to lie low when I get there, and wait for the police to come along. That's what that note's for."

Meade looked dubious. But he knew that if Perrin had set his mind to a thing, it was quite useless to try to dissuade him from it. He merely shrugged his shoulders. "All right," he said. "Philpott and I will organize a search party for you if you don't turn up in the morning. But you might leave me a clue to where you're going."

"I don't know myself," replied Perrin. "Somewhere between Ware and Buntingford, that's all I can tell you. A man who knows where the house is, is going to drive me there. He owns a car, lives out Barnet way, has a telephone and his name is Quentin. He was here this morning."

"Here, let's make a note of that," said Meade, reaching for the telephone directory. "Qua—Que—here we are. This must be the chap. 'Quentin, John, cars for hire.'" He made a note of the address and number. "That's better," he continued. "We shall know where to start now, at all events."

Perrin laughed. "You'll be disappointed, I'm afraid," he said. "It won't come to that." And he went back to his own room.

He dined comfortably in his own flat, and at a quarter to eight started for his rendezvous, taking the route across St. James's Park. This gave him an excellent opportunity of seeing whether he was followed. By the time that he reached the foot of the Duke of York's steps, he was quite satisfied that he was not. Either those who had watched him on a previous occasion were satisfied that he had abandoned the trail, or they believed that he could now do no harm. Encouraged by this reflection, he mounted the steps, and looked round for Quentin.

A light grey car was standing at the corner of Carlton House Terrace, and Perrin walked towards it. As he approached, the driver touched his cap, and he recognized Quentin. "Right on time, sir," said the latter. "I've only been here five minutes, and Big Ben is striking now."

He held the door open and Perrin entered the car. "I'll sit beside you, Quentin, and you can show me the way," he said.

They drove in silence through Central London, and not until he saw the road comparatively clear before them did Perrin speak. "There's one thing I forgot to ask you this morning, Quentin," he said. "Do you remember if the gentleman you picked up in Harley Street had an attaché-case with him?"

"I believe he had, sir, now you come to mention it. Yes, I'm sure he had, I remember it now. The gentleman I took to be a doctor put it into the car when we started. And I handed it out to your gentleman when we got to the end of the journey. I remember thinking that it was very heavy for its size."

Perrin wondered what the attaché-case could have contained. Something more than papers perhaps, to account for its weight. And what had become of it? Had it been left at the mysterious house? Or had it been deposited in the pavilion with Solway? If so, Rushburton must have removed it when he found the body. Was his concern over the non-return of his secretary due to the contents of that attaché-case?

The answers to these questions probably lay hidden at his destination. The car worked its way out of London, then through Enfield, Broxbourne and finally Ware. A couple of miles or so beyond the latter town Quentin slowed down. It was then twenty minutes past nine. The evening was overcast and a light drizzle was falling. The sun could have only just set, but it was darker than usual for the time of year. Perrin was rather pleased than otherwise. It was all in his favour.

"I don't want to miss the turning, sir," remarked Quentin. "I've only been down it once, that time I brought your gentleman. But I think it is a mile or so further on, yet."

They went along quietly for a little, and suddenly Quentin uttered an exclamation of satisfaction. "That's it, sir! I recognize it now, right enough. The gate isn't more than a mile or so further on, now."

They turned to the left, down a road which appeared to be little used, since in places it was grass grown.

In two or three minutes they came to a massive wooden gate and Quentin pulled up. "This is the place, sir," he said triumphantly.

"I'm very much obliged to you, Quentin," replied Perrin. "Here's your other five pounds, and an extra thirty shillings for your fare. That's what the other gentleman gave you, isn't it?"

"I'm sure I'm much obliged to you, sir, and I hope I may have the pleasure of driving you again. But wouldn't you like me to wait for you, sir? How are you going to get back to London?"

"Oh, I shall probably stay here the night," replied Perrin hastily. It would never do for the car to remain at the gate. Anyone seeing it would guess that it had brought a visitor, even if they did not question Quentin. And Perrin was particularly anxious that his visit should be unannounced. "Don't you wait for me, you get back home. And whenever I want a car you may be sure I'll ring you up."

"Thank you kindly, sir. Five shillings an hour and distance no object. That's my motto. Good night, sir."

Perrin stood by the roadside until Quentin had turned the car and driven off in the direction of the main road.

When the car had disappeared round a bend in the road he approached the gates. They were just as Quentin had described them, a wide one for vehicular traffic, and a smaller one at the side for pedestrians. The wider one was secured by a massive chain and padlock, but the other was fastened with an ordinary latch.

Perrin felt in his pockets to assure himself that his automatic pistol and electric torch were ready to his hand. Then he stood still for a minute, listening and taking stock of his surroundings. It was very still, the only sound that came to his ears was the faint swish of the drizzle in the leaves of the trees which stood up all round him. Beyond the gates he could see the first few yards of the drive, winding away towards the hidden house.

He approached the narrower gate, and examined it very carefully. He was taking no risks. If, as he suspected, the occupants of the house relied on their seclusion, it was quite possible that the gate was fitted with an electrical device which rang a bell in the house when it was opened. But he could find no sign of anything of the kind, and he decided to risk opening it, especially as a thick quickset hedge, impossible to climb over or to scramble through, stretched on either side of it. Very cautiously he opened the gate, and was relieved to find that his fears were unfounded. There was no attachment to it of any kind.

Having closed the gate softly behind him, he entered the drive. Here, under the trees, he was in deep shadow, so deep that when he stood still, wearing a grey raincoat, he was practically invisible against the background. The drive was graveled, but on either side of it was a margin of grass. He walked cautiously along this, counting his paces. At the end of three hundred yards or so, the trees suddenly ceased and he saw the outline of a building before him.

Keeping carefully under cover, he reconnoitered the position in front of him. From where he stood, a wide lawn stretched up to the house, perhaps a hundred yards distant. The house seemed to be of medium size, and was a square, rather unlovely structure. But what struck Perrin most was that not a light showed from any of the windows. The house stood up grim and forbidding, like a rock in the midst of a green sea of lawn.

For fully ten minutes Perrin stayed where he was. But not a sound reached his ears, and the house betrayed no sign of life. He began to wonder whether it could have been abandoned by its occupants after Solway's death. But he could not decide this without closer inspection. It was, of course, just possible that the absence of lights was due to everybody having gone to bed, or to the occupied rooms being at the other side of the house.

But how was he to get near enough to make a closer inspection? It would be madness to cross the open stretch of lawn, he would be clearly visible to anybody who might happen to look out of the window. It is never quite dark on a June night in English latitudes, and anything moving across the open could be detected at once.

Perrin began to work through the wood, parallel with the edge of the lawn. To his delight he discovered that the lawn was bounded by a yew hedge, beyond which was a kitchen garden. Very cautiously he left the shelter of the wood, and crept up under cover of the hedge, along the side of which ran a path surfaced with well-rolled ashes. The path was hard, and would leave no tracks of his rubber-soled shoes.

The path ended at an iron gate leading into a courtyard at the back of the house. Once more Perrin peered out cautiously before leaving his place of concealment. From where he stood he could see the back and one side of the house. Still no light, or any sign of human occupation.

He began to feel sure that the house was empty, or at the worst that it had been left in charge of a caretaker who had gone to bed. Dare he try to enter it? That was the question. Everything was silent as the grave, but the least noise on his part might be fatal to his plans. He looked at the iron gate with misgiving. It probably creaked most damnably. And what if there was a dog asleep in one of the outhouses enclosed within the courtyard? On the other hand, if he went no further, he would be as ignorant of the occupants of the house as he was before.

Perrin decided to risk it. The darkness of the night was in his favour. If his presence were detected, he knew that he was fleet enough of foot to escape to the shelter of the trees before he was caught. As for getting into the house, that presented very little difficulty. He knew that there are very few houses into which an active man cannot break if his mind is set upon it.

He laid his hand upon the latch of the gate, raised it, and very cautiously opened the gate a few inches. It moved comparatively silently on its hinges, but even so, the slight grating seemed to fill the courtyard with echoes. He stood motionless as a stone figure, and listened. The grating produced no responsive sound. Had there been a dog about he would certainly have barked by now.

Perrin slipped through the gate, and immediately took cover behind the projecting wall of an outhouse. The courtyard was not very big and was enclosed on three sides.

Immediately in front of him was the back door of the house. He edged his way round the courtyard towards it. Close beside the door was a cellar flap secured by a heavy padlock. He tried this and found it securely locked. Nor was he more fortunate with the back door. This was also locked, and, so far as he could ascertain by leaning his weight upon it, bolted top and bottom.

Well, he hardly expected to find a door open ready for him to walk in. He turned his attention to the windows which, on this side of the house, were probably those of the kitchen premises. But they were distinctly unpromising. Their fastenings might have yielded to his persuasions, but they were guarded outside by massive iron bars, too closely set for him to be able to worm his way between them.

It began to look as though the fortress would baffle his attack. There was clearly nothing to be done at the back of the house. Perrin began to creep round the wall, through the open end of the courtyard, and round the corner to the side of the house. Here, as in the front, was an open stretch of lawn, with a wide flowerbed between it and the house. There were several windows within easy reach of the ground, but to approach them it would be necessary to cross the flower-bed, and Perrin had no intentions of leaving tell-tale footprints behind him if he could help it. However, these windows might come in useful as a last resort. He decided first to explore the front and the remaining side. So convinced was he by now that the house was unoccupied that he was prepared to take risks. He ran lightly across the lawn till he gained the front of the house. Here the windows were higher up and would be awkward to reach. But he crept to the front door and tried it. It was of massive construction and fitted with a Yale lock. Although he leaned his whole weight against it, it did not yield in the slightest. Bolted and barred inside, no doubt.

Only the remaining side was left to explore. Here a gravelled path ran along the wall, and Perrin ventured upon it cautiously. His heart gave a throb of excitement as he saw a french window opening on to the path. He made his way up to the window, and peered in. A heavy curtain was drawn across it, but through the crevices of the curtain he could see that all was dark within. This he decided was where his attempt should be made.

He put his hand out to touch the window and feel whether it was fastened top and bottom, or only in the centre. Beneath the pressure of his hand it yielded with a gentle click, and swung open.

This was amazing. How came it that the rest of the house was securely fastened and this window left unlocked? Oversight, no doubt. Probably, since the house was almost certainly unoccupied, somebody visited it every day to see that all was well. And that somebody must have inadvertently left this window open.

Very gently Perrin pushed the window back and stepped in. The curtain still hung between him and the rest of the room, but he felt for the edge of it and drew it aside. It was, of course, pitch-dark within and he could discern nothing. But it struck him that the slight sound made by the withdrawal of the curtain produced a curiously empty echo. He took out his torch and flashed it round the room. It was wide and lofty, with a parquet floor. But of furniture there was not a vestige. The room was utterly bare and empty.

So the house was not only unoccupied, but unfurnished. Perrin walked into the room, drawing the curtains behind him. He realized that he had been fooled. Suddenly, the explanation of why Solway, having carefully hidden his destination from everybody else, had apparently not troubled to conceal it from Quentin, occurred to him. He had driven up to this empty house, gone up the drive out of sight, and waited for Quentin to drive away. Then he had come down again and proceeded to his true destination. Perhaps another car had met him at the gate.

In spite of his annoyance at having been misled so easily, Perrin could not resist a smile. His first impulse was to abandon the fruitless adventure at once, walk back to Ware, and hope to arrive there in time to catch the last train to London. Failing that, he would try to get a car at some garage. But he reflected that a few minutes more or less could hardly make much difference. He might just as well explore the rest of the house while he was at it.

There was, of course, still the possibility that there might be a caretaker somewhere upstairs. He did not relax his precautions, but switched off his torch and walked silently towards the door of the room. As his eyes became accustomed to the gloom, he found that the darkness was not absolutely complete. The faintest possible glimmer filtered into the house from without. He opened the door, and found himself in a large but empty hall.

He paused to take his bearings. On his right was the front door with a fanlight over it which made the outline of the hall dimly visible. To his left was the foot of the staircase leading to the upper floors. Almost directly in front of him was another door, leading apparently into a second room. This door was ajar and he determined to see what lay beyond it.

He crossed the hall, pushed the door open and walked in. To his astonishment, he felt a soft carpet beneath his feet. This room, then, was probably furnished. He made a cautious step forward. As he did so a blinding light flashed into his eyes, and a harsh voice uttered a sharp command: "Hands up!"

CHAPTER XVII

ALTHOUGH completely taken by surprise, Perrin's presence of mind did not desert him. In an instant his hand dived towards the pocket in which lay his automatic. But before his fingers could grasp the pistol a sharp report rang out and a bullet sang past his left ear, to bury itself with a thud in the wall behind him.

"Now then, no nonsense!" said the same harsh voice. "Up with them! That's better. Now, what have you got to say for yourself?"

The light in front of him ceased to shine directly in Perrin's eyes, and he perceived that it came from a powerful reading-lamp, the shade of which had that instant been lowered. He was able to take stock of his surroundings. He was in a room of much the same size as the first he had entered, but in this case it was completely furnished as a library. Perrin found that he stood facing a massive table set in the centre of the room. Seated in the further side of the table was the man with the harsh voice.

The first thing that caught Perrin's eyes was the wicked-looking automatic, with a faint curl of smoke still issuing from its muzzle, which the man held in his right hand. In fact Perrin could hardly help noticing it, for it pointed unswervingly towards the centre of his forehead. From the pistol his eyes wandered to the man's face. He felt a queer shock as he did so. For an instant he had the impression that he was looking into the face of a sheep-dog. The man was almost incredibly hairy, so much so that his features were hardly visible. His head was covered with a shock of white hair, rough and coarse like a mane.

A flowing white beard hid the lower part of his face, running up on either side in long white whiskers till it met the hair above. To complete the extraordinary effect a pair of bushy white eyebrows almost concealed the eyes which flashed at Perrin from under their shelter.

The table in front of this amazing individual was littered with books, and one heavy-looking tome lay open in front of him. In spite of his unpleasant predicament, Perrin could not help wondering what the man had been reading. And then the man spoke again in the same harsh, impatient tone. "Come on, let's hear your voice. I'm asking you what you've got to say for yourself?"

It occurred to Perrin that he had remarkably little to say for himself. He was fairly caught and he knew it. The next move clearly lay with his captors. However, in spite of that, he felt impelled to say something, and it was with a faint smile that he replied, "I assure you that I did not come here with any intention to steal."

"Confound you!" roared the other. "Don't stand there grinning at me like that. And don't try to move, either. I've got you covered, and I've always been reckoned a crack shot. And let me tell you this. You won't find lying any good here. What the devil did you break in for, if you aren't a burglar? We'll soon see about that."

He nodded towards the shadows behind Perrin's back and for the first time the latter perceived that they were not alone in the room. Two men dressed in black stepped up to him, and took up their position, one on either side of him. "Go through his pockets," said the hairy man curtly.

Perrin stood there helpless, his hands above his head, while the two men ransacked his clothes with clumsy fingers. But his thoughts were busy. Was this indeed the headquarters of the syndicate, and was the hairy man a member of it? If so, his own fate was sealed as soon as he discovered his identity. But unless he were shot out of hand where he stood some opportunity for escape might yet occur.

The first objects the searchers laid their hands upon were his automatic and electric torch, and these they laid upon the table. The hairy man glanced at them grimly. "So you're not a burglar, eh!" he said with bitter irony. "I wonder how you'll explain to the magistrates what these things are for? Come on, you two, don't be all night about it. What else has he got?"

A clasp knife, a cigarette-case, a silver match-box, and finally Perrin's wallet were in turn laid upon the table. The hairy man picked up the wallet, and Perrin's heart stood still as he opened it and glanced at its contents. He drew out a wad of notes, counted them and put them back. Perrin could hardly restrain a gasp of relief as he closed the wallet without examining it further and threw it down. "Put that back in his pocket," he said. "I don't know how far we are justified in taking his money from him. Not that he'll want it again for some little time."

He paused and turned to his captive. "Now, my man," he said menacingly, "we've caught you this time, and we're not going to let you go. I suppose you won't have the nerve to deny that you're the fellow who made his way into this room, just a fortnight ago, in broad daylight and went through my things?"

Perrin was so taken aback by the unexpectedness of this question that he made no reply. "So you won't answer, eh!" continued the hairy man. "Well, you wouldn't be likely to incriminate yourself, I suppose. We shall see what sort of a yarn you'll spin to the police. We've been waiting for you every night for some time, now."

Again he paused and seemed to be considering. "It's rather a nuisance for you that we haven't got a telephone," he continued. "If we had we could have sent you straight off to spend a comfortable night in the cells. As it is you'll have to put up with our hospitality for an hour or two. Take him away and lock him in the coal-cellar. He'll be safe enough there. And then one of you go down to the village and see if you can find the policeman. Tell him he'd better bring a pair of handcuffs with him."

The two men laid hold of Perrin, each grasping one of his arms and spun him round. Perrin made no resistance, nor did he attempt to speak. He was too bewildered as yet to decide upon any course of action. The two men led him out of the room and across the hall, switching on the lights as they went. They took him along a stone-flagged passage, then down a flight of steps, at the bottom of which was a heavy door with a key in the lock. One of them opened the door and they thrust Perrin unceremoniously inside. Then, without a word, they left him. He heard the key turn in the lock and realized that he was a prisoner.

A prisoner, certainly. But who were his captors? Who, above all, was the hairy man who spoke so confidently about the police? Perrin felt as though he were in the middle of some meaningless nightmare. A few minutes before he had fancied himself to be face to face with instant death. Now, he found himself an ignominious prisoner in a coal-cellar. An infinitely preferable position, no doubt. But what on earth was the explanation of it?

The more Perrin racked his brains the less he understood it. The hairy man had made no attempt to ascertain his identity. He apparently assumed that he was the same as some person who had entered the house just a fortnight ago in broad daylight. And then suddenly it occurred to Perrin that it was just a fortnight ago that day that Solway had driven from Harley Street to this house in Quentin's car.

Was it conceivable that Solway was the person referred to? Had the journey which he had kept so secret been for the purpose of exploring the contents of the house? He might have discovered in some way that there would be nobody about on that particular day. But would he have undertaken such an enterprise carrying a heavy attaché-case? Again a light dawned upon Perrin. What if the attaché-case had contained a set of burglar's tools?

The idea of Rushburton's secretary adventuring as a burglar was utterly bizarre. But so, for that matter, was Perrin's own predicament. There was no doubt about his being a criminal in the eyes of the law. He had entered the house without authority and with firearms in his pocket. The hairy man was perfectly justified in handing him over to the police, who would undoubtedly take a very serious view of the offence.

What was to be done about it? The more Perrin considered the matter, the more repugnant it appeared to him. It dawned upon him that he had made a complete and utter fool of himself. He had set out to reconnoitre the lair of a mysterious and sinister syndicate and the outcome had been that he had himself been ensnared by the simplest of tricks. Why hadn't he had the sense to suspect that window, left so invitingly unfastened? And instead of unearthing a syndicate, he found a very self-possessed and incredibly hairy old gentleman, apparently of literary tastes.

It was all very well for him to comfort himself with the thought that as soon as he was taken to the police-station he would persuade whoever was in charge there to ring up Inspector Philpott. But, after all, what could the inspector do? He could vouch for his respectability and explain his motive, certainly. But it was more than doubtful whether he could prevent his appearance in court before the magistrates, and then the cat would be out of the bag with a vengeance. How the papers would revel in the story! "Detective imprisoned in coal-cellar."

"Private investigator charged with burglary!" He would be the laughing-stock of London. And, more serious still, the reputation of Perrins, Investigators, would fall to zero.

For a moment the idea of giving a false name and letting things take their course occurred to him. His fingers were already feeling for his wallet, for the purpose of taking out the cards, and other evidence of identity which it contained, when he remembered the note which he had left with Meade. When he did not turn up at the office in the morning, Meade would get hold of Philpott and they would set out to look for him. Quentin could bring them to the house, where they would learn what had happened. Perrin had a momentary vision of the inspector's face when he heard that his friend had been committed to jail for attempted burglary.

And yet there was another alternative, escape! If he could somehow get away before the local policeman arrived, he could contrive to make his way back to London. Once there he could probably put matters right. Perrin, who had been standing motionless just inside the door of the cellar, began to put his wits to work. He was in pitch-darkness and both his torch and his matches had been taken from him. If he was to explore his prison he must rely upon his sense of touch.

The door he dismissed as hopeless. It was heavy, was fitted with a massive lock and opened inwards. Without a crowbar or something of the kind, it would be folly to attempt to open it. But he had taken careful note of the passage along which he had been led, and he reckoned that he was at the back of the house. If that were so, the cellar in which he was confined was almost certainly the one into which the cellar flap which he had previously noticed opened.

His heart sank as he remembered the padlock which secured it. No chance of breaking that. But it was just possible that the fastenings were rotten and that he might be able to force them. He stretched out his hands and began to make a tour of the walls. The coal crunched beneath his feet as he progressed. At last he stumbled and put out his hands to save himself from falling. They came into contact with a heap of loose coal.

This must be the heap which had remained under the flap when the last load was delivered. Not without difficulty he scrambled up the heap and felt above his head. His fingers came in contact with the wooden doors of the flap. They were just so far above him that he could get his shoulders under them comfortably. Setting his feet as firmly as he could on the shifting coal he bent his head and exerted all his strength. The doors of the flap lifted a trifle and then resisted. He exerted a mighty effort. The flap groaned and rattled, but not an inch further could he move it.

It was not until he was utterly exhausted that Perrin desisted. Then he sat down on the coal heap feeling acutely discouraged. There was no escaping from the prison to which he had been consigned. The hairy gentleman had known that well enough, confound him! There was nothing to be done but to await the arrival of the policeman and the ignominious sequel that must follow.

All at once the sound of stealthy footsteps broke the complete silence. This must be the policeman, thought Perrin. But as he listened he located the footsteps coming, not from the staircase leading to the door, but from the courtyard into which the flap opened. They stopped, and Perrin heard a rattling sound on the flap itself. A key grated in a lock and flap slowly opened, leaving a square patch of faint grey.

The patch was obscured by the outline of a man's head and shoulders. "You there, guv'nor?" came a hoarse whisper.

"Yes, I'm here all right," replied Perrin, in the same tone. "What do you want?"

He was just under the flap, and had already gathered himself together for a spring. If the man was alone, he might manage to bowl him over and make a dash for freedom. But he had no time to act. "Stand clear then, I'm coming down," replied his unknown visitor. And almost before Perrin could move out of the way, a heavy form dropped on the coal beside him.

"Now see here, guvnor, no nonsense," came the same hoarse whisper. "I've got an iron bar here and I wouldn't be afraid to use it. Hear that?" A dull clang ran out as the man struck the wall with the bar.

Perrin retreated until he felt himself to be out of range. "Yes, I hear it," he said calmly. "What's the game? Who are you?"

"I'm one of the chaps what brought you down here just now. The other chap is just gone down to the village to fetch the cop.

He won't be back inside half an hour or so. He's the inside man. I'm the under-gardener. See here now, guv'nor. I watched the Admiral count them notes you've got in your pocket."

So the man with the bar was intent upon robbery with violence, thought Perrin. Well, a scrap in the dark wouldn't come amiss. It might lead to a possibility of escape. "Well, my friend, what about those notes," asked Perrin cheerfully, maneuvering so as to keep the outline of his visitor against the faint glimmer of light that came through the open flap.

"Why this, guv'nor. You hand me over them notes, and you can slip out of this here cellar before the cop comes, twig me?"

Perrin hesitated. This might be a ruse designed to disarm his suspicions. But the thought struck him that if the man intended violence, he would have to account for it when the police came. "What have you brought that bar for?" he asked cautiously.

"Why, to smash the hasp of the flap with, after you're gone. What do you think? You don't suppose that I'm going to let the Admiral know that I let you out, do you? Why, he'd sack me on the spot. Terrible fierce old bloke the Admiral is when he's roused, I tell you. When they finds the hasp broke they'll think you burst it from below, see?"

There was something in the man's voice that gave Perrin confidence. He had a peculiarly cunning way of speaking, and Perrin put him down as a man who would do anything for money as long as it involved no danger to himself. To a man of this stamp the dozen or so pounds he had in his wallet would be an irresistible temptation.

"All right, you shall have the money," said Perrin. He felt for his wallet, took out the notes and held them out. "Here you are."

The man's hand fumbled for his and their fingers met. The notes changed hands and Perrin could hear the rustle of them as the man counted them. "Pity you hadn't got a few more, guv'nor," he said avariciously. "Now, the best thing you can do is to hop it as quick as you can. The Admiral's still in the library waiting for the cop. He won't move till he comes and there's nobody else about. You keep to the hedge beside the kitchen garden and go down through the wood to the gate. Then you'd best cross the road, and get to Ware over the fields. What you do then is your business, but I wouldn't hang about around here, if I was you."

"I certainly shan't," replied Perrin. "Once I'm out of here I'll get away all right, don't you worry. What's the time?"

"Just gone half-past eleven. See here, it'll be dark for a bit yet, and they've taken your matches and torch. Better take this."

Again their fingers met, and Perrin felt a metal box pushed into his hand. "There's matches in there," continued the man. "Mind you don't lose them. The spring of the box is broken and there's a rubber band round it. If that comes off, the lid'll come open, and you'll drop the matches. And don't you get striking any of them till you're well clear of here. The Admiral will have every soul in the place after you when he finds you're gone."

Perrin put the matches in his pocket and, assisted by his unexpected rescuer, clambered up the coal and hoisted himself out of the opening. Once he felt the stones of the courtyard beneath his feet he lost no further time. He took to his heels, and, guiding himself by instinct more than anything else, ran silently down the yew hedge until he gained the shelter of the trees.

There he perforce slackened his pace. Out in the open there was a certain amount of light, but under the trees it was almost as dark as it had been in the cellar. The drizzle had ceased, but the sky was still thickly overcast. It seemed to Perrin almost incredible that it was not yet midnight. It seemed an age since he had parted from Quentin at the gate.

No doubt his rescuer's advice to get away from the neighbourhood as soon as possible was sound. Perrin smiled to himself as he pictured the search that would ensue when his escape was discovered. The Admiral would head it, armed with his automatic, no doubt. Bloodthirsty old boy! Perrin wondered who he was, and what possible object Solway could have had for paying him that mysterious visit.

All this time he was moving swiftly among the trees. He gained the gate, and glided like a shadow across the road into the wood beyond. It was all very well to say keep on over the fields to Ware. There was not a star to be seen and Perrin knew that he would have to depend upon his own sense of direction. He plunged on through the wood, making slow progress thanks to the undergrowth which wound itself about his legs. Better this than venturing upon the open road, though.

He had plenty of time to realize the problem before him. He could guess pretty well what would happen. The Admiral would insist upon an immediate hue and cry. Perrin felt that if it came to a hunt he could easily outwit any of the followers who were likely to join in it, especially in the dark. His real source of danger would be the local policeman. If he had his wits about him, he would go to the nearest telephone and warn all the police in the district. Perrin realized that unless he managed to get to Ware before the alarm was circulated, he would almost certainly be arrested when he arrived there.

Even if he succeeded in this, what was he going to do? It was unlikely that there would be any train back to London that time of night. His original idea had been to find a garage and hire a car. But now that he had parted with the notes in his wallet he realized that he had only a few shillings about him. And it suddenly struck him that nobody was in the least likely to take him on trust. By this time his appearance must be worse than disreputable. His exploration of the cellar must have covered him all over with coal dust. And he was painfully aware that not only his clothes but his face and hands also were torn by the brambles through which he had forced his way.

It was a ridiculous situation, and the more Perrin considered it the more annoyed he became. He must get back to London before he was arrested. But how? He dare not show himself in his present condition for fear of arousing suspicion. It began to appear that he was very little better off than he had been in the coal-cellar. Perhaps, after all, if he had had a chance of explaining matters to the hirsute and fiery Admiral, he might have persuaded him to see reason.

The wood came to an end at last, and a stretch of open country spread before him. He made rapid progress across this, walking quickly in what he assumed to be the correct direction. Then he came to a second wood. He dare not waste time trying to find a way round it. So he plunged in over a barbed-wire fence, which tore a great rent in his raincoat, and found himself once more in almost complete darkness.

Here once more it was very difficult going. More than once he stumbled over unseen obstacles. And then when he had penetrated some considerable distance into the wood his foot caught in what appeared to be a fallen branch. He made a desperate effort to save himself, but he could not recover his balance. He fell heavily to the ground, almost knocking the breath out of his body.

Painfully he picked himself up and felt in his pockets. The wallet was still there, but the metal box, so thoughtfully provided by his rescuer, was gone.

He could not afford to lose this, he might be in desperate need of a match before dawn. He went down on his hands and knees, and felt about all round the place where he had fallen. The box was nowhere to be found, but just as he was about to abandon the search in despair, his fingers came in contact with something that felt like a match.

Yes, it was a match, without a doubt. With supreme care, and after one or two attempts, Perrin managed to strike it on the seat of his trousers. By the light of its flickering flame he resumed his search for the box. He saw it at once, almost out of his reach under a fallen trunk. The rubber band securing the lid had come off in the fall, and box was open. The match he had picked up had evidently fallen out of it.

Perrin stretched out his hand, still holding the match, towards the box, hoping that the light might reveal some of its scattered contents. As he did so the flame came in contact with the metal. But before he had time to draw it away something struck Perrin a violent blow, seeming to lift him clean off the ground and fling him back upon it with shattering force.

He lay there, prostrate and senseless, his arm still outstretched beneath the fallen trunk.

CHAPTER XVIII

ON TUESDAY morning David Meade went to the office earlier than usual. He had not been deceived by Perrin's assurance that the enterprise he was about to undertake was utterly devoid of danger. He knew his partner too well for that. If it had been merely a matter of ordinary investigation, he would have allowed Meade to go with him.

As the minutes passed, and no message came from Perrin, nor did he put in an appearance, Meade felt that his worst fears were realized. He rang up Perrin's flat, to learn that he had not been seen there since the previous evening. Then, unable to control his impatience any longer, he rang up Scotland Yard.

He was put through to Inspector Philpott, and in a few hurried sentences explained the situation. "Perrin's left a note for you here," he concluded. "If you can manage to come round, I'll send for Perrin's car, and it'll be ready for us if we have to go anywhere."

"It seems to me that it isn't the first time that I've had to go chasing round after Perrin," grumbled the inspector. "All right, I'll come round."

He was as good as his word. Not many minutes passed before he reached Hanover Square. Snatching up the note he tore it open, and read it with an expression of growing interest, then he tossed it across to Meade. "What do you make of that?" he asked.

Meade in his turn read the note.

DEAR PHILPOTT,—

I believe that I am on the track of certain people who know something about the death of the Prime Minister. I cannot be more explicit than that, for I have no facts at present, and I may be on the wrong track altogether. I am going tonight to reconnoitre a house, of which all I know is that it lies somewhere to the left off the road between Ware and Buntingford.

I know this, because I have traced the car which I asked you to make inquiries about. It belongs to a man called Quentin, who lives in or near Barnet, and drives this car for hire. He took Solway to the house on the third and he is going to take me there this evening.

I shall, of course, take every precaution not to be seen and recognized. But if I don't turn up on Tuesday morning it will probably mean that something pretty serious has happened to me. In that case, Meade has instructions to give you this note. What steps you may take must be a matter for you to decide.

Yours,

CHRISTOPHER PERRIN.

Meade became deadly pale as he read the note. "Something pretty serious!" he exclaimed. "He swore to me that he wasn't going to do anything rash. I don't know what you mean to do, inspector, but I'm going off after him."

"You'll probably get knocked on the head if you do," said the inspector calmly. "And, since I can't stand by and see a man set out deliberately to commit suicide, I suppose I'd better come with you."

"Good man!" exclaimed Meade fervently. "I've got the car waiting outside. And I've got this chap Quentin's address. I looked him up in the telephone book yesterday. We'd better get hold of him and make him take us to the house."

The inspector nodded, and they set out at once. During the journey they exchanged notes of what they knew of Perrin's intentions. "As far as I can make out, the line Perrin was following was this," said the inspector at last. "He believed that the people whom Solway went to see after he left the specialist chap in Harley Street are the people behind the death of Wedderley. He already believed that the murder of Ben Hammerton was a warning to himself. If he's right, and he's let himself be caught by these folk, it's a pretty poor lookout, from what I can see of it."

It was in this gloomy state of mind that they reached the address which Meade had taken from the telephone book. They saw a fair-sized garage, with a house attached. A couple of men were working in the garage, and the inspector went in and addressed the first he came to. "Is Mr. Quentin about?" he asked.

The man raised his head from the gear-box which he was inspecting. He was big and burly, with a red face.

"That's me, sir," he replied readily, wiping his hands on a rag. "Is there anything I can do for you?"

"I want some information from you, Mr. Quentin. I'm Inspector Philpott from Scotland Yard, and a friend of Mr. Perrin. And I want to know exactly where it was that you took him yesterday evening?"

A look of blank astonishment spread over the man's face. "I haven't the least idea what you're talking about, inspector," he replied. "Here, come along into the office, and we'll try to get this right."

He led the way into the house, and Inspector Philpott beckoned to Meade to join them. "This is Mr. Meade, Mr. Perrin's partner, Mr. Quentin," said Philpott.

Meade and Quentin stared at one another. Meade was the first to speak. "There's some mistake!" he said. "This isn't the Mr. Quentin that come to the office yesterday. I saw him as he left Perrin's room."

"I'm afraid you gentlemen have come to the wrong place," replied Quentin. "I don't know anybody of the name of Perrin."

The inspector frowned. "I don't get the hang of this," he said. "You've got a car for hire, haven't you, Mr. Quentin?"

"That's so," replied Quentin. "I've got two for that matter. A limousine and an open four-seater. To say nothing of a small char-à-banc."

"What colour is the limousine?"

"Dark blue, a Daimler. You may have noticed her in the garage just now. The open car is black. She's out just now with my son driving her. He'll be back any moment."

"You're quite sure you haven't got a biggish saloon painted light colour, and driven by a chap in livery?"

"Quite sure. I haven't got a saloon at all, though I'm thinking of getting one. And as for a chap in livery, there are only three of us here altogether. Myself and my son, who's a lad of twenty, and the mechanic you saw in the garage just now. My son Bob and I do all the driving. There's Bob coming in now."

Through the window they could see a fresh-faced youth in the driving-seat of a rather aged open car of American aspect. The inspector glanced at Meade, who shook his head. This was certainly not the man he had seen at the office the day before.

"I don't understand this at all," said the inspector. "I have it on very good authority that somebody who gave his name as Quentin, and said he lived near Barnet and had a car for hire, called at Mr. Perrin's office in Hanover Square yesterday morning. The same man had driven a gentleman from Harley Street to a house somewhere between Ware and Buntingford on the third of this month. Yesterday evening he picked up Mr. Perrin somewhere in London and drove him to the same house."

"Well, it wasn't me," replied Mr. Quentin. "I haven't picked up anybody in London this year, that I can remember. My work's mostly round about here, except when there's a football match, and then I take the charry. And neither Bob nor I were out all day yesterday, as it happens. We were busy in the garage."

"Is there anybody else about here with the same name who has a car for hire?" asked the inspector.

Mr. Quentin shook his head. "I've had this place for the last ten years and more, and I've never heard of one. It's not a common name about here. I don't believe there's another anywhere round."

The inspector felt satisfied that he was speaking the truth, especially since he had nothing to gain by denying his knowledge of Perrin. He and Meade left the place, and returned to their car. Meade looked very anxious. "What do you make of it?" he asked.

"I don't like it," replied the inspector. "The man who called at your place yesterday gave Quentin's name in case inquiries should be made. He had to give the name of some garage, in case anybody looked it up, as you did yourself. Actually, I suppose, he was in league with the fellows Perrin was after, if he wasn't actually one of them himself. I wish I knew where to lay hands on him."

"I'm not interested in him for the moment," said Meade impatiently. "We've got to find Perrin, that's all that matters.

And I don't know how the devil we're going to set about it. This fellow may have taken Perrin off anywhere. How do we know that the house was actually between Ware and Buntingford? It's probably in the opposite direction."

The inspector shook his head. "I think not," he replied. "If the false Quentin told Perrin the direction of the house, he must have driven him out that way. If he'd gone in any other direction, Perrin would have become suspicious at once. I think that the best thing we can do is to drive to Ware, and have a word with the police there."

Since this seemed to be the only reasonable course, Meade agreed. They drove to the police station at Ware, where they introduced themselves to a sergeant, who was much impressed by his visitor from Scotland Yard. Philpott told him as much as he thought fit of the contents of Perrin's note. "Now, sergeant," he continued, "we've tried to trace this man who calls himself Quentin, and failed. Perrin had reason to believe that the people who lived in this house were suspicious characters. Can you give us any hint as to where the house could be?"

The sergeant looked doubtful. "I'm afraid I can't, sir," he replied. "It's a bit vague, somewhere to the left off the road between Ware and Buntingford. There are a lot of gentlemen's houses that might apply to. But they're all respectable people, as far as I ever heard. It's what you'd call a very quiet neighbourhood, sir."

"You've heard no report of anything out of the ordinary having happened last night?"

"No, I've not, sir," replied the sergeant.

Then Meade had an inspiration. "Do you happen to know if Sir Ethelred Rushburton owns any property in this direction?" he asked.

"Not to my knowledge, sir, and I've been about these parts for a good many years."

"Or perhaps Lord Brimstoke?" persisted Meade.

"Lord Brimstoke, sir? Yes, he did buy a house some years back. Leighton Grange, it's called. A nice place, sir, and they say he bought it cheap. But he's never lived in it. It's let to another gentleman who's been there a couple of years or more."

"What is the gentleman's name?" asked the inspector quickly.

"I couldn't say, sir. It's a bit outside my district. But I believe that he's a professional gentleman of some kind who is in business in London and isn't often at Leighton Grange except at the weekends."

"Where is the house?" asked Meade eagerly.

"I could show you on this map, sir. You drive on towards Buntingford, and there's a narrow lane turns off just here. You go down that lane about a mile or so, until you come to a drive gate, and that's Leighton Grange. But that can't be the place you mean, sir."

It was quite clear that the sergeant could not contemplate a titled gentleman like Lord Brimstoke letting a house to anybody in the slightest degree suspicious. But the inspector had caught Meade's eye. "No, I don't suppose it is, sergeant. But I think that we will start our explorations there. How does one recognize this lane when one comes to it?"

"There's a clump of trees just before you come to it, sir, but then there are several clumps along that road and if you don't know it, you might pick on the wrong one. I tell you what it is, sir. I'll send a man with you to show you the way, if you like."

"That's very good of you, sergeant. Just as well to have a guide, in case we lose our way. We'll go out to the car, and wait there till the chap's ready."

"Just as well to take a local man with us," remarked the inspector, as soon as they were outside the police-station. "We haven't any idea of what we may be up against. It's only a chance, trying this place Leighton Grange, anyhow. We don't know that it's the place Perrin meant."

"I'm pretty certain it must be," replied Meade. "For one thing, the sergeant pointed it out to me on the map, and it complies with Perrin's description of its position. I'm not denying that that applies to dozens of other houses as well. And, for another, it's a queer coincidence that it belongs to Lord Brimstoke. Perrin's convinced that he's got a hand in this business."

"Hope we shan't meet his Lordship," grumbled the inspector. "I didn't enjoy my last interview with him."

"According to the sergeant, there's not much likelihood of his being there. What are we going to do when we get to Leighton Grange?"

The inspector shrugged his shoulders. "Use our wits, I suppose. We can't insist on searching the place; I should want more evidence than we've got, even to apply for a warrant. Better leave it to me. We'll see who we find there, and act accordingly. Hullo, here's our man, I think."

A constable appeared from the police station, and reported to the inspector. "Constable Gurley, sir."

"Right, Gurley, jump into the car, and show us the way to Leighton Grange."

Under Gurley's guidance they arrived at the gates to which the false Quentin had driven Perrin the previous evening.

"We won't drive up to the house," the inspector decided. "You stay here with the car, Gurley. Come on, Mr. Meade, let's go and pay our call."

They walked up the drive until they came in sight of the house. Seen by daylight, there was nothing particularly striking about it. They went up to the front door, without seeing anybody about, and rang the bell.

It was answered by a trim maid, who looked at them inquiringly. "Can I see the occupier of this house?" asked the inspector.

She looked at the pair of them doubtfully and evidently arrived at the conclusion that they were canvassers or something of the kind. Rather grudgingly she admitted them to the hall. "If you'll wait here for a minute, I'll go and see," she replied, ungraciously.

The inspector glanced rapidly about him. "Bare-looking place," he whispered. "Doesn't look furnished to me."

Before Meade could reply, the maid reappeared. "Will you come this way, please?" she said. She led the way upstairs and into a room, half drawing-room and half boudoir. An elderly woman, with grey hair and a pleasant expression, rose to greet them.

The inspector produced a card and handed it to her. "I am Inspector Philpott, of Scotland Yard, and this is Mr. Meade, a friend of mine," he said politely. "We have called to ask if you can give us any information about a matter we are investigating."

"Sit down, inspector, and you too, Mr. Meade," she replied hospitably. "I shall be pleased to give you any information I can. My name is Mrs. Clarke."

"Thank you, Mrs. Clarke. In the first place, may I ask if you are the tenant of this house?"

"No I am not," she replied. "Mr. Hardcastle, who is a specialist in Harley Street, is the tenant. I am his housekeeper."

Both Meade and the inspector stared at her in amazement. The true Quentin's denial that he had ever seen Perrin was startling enough. That Perrin should have been driven to Mr. Hardcastle's house was sheerly incomprehensible. "Do you mean that Mr. Hardcastle lives here?" asked the inspector at last.

"It would hardly be correct to say that he lives here," replied Mrs. Clarke. "The house in Harley Street where he has his consulting-room is his, and he lives there during the week. But he comes here nearly every week-end. I expect him on Friday evening, for instance."

"Was Mr. Hardcastle here last night?"

"No, he hasn't been here this month. As a matter of fact, there was nobody here last night. The house was empty, and had been for three weeks. The servants and I were having our holidays, and we only came back this morning. The place has been shut up all that time. That's why you find it rather untidy, I am afraid."

"The house has been unoccupied for three weeks!" exclaimed the inspector. "That is very curious, Mrs. Clarke. We have information that at least two visitors have called here during that time. One on the third, and the second yesterday evening."

"Then they can have found nobody at home," she replied decisively. "I arrived here this morning, before the servants, and unlocked the house. I found it exactly as I left it. Besides, if Mr. Hardcastle had been here while I was away he would have told me. I saw him at Harley Street yesterday afternoon."

"This is really most extraordinary, Mrs. Clarke. We have every reason to believe that a Mr. Perrin, who knows Mr. Hardcastle personally, came to this house yesterday evening. We have most urgent business with him, and since he had not returned to London this morning we came here to look for him."

"Well, I assure you he isn't here," replied Mrs. Clarke with a trace of asperity. "As I tell you, the house was all locked up when I got here. But if you care to look for yourself, I have not the slightest objection."

"I am afraid you'll think it very impertinent of me, but I should like to accept your offer. You see, it's just possible that Mr. Perrin got in somehow and is lying hidden somewhere."

"If you think that is possible, I should be very glad if you make a search, inspector," she replied hastily. "I don't at all like the idea of a strange man being hidden in the house. If you will come with me, I will show you all the rooms."

They began on the ground floor. The first door which Mrs. Clarke opened was that of the empty room with the french window. "This is really the drawing-room," she explained.

"But Mr. Hardcastle never furnished it. When Lord Brimstoke first showed him the house, he said the room was too big and comfortless for him to use. As you will see when we go upstairs three or four larger bedrooms are not furnished either. It's really a bigger house than Mr. Hardcastle wanted, but Lord Brimstoke was very keen on his taking it, and he agreed to do so, as except for its size he was very much taken with it."

"Lord Brimstoke is a friend of Mr. Hardcastle's, I suppose?" remarked the inspector.

"Well, hardly a friend. They only meet professionally. You see, Lord Brimstoke is one of Doctor Hardcastle's oldest patients. Nobody could hide in here, as you see. Now, this is the room that Mr. Hardcastle uses most when he is here."

She opened the door of the library and they walked in. Everything was in perfect order, with books neatly arranged upon the shelves. The inspector noticed that they were almost without exception medical and scientific works in many languages. But of Perrin there was no trace.

It was the same in every other room of the house, each of which the inspector entered. Even the coal-cellar was inspected without result. Only one room remained unentered and that was at the top of the house. "This is Mr. Hardcastle's laboratory," she explained. "He keeps the key himself and does not like anybody else to go into it."

The inspector nodded, but he was not satisfied. To search the house and leave one room unexamined seemed to him the height of folly. But it was not until they had gone outside to inspect the outhouses and his eyes fell upon a long ladder hung up against a wall that he returned to the matter. "Do you think, if we put that ladder up against the house, we could see into the laboratory?" he asked.

"I really don't know, but I see no harm in your trying," replied Mrs. Clarke. The inspector and Meade between them carried the ladder to the side of the house, and raised it beside the window which Mrs. Clarke pointed out. The inspector mounted it with agility. He found that by standing on the upper rungs he could see the whole room through the window. It was undoubtedly a laboratory, fitted with instruments of all kinds. The inspector glanced at them, wondering what purposes they could serve. Then having satisfied himself that Perrin could not possibly be concealed there, he descended the ladder.

"Well, inspector, I think you've seen pretty well everything now," said Mrs. Clarke, as he reached the ground.

"I think we have and I'm very much obliged to you," replied Philpott. "There's certainly nobody hidden about the place. We needn't trespass on your kindness any longer."

They took their leave of Mrs. Clarke and walked slowly down the drive. "We're off the track, Meade," said the inspector gloomily. "This can't have been the house that Perrin came into. And yet it's a most extraordinary coincidence that it should belong to Lord Brimstoke and be rented by this specialist chap, Hardcastle. Did Perrin know that, I wonder? Confound it, I wish he'd been more explicit in that note."

"I wish he had," agreed Meade. "I can't see any sense anywhere. It's that car I can't understand. Of course, it's pretty clear now that Solway didn't really drive out here. He wouldn't have gone from Harley Street to Hardcastle's country house, especially since it was empty. There wouldn't be any point in it. All I can suppose is that Perrin was driven out here last night on a wild-goose chase, but what's become of him, that's the point. There's no doubt that the house really was empty last night."

"I shouldn't think so," replied the inspector. "Mrs. Clarke seemed to be a perfectly honest and respectable person. In any case, she wouldn't tell a yarn like that if it wasn't true. It would be too easy for us to disprove it by making inquiries, which I propose to do, if necessary. Now, the only thing to do is to consult Gurley, who evidently knows the district and find out what other houses agree with Perrin's description."

Chapter XIX

As THEY reached the gates, a remarkable spectacle confronted them. Constable Gurley had leaped from the car, and was coursing down the road after an incredibly tattered and grimy figure. The quarry was obviously very near the end of his tether. He swayed from side to side as he shambled on, and stumbled at every other step. At last he fell headlong, and the policeman bent down to inspect him.

The inspector and Meade hurried to the spot. "What's up, Gurley?" shouted the former.

"I don't know, sir," replied Gurley, breathing heavily. "I was standing by the car waiting, when this chap crept out of the hedge and began to walk towards the car. He didn't see me at first, but when he did, he turned and took to his heels. I guessed he was up to no good, sir, so I went off after him."

The tattered figure lay face downwards on the road, making no attempt to rise. As the inspector and Meade approached, they saw that a handkerchief soaked in blood was wrapped about his right hand. Suddenly Meade uttered an exclamation, and started to run. He reached the prostrate man, and knelt down beside him. "Why, good Lord! it's Perrin!" he exclaimed.

The prostrate figure turned over and opened his eyes. The first thing he saw was the uniformed policeman. "Well, you've got me all right," he said feebly, with a faint smile. "I don't know how you're going to get me to the police station, for I can't walk. I'm pretty well all in by now."

Meade imagined that his partner was delirious. "It's all right, Perrin," he said soothingly. "We've got your own car here, and we're going to drive you home." He bent down, and tenderly raised Perrin to his feet.

"Hullo, David, so you've got here, have you?" said Perrin, in a dazed way. "And you too, Philpott? You're real pals, you are. But I'm afraid we can't go home just yet. Ask the constable here."

Meade and the inspector glanced at one another. "It's all right, old chap," he said. "You stay here, and I'll bring the car along. Then we'll have you back home in bed, in no time."

"That's right, sir," said Gurley encouragingly. "Just you lean on me till we get you into the car."

"But what about the Admiral?" replied Perrin. "He'll raise Cain if you let me go off like this."

A look of complete bewilderment spread over Gurley's honest face. "The Admiral, sir?" he asked. "What Admiral?"

"Why, the hairy old boy who locked me up in his coal-cellar. You're the local man he sent for, I suppose?"

Gurley was about to reply, but the inspector restrained him with a look. Naturally, he could not make head or tail of what Perrin was talking about. He could only suppose that he had been through some extraordinary adventure, which had temporarily unhinged his mind.

By this time Meade had brought the car up, and they hoisted Perrin into it. He settled himself in the back, where he relapsed into a sort of stupor. They drove back to Ware, where they dropped Gurley, and then went straight on to Perrin's flat in Victoria Street. Perrin was conscious by that time, and apparently disposed to talk. But they would not listen to him. He was put to bed and his own doctor sent for.

Meade and the inspector waited for the doctor's report. It proved to be more reassuring than they had dared hope. "There's nothing very serious the matter with him," said the doctor. "I can't get much out of him. He says that he had a severe blow, which knocked him out. There are no signs of a bruise anywhere about him, but he's undoubtedly had a severe shock of some kind. And his right hand is pretty badly cut about, but I don't think there'll be any permanent injury. He's very restless and anxious to see you two, but he'll have to rest for a few hours first. I've given him an injection that'll keep him quiet for the rest of the afternoon. But you'd better come round and see him about six o'clock. He'll worry himself to death if you don't."

"This business gets queerer and queerer as we go along," said the inspector when the doctor had gone. "I'm anxious to hear more about this Admiral and his coal-cellar, that is, if Perrin wasn't dreaming just now. I'll meet you here at six, then."

By six o'clock, when Meade and the inspector reached the flat, Perrin had practically recovered. They found him up and dressed, and impatiently awaiting them. Brushing aside their inquiries, he plunged straight away into an account of his adventures, from the time he met the so-called Quentin at the head of the Duke of York's steps, until his fall in the wood and its sequel.

"Something knocked me clean out," he continued. "When I came round, it was well on in the morning, as I could tell by the sun. My hand was badly cut about, and I had lost a lot of blood. I felt pretty rotten, and so weak and shaky that I could hardly drag myself along.

"I didn't know what the deuce to do. I was certain that if I showed myself I should be arrested, for by that time the police would be looking out for me. I found I had only a hazy idea of the way I'd come from the Admiral's place. I began wandering about, keeping under cover as much as possible, trying to find out where I was. And then, after a goodish bit, I saw a road with a car standing in it. When I got closer, I saw it was my own car, and guessed that you two had come out to search for me. Quentin, of course, had put you on the track. There was no sign of you, but I thought you couldn't be far off. And then, all at once, I saw that policeman of yours, and I started to make a bolt for it. I was afraid he'd carry me off before I had a chance to have a word with you."

The inspector shook his head in a puzzled way. Perrin's story sounded like pure fiction. "What was the name of the house where you had all these adventures?" he asked.

"Lord knows. I didn't stop to ask. It was a square barrack of a place, with lawns in front and one side of it, and a kitchen garden with a yew hedge on the other. A drive with wooden gates at the end runs up to it through a small wood. As I tell you, I went in through an empty room, across a hall, and into a library. I wasn't given an opportunity of seeing the rest of the premises, except the coal-cellar."

"Look here, Perrin," said the inspector, gravely. "You've had a severe shock, the doctor says. Are you absolutely certain that you didn't dream all this about the Admiral and the coal-cellar?"

"I've been delirious more than once in my time," replied Perrin with equal gravity. "On those occasions, I've had some pretty bad dreams. But never in the worst of them have I imagined anybody so appallingly hairy as the Admiral. No, everything I've told you happened right enough, I can assure you."

"Well, I can only say that Meade and I spent a couple of hours in that house this morning, and saw no trace of this Admiral of yours, or of any other man, for that matter." The inspector went on to describe the events of the morning, to which Perrin listened with the deepest attention.

"So my Quentin wasn't the real Quentin," he said thoughtfully when the inspector had finished speaking. "That's where I came unstuck at the very beginning, of course. Then you say that the house belongs to Lord Brimstoke? 'Pon my word, I'm beginning to see daylight, I do believe. And this Mrs. Clarke told you that the house had been unoccupied for three weeks until this morning?"

"She did," replied Inspector Philpott. "What's more, I rang up the police at Ware this afternoon and got them to make inquiries. Her story's true, right enough."

"Well, then, let's try to put two and two together. Brimstoke owns the house, and therefore knows his way about it. Hardcastle, who took it, mark you, owing to Brimstoke's persuasion, sends his housekeeper and servants away on holiday for three weeks, and shuts up the house. Brimstoke is one of his patients, and he mentions this to him in the course of conversation.

"Right. Now Brimstoke is up to some dirty work or other, and wants a secluded spot in which to meet his associates. It strikes him that Leighton Grange will suit him admirably. I expect he's got a duplicate key of it, unknown to Hardcastle. He appoints a rendezvous there with Solway, probably as Rushburton's representative. He sends the false Quentin, who is one of his creatures, no doubt, to drive him there. What he did with Solway when he found he was a dying man, I don't know. Put him in that confounded coal-cellar, perhaps. Any objection so far?"

Meade and the inspector shook their heads, and Perrin continued. "Like a fool, I went to Brimstoke's office on the Monday after Solway's death, and made inquiries about him. From that moment I was watched. Whoever was on my trail saw me talking to poor Ben Hammerton, followed him, and saw him questioning Rushburton's chauffeur. Ben, as he went home that evening, was knifed, and the post-card put in his pocket, as a gentle warning to me to keep out of mischief.

"But I didn't. I began making inquiries about the false Quentin and his car. Very well, says Brimstoke to himself, if the idiot wants trouble, he shall have it. The false Quentin rolls up in due course, and pockets my ten pounds for his valuable information, confound him! How he must have chuckled to himself when he dropped me at the gate.

"Brimstoke's people were waiting inside for me, all right, while I was scouting round the premises. And, of course, they got me. If I hadn't walked into the house, they'd have come out after me. And that preposterous Admiral! I tell you, Philpott, he was a masterpiece! I never suspected him for a moment. Of course, I see now that all that hair was artistically stuck on.

"I'd give a good deal to find out who he really was. It wasn't Brimstoke himself, or Rushburton, or anybody I know at all well, I'll swear to that. But I've an idea that I've heard his voice before. Only once, just two or three words. And that comparatively recently. Somebody who has spoken to me for an instant. There's just a chance that I may remember who it was.

"However, that's beside the point. We can assume for the present that he was one of Brimstoke's people, and that his particular job last night was to do me in. But not at Leighton Grange. Bodies are deucedly awkward things to dispose of, and what would your charming friend Mrs. Clarke have thought if she had come back this morning to find a deceased private investigator in her cellar? It was all right in the case of Solway, he could be dumped at Oldwick Manor, and Rushburton could be trusted not to ask too many questions. But if I were to be found at all, it must be as far as possible from Leighton Court.

"Hence all that foolery with the coal-cellar. The idea was to put the wind up me about the police, and so to make me anxious to escape. Then enters the second villain, who relieves me of the rest of my cash and lets me out. He and the false Quentin must have thought they had caught a mug this time, and no mistake. Not only does he open the flap for me, but obligingly suggests a route for me to follow. Of course, one of the gang followed me in my ramblings and took the opportunity, when I was grovelling under that tree-stump, of giving me a clout from behind.

"Neat, wasn't it? My lifeless corpse was to be found, sooner or later, in that confounded wood, a long way from Leighton

Grange. And there wouldn't have been a scrap of evidence that I'd ever been near the place. You didn't believe it yourself, just now. For, as soon as I'd gone, the Admiral and his gang cleared out—in the false Quentin's car, I expect—leaving everything nice and tidy behind them. It would have been another unexplained murder for your people to worry about, Philpott."

"I dare say that you're right," agreed the inspector, "but if I may say so, Perrin, it doesn't explain quite a lot of things we want to know."

"It explains nothing," replied Perrin, with a smile. "It merely suggests that we are up against as amazing a set of ruffians that it has ever been my good fortune to meet. But we'll have them yet, never you worry."

"For the moment I don't exactly see how. You don't propose to confront Lord Brimstoke with this story, I suppose?"

"My dear Philpott, I don't propose to confront anybody with anything, at present. Let everybody concerned think that I'm lying dead in the wood. I want some more facts before I take any action."

"Well, I hope you'll get them. But you understand that, from my aspect, this is all beside the point. You hinted in your note that you expected to learn something about the Prime Minister's death. But I fail to see that you've established any connection between that and this gang of yours."

A shade passed across Perrin's face. "Perhaps I was a bit hasty there," he said in a voice which seemed suddenly to have become tired. "Anyhow, my brain isn't equal to coping with that problem for the moment. That confounded stuff the doctor gave me hasn't worked off yet, quite. I'll see you tomorrow, when I feel a bit fresher."

The inspector rose to take his leave, and Meade followed his example. But Perrin detained him. "Don't go for a minute, David," he said languidly. "I want a word with you."

He waited until the inspector had left the flat, and then turned to Meade. "Poor old Philpott!" he exclaimed, and all the usual energy had returned to his voice. "It's a shame not to take him completely into my confidence, after all he's done, but, if I did, he'd think that I'd gone completely off my head for good and all. And I don't want to be certified as a raving lunatic just yet. Now, my lad, I've got a job of work for you. You've got to be up bright and early tomorrow, by four o'clock at the latest. Get out the car then, bring it round here, and we'll go for a jolly little spin in the dawn. You've no idea what a lot of good it'll do you."

"I'm game," replied Meade. "But what about you? Are you fit for that sort of thing?"

"Perfectly. You can drive, and I'll be the invalid, enjoying the fresh morning air. Now you run along and play. I'm going back to bed, and after I've had a good sleep, I shall be fit as a fiddle. This hand's a damned nuisance, though, I shan't be able to use it properly for a long time to come."

It was soon after four o'clock next morning when Meade brought the car round. Perrin joined him, looking considerably paler than usual, but in the best of spirits. Meade could tell from his manner that he was in a state of suppressed excitement. But he made no comment. "Where are we bound for?" he asked.

"We'll follow the example of John Gilpin, and take the road to Ware," replied Perrin. "No, we're not going to call on any of your friends of yesterday. We're going to take a little country walk."

He refused to be more explicit, and they drove to Ware in silence. "Keep right on along the Buntingford road," said Perrin. "But stop short a mile or so before the turning to Leighton Grange. We'll find a nice quiet spot by the roadside to park the car."

They found the required spot, and both descended from the car. Perrin took a large-scale map from his pocket and opened it out. "I was studying this after you left me yesterday evening," he said. "I think I've identified the wood where my adventure ended. I must have come back on my tracks yesterday morning, and lucky for me that I did, as it happened. I want to have another look at that wood, but we won't approach it from the Leighton Grange direction. I don't want to be seen alive and well just yet. Not that there's much risk at this time in the morning, but there's no point in taking risks. If we strike over the fields from here, we ought to reach the place in a mile or two."

Perrin leading the way, map in hand, they set off. After crossing several fields and scrambling over gates they reached a large coppice. "This must be the place, I fancy," said Perrin. "I'm not going to say I recognize it, for I merely blundered into it in the dark, from the other side of course. We'd better start our exploration from there."

They worked round the wood, and Perrin uttered an exclamation of satisfaction. "This is it, all right!" he said. "I remember the barbed wire along this side. I dare say if we were to look closely enough, we should find a bit of my coat hanging on to it somewhere. But we won't wait to do that. I don't care about hanging round in the open too long. We'll get under cover and start to work through the wood."

"What, exactly, are we looking for?" asked Meade.

"Why, the place where I fell over the log," replied Perrin. "You'll know it by the blood you'll find about. My hand must have bled like a fire-hose. You start here, and I'll keep level with you a few yards to your right."

They penetrated the coppice until they reached the further end, then, shifting their positions slightly, came back again. It was not until their third attempt that Meade thought he noticed traces of someone having forced their way through the undergrowth. He followed these up, and came to a fallen log. On this and the surrounding ground were dark stains which might have been blood.

He shouted to his partner, who made his way up to him. "That's the place!" exclaimed Perrin. "Now, I wonder!"

He dropped on his hands and knees, and stared intently under the log. After a minute or two, he picked up a small object and handed it to Meade. It was an unburnt match. Perrin looked about, and picked up three or four more. Then he beckoned to Meade. "Kneel down, and look under this log, just here," he said. "What do you see?"

"I see a hole in the ground, about the size of a large pudding basin," replied Meade. "Just as if someone had scooped out the earth. And above that, a bit of the bark has been ripped off the log, and there's a big dent in the wood where the bark came from. I can't see much else."

"There was the metal match-box that chap up at Leighton Grange gave me, exactly in that spot," said Perrin quietly. "I saw it, in fact I almost touched it, when I lighted that match!"

"Well, it's not there now," replied Meade, after a careful scrutiny. "The chap that hit you must have picked it up and taken it away."

Perrin shook his head. "I think not," he said slowly. "Who picked up the pencil that Wedderley was sharpening when he died?" He smiled at Meade's puzzled expression, but did not wait for an answer. "I never really believed that I was followed, or that anybody hit me," he continued. "I only said that to give some sort of explanation to Philpott yesterday evening. For one thing I've got no bruises anywhere, and for another I believe that there's some other explanation. But before we jump to conclusions, let's see if that match-box is anywhere about."

They did not desist from their search until Perrin was satis-fied that the match-box was nowhere within a radius of several feet. He seemed in no way disappointed, rather the reverse, in fact. "Let's get back to the car," he said.

They returned to the road without further adventure. "Jump in and drive us home, David," said Perrin. "I'll sit beside you and expound a theory I've got. I can't explain it, but perhaps you can."

He settled himself into the car, and as soon as they were under way, began his exposition. "I want you to compare what happened in the Prime Minister's room a week ago with what happened to me on Monday night. Wedderley was killed and Durrant knocked out, by a shock which nobody has ever been able to explain properly. The same thing occurred in my case. I was conscious of a shock which knocked me out, yet I have no injuries except this damaged hand. Wedderley's left hand was also lacerated.

"Wedderley, when he received the shock, was sharpening a pencil which could not be found afterwards. I was looking for a metal match-box, and had my right hand holding a match within an inch or so of it. That match-box is not to be found. Wedderley was holding the pencil in his left hand. Both my right hand and Wedderley's left were lacerated.

"The various objects standing on Wedderley's desk were swept on to the floor, and the desk itself was slightly damaged. Beyond that, there were no signs of disturbance in the room. As you have seen for yourself there was a hole in the ground where the match-box lay, and above it the log was damaged. Nothing else round about was disturbed. Neither in Wedderley's room nor at the spot where I fell was there any sign of burning or anything else that would indicate that an explosion had taken place.

"Wedderley is reported to have said that the pencil he was sharpening was left behind by Lord Brimstoke. We have been unable to prove this, but, on the other hand, we have never actually disproved it. The matchbox was given to me by a rascal whom I strongly suspect of being one of Brimstoke's agents, and who cautioned me particularly against striking a match anywhere near Leighton Grange. Now, what is your deduction from these facts?"

Meade shook his head. "I don't know," he replied. "You say yourself that in neither case was there any explosion. Therefore the pencil and the match-box cannot have contained explosives."

"No, but I believe that both of them had the power of disruption, with the production of severe shock, and a very limited local destructive effect, extending to a range of only a few inches. They disrupted without explosion in the true sense, without the production of fumes or heat, that is. The pencil, I imagine, disrupted under the friction of the penknife. The match-box disrupted when I touched it with the flame of the match. That, of course, was a pure accident. My friends at Leighton Grange counted on my holding the matchbox close to my body, and striking a match on the bottom of the box, which was specially roughened for the purpose. That would have disrupted the box and I should have received the full effects of the shock."

"Oh, dash it all, Perrin, that's outside the range of human experience!" protested Meade. "I have enough elementary science to know that there is no substance which can be made to disrupt in the way you describe."

"No substance known to us," corrected Perrin. "But I have a dim idea of how such a thing might become possible. It's only very dim, for science has got beyond the range of the ordinary man's understanding in recent years. But I'll find out, you mark my words!"

He relapsed into silence and did not speak again until they were nearly home. And then suddenly he leaped in his seat with such violence that Meade applied the brakes abruptly. "What's up?" he asked anxiously.

"It's all right," replied Perrin. "Carry on. Sorry I startled you. It's just come back to me where I heard the Admiral's voice before. Good Lord, what a blind idiot I've been! Tell you what, David my lad, the best thing you can do in your own interests is to buy me out of partnership. Then you can get somebody into the firm who has got some sense in his head."

Chapter XX

No sooner had they arrived at the office than Perrin set out again. He was in a state of feverish excitement, which he could scarcely repress. He called upon a certain eminent scientist whose name was a household word, and who was generally acknowledged to be one of the leading physicists of the day.

With him Perrin spent a couple of hours. In the course of this interview he acquired an outline of the latest research into the constitution of matter. It would be difficult to say whether he or the scientist enjoyed the interview the most.

"What you suggest has long been known to be possible," said the latter to him as they parted. "In fact, on an incredibly minute scale, it has already been done. But, up till now, nobody has succeeded in controlling the experiment, or in reproducing it on a larger scale. I need not tell you how eagerly I await any further particulars that you may have to give me."

From the scientist Perrin went to Scotland Yard. He asked for Inspector Philpott, and persuaded him to secure him an interview with the assistant commissioner. Here, again, the interview lasted a long time, and Perrin had the greatest difficulty in overcoming the assistant commissioner's scruples.

"I can't act on my own responsibility in a matter like this," said the harassed chief of police at last. "I'd do practically anything to clear the mystery of Wedderley's death, except this. There are too many prominent people involved. The only thing I can suggest is that you come with me and see the Home Secretary, Mr. Perrin."

So they adjourned to the Home Office, and there, after much persuasion, Perrin got the Home Secretary to sanction his plan. "As I see it," said the Minister, "it all depends upon what happens this evening. If what you expect occurs, well and good. You can trust the police to play their part. But if it doesn't, your blood is on your own head. We wash our hands of you officially, and you'll have to stand the consequences. You understand that quite clearly, don't you, Mr. Perrin?"

"I'll take it on those terms, sir," replied Perrin cheerfully.

So it came about that Perrin and Inspector Philpott drove down to Oldwick Manor that evening. "We shall find Rushburton at home all right," said Perrin cheerfully. "It's been given out that he is suffering from a slight indisposition and he hasn't been in the House since Wedderley's death. All you've got to do is to introduce me and then let me do the talking."

Pearson first declared that his master would receive nobody. But on the production of the inspector's card, he at length agreed to inquire if Sir Ethelred would see them. After a long wait they were shown into his study, where they found him hunched up in an arm-chair. If he had looked perturbed on the occasion of their first visit, he looked perfectly ghastly now. He seemed to have aged ten years, his face was drawn, pallid and unhealthy. As he laid down the book he had been reading Perrin noticed that his hand shook uncontrollably.

Rushburton looked up as they came in. "Well, what is the reason of this intrusion?" he asked, in a voice that had lost nothing of its tone of command.

"I came here to introduce this gentleman, sir," replied the inspector respectfully, and as he spoke Perrin came forward. Rushburton looked him up and down. "I've seen you before somewhere," he said. "Yes, I remember. You were here with the inspector a week ago last Saturday. Well, what do you want? First of all though, what's your name?"

"My name is Perrin, Sir Ethelred," was the quiet reply. Yet quiet as it was it produced the effect of a bombshell on Rushburton. His eyes started out of his head, and he grasped the arms of his chair as though to pull himself up. Then with a visible effort, he controlled his agitation and let himself sink back again.

"I never heard of you before," he growled. "Make haste and tell me what you want."

"I think you must have heard of me, Sir Ethelred," replied Perrin easily. "Surely Lord Brimstoke or Mr. Hardcastle must have mentioned my name to you? However, it hardly matters. I've come to ask you a few questions about your late secretary, Mr. Solway."

"What business is it of yours? And what right have you got to come here and talk to me like that?"

"No right at all. But I think you will not refuse to answer me, Sir Ethelred. Would it come as an unexpected shock to you to learn that Mr. Solway was murdered?"

A tremor shook Sir Ethelred's massive frame, and the look of terror which Perrin had noticed before came into his eyes. "Murdered!" he exclaimed wrathfully, but his voice shook. "What the devil are you talking about? Why, the highest possible medical authority certified that his death was due to natural causes!"

"Nevertheless he was murdered," persisted Perrin. "How could a man, living the life he did, acquire the parasites which caused his death? Those parasites were injected into his blood in order to kill him. And you know why, Sir Ethelred."

Rushburton made a final attempt at bluster. "I really cannot continue this conversation, Mr. Perrin," he said, loftily. "If you have any more of these ridiculous accusations to make I must refer you to my solicitor."

He stretched out a trembling hand to reach the bell, but Perrin took a step forward. "Believe me, Sir Ethelred, it will be to your advantage to be frank with me. Indeed it is your only chance to escape complete ruin and disgrace. You will understand this perhaps when I tell you that I know how Mr. Wedderley was killed, and who conspired to murder him."

Their eyes met, and for many seconds Rushburton stared at Perrin as though fascinated. Then his head dropped and his fingers fumbled in his waistcoat pocket. Before he could withdraw them, Perrin leaned swiftly over him and clutched his arm. "Not that way!" he said firmly but not unsympathetically. "Allow me." He felt in the pocket, and removed a tiny glass tube containing three or four white pellets, which he handed to the inspector. Rushburton, his resistance completely broken, fell back limply in his chair.

"I assure you, Sir Ethelred, that I know too much for you to attempt a denial," continued Perrin. "I have the authority of the Home Secretary to tell you that if you will make a full and complete confession no proceedings will be taken against you. I have reason to know that you took no active part in the murder of Mr. Wedderley and your secretary or in the attempted murder of myself. Also I know that ten days before the murder of the Prime Minister you had resolved to have nothing further to do with the conspiracy. Why did you send Mr. Solway to see Lord Brimstoke and Mr. Hardcastle on the third of this month?"

There was a long pause before Rushburton replied. "I sent him to tell them that I had decided to go no further in the matter," he replied at last, in a voice shaken with emotion. "I didn't know till then that they meant to go as far as murder. I thought they would be content to wait till the government fell in the ordinary course, and I should be able to help them."

"That is exactly what I supposed. And Solway was murdered as a warning to you, in the same way that Ben Hammerton was murdered as a warning to me. But how was it that Mr. Solway allowed Mr. Hardcastle to inject the parasites of that terrible disease into his blood? What is the secret of Mr. Hardcastle's power over his patients, Sir Ethelred?"

Rushburton drew back the sleeve of his left arm. It was covered with the traces of minute punctures. "That is what his patients went to him for," he replied in a low voice.

"I guessed as much, but I had no proof of it. He created the craving for drugs, and so placed his patients at his mercy. And of course, when he offered Mr. Solway an injection, he had no idea that it contained anything but the usual dose of morphia or cocaine. When he did not return that evening, you must have guessed what had happened to him."

"I didn't know for certain, I swear it. I didn't dare face Brimstoke and Hardcastle myself. That's why I sent him. He didn't know what he was carrying, he merely gave them letters from me. I thought that they wouldn't trouble to touch him. When he didn't come back, I didn't know what to think. But I knew that he had fallen into their clutches. It was not until Brimstoke came here on the following Friday that I was told the truth."

Rushburton paused, but Perrin made no comment, and at last he continued: "Brimstoke told me that day, as we were sitting in the pavilion after lunch. He said that Solway was dying, and could not live many hours. And he told me that his death was a warning to me of what my own fate would be if I played them false. The great scheme must be put into operation at once. Brimstoke said frankly that he dare not risk the passage of the War Debts Bill. Once it was certain that it would become operative, the London and Provinces Bank would be ruined, and he with it. Then it would be too late to go on with the scheme. He insisted that the only course was to remove Wedderley, and that within the next few days.

"I asked him what had happened to Solway, and he told me. He said that as soon as he had read my letter, which Solway had brought him, he rang up Hardcastle and they decided that I must be taught a lesson. Hardcastle received Solway quite amiably, read the letter he brought him, and told him to tell me that I must please myself. Then he offered him the usual injection of the drug. Solway accepted, but the injection contained not only the parasites, but also a further drug which rapidly deprived him of the power of speech or motion. In that condition he was taken down to Hardcastle's own car, which was waiting, and driven to Leighton Grange, where further injections of the parasites were administered. Leighton Grange was unoccupied at the time. Solway slept through the day, and Hardcastle visited him only at night."

Perrin could hardly restrain a shudder at the coldblooded and devilish cruelty of the proceeding. "And Lord Brimstoke told you how his body was to be disposed of?" he asked.

"He said that when Solway's death was imminent he would be brought here and placed in the pavilion. He told me that it would be better for everybody concerned that I should be the one to find it. My position would prevent too many awkward questions being asked. In any case, his death could not be traced to Hardcastle."

"And you accepted the warning and did nothing. Not only were you afraid of what might happen to you if you spoke, but you stood to gain considerably by the scheme which was to be put into operation. There was an epoch-making discovery out of which an enormous fortune could be made to be shared between you, Lord Brimstoke and Mr. Hardcastle. And I know now what that discovery was."

Even from the depths of his misery Rushburton evinced a feeble incredulity. "You know!" he exclaimed. "How could you?"

"Mainly because I was myself made the subject of an experiment as to the efficacy of the discovery," replied Perrin. "Mr. Hardcastle has solved the problem at which the scientists of the world have been working for years. He has discovered how to control at will the disintegration of the atom. He is able to produce a substance which, under certain circumstances, will disrupt of itself. And such a substance is the most efficient weapon for murder which has yet been devised."

"Murder," repeated Rushburton dully. "Yes, I admit that the first use which has been made of the discovery was murder. Man, don't you realize what Hardcastle's discovery means?"

"I fully realize it. I understand that it puts the possessor of the secret in possession of such vast sources of power that the human mind can scarcely contemplate it. All sources of power hitherto known must become obsolete. Coal, oil, water power become cumbrous and ludicrously inefficient. So great an authority as Sir J.J. Thomson said years ago, that the atomic energy stored in an ounce of chlorine would keep the *Mauretania* going at full speed for a week. Yet, now that the secret of liberating that energy is discovered, the first use made of it is to murder an honest and kindly gentleman!"

Rushburton writhed beneath the scorn of Perrin's voice. "The idea of the murder was not mine," he replied feebly. "I assure you that as soon as I heard it was suggested, I sent Solway with those letters saying that I would have nothing further to do with the business."

"Yes, you sent Solway and the poor devil was murdered in consequence. And even then you hadn't the pluck to tell the truth! So Mr. Wedderley was killed, and still you kept quiet. Not exactly the conduct one might expect from the Champion of English Liberty, is it, Sir Ethelred?"

Inspector Philpott, watching the scene from the background, felt his brain reeling. The established order of things seemed to be crumbling about his ears. Sir Ethelred Rushburton, a name to conjure with, the future Home Secretary, had collapsed like a pricked bladder. He sat hunched up in his chair, unable to say a word in reply to Perrin's indictment.

After a long pause he made an attempt to justify himself. "If I had said a word, if I had dropped the least hint, they would have killed me," he said in a low voice. "I wouldn't have minded taking an ordinary risk perhaps, but Hardcastle had at his command weapons which nobody could guard against. And he would not have hesitated to use them. He was a man of one idea, and nothing in heaven or hell would have diverted him from it. He got hold of Brimstoke, years ago, through his infernal drugs and made him finance him. Leighton Grange and his laboratory there, the consulting-rooms in Harley Street, the men he employed, all these were paid for by Brimstoke."

"And what exactly did Lord Brimstoke hope to get out of all this?"

"Hardcastle had convinced him that he was on the verge of being able to control the disruption of the atom. Brimstoke knew that this secret if discovered would be of inestimable value. As you suggested just now, it would provide a source of power which would cost practically nothing. Brimstoke and Hardcastle were to share the profit of the discovery. But the results would be so revolutionary that no ordinary commercial organization could deal with them. There was only one source from which the millions that the secret would be worth could be derived, the nation itself. Brimstoke realized this and decided that it would be necessary to include in the syndicate some member of this or a future government who could influence the negotiations. I was already a patient of Hardcastle's and seemed to be the person indicated."

"Another argument in favour of approaching you was that your scruples were not likely to prove an obstacle," remarked Perrin icily. "So Lord Brimstoke supplied you with certain information, which enabled you to make money on the stock exchange, and Hardcastle, I expect, gave you to understand that he would withhold the supply of drugs unless you consented to come in. But I don't expect that much pressure was necessary. From your point of view you had everything to gain and nothing to lose. A very pleasant prospect, Sir Ethelred."

"I saw no harm in it then," replied Rushburton. "Besides, I did not share Hardcastle's confidence to the same extent as Brimstoke. And when one day a couple of months ago, Hardcastle invited Brimstoke and myself to Leighton Grange, he said that he had something to show us. He took us up to his laboratory, which was full of apparatus, and he told us that at last he had discovered the secret to which his life had been devoted.

"He saw that we were both a trifle sceptical and he told us that he had brought us to Leighton Grange in order to demonstrate the truth of what he said. He asked us to examine a piece of machinery which stood in the centre of the room. It consisted of a drum, round which was wound a few turns of rope. The other end of the rope passed over a pulley in the ceiling and then down a metal weight which stood on the floor.

"He showed us how, by turning a handle fitted to the drum, it was possible to raise the weight from the floor to the ceiling. The weight was two hundred pounds and the height to which it could be raised was ten feet. The effort exerted in raising it the full distance was two thousand foot-pounds. One horsepower, he said, would therefore raise the weight from the floor to the ceiling in approximately four seconds. He made us each try the handle of the winch, and we found that we could not raise the weight in anything like that time.

"Then he showed us a minute fragment of some substance which looked like a lead pellet, not much larger than a pin's head. He put this into a box attached to the spindle of the winch, and directed the rays from what looked like an X-ray tube upon the box. The winch immediately revolved, and the weight was carried up to the ceiling in less than two seconds. This was done repeatedly without the tiny piece of active substance being replaced. Hardcastle told us that it contained enough energy to continue the action for several days.

"Brimstoke was still skeptical. He thought that there must be a hidden motor of some kind connected with the winch. Hardcastle let him examine it as he pleased, and at last he was satisfied that the winch had been operated by the energy contained in the substance alone.

"We asked what the substance was and he told us that it was derived by actual transmutation from lead. This transmutation, he told us, was a comparatively simple process, on any scale. The piece we had seen would exert two horse-power for several hundred hours before all its atoms were disintegrated. Or it could be caused to liberate all its energy at once. In that case he told us something like an explosion would take place. The atoms of the substance would be suddenly resolved into protons and electrons, with a very limited disruptive effect, but causing a shock, due to the impact of the highly charged particles of an electrical nature. This shock would be felt over a slightly wider area. He offered to demonstrate this to us, but we told him we had seen enough and were quite satisfied."

"Your caution was fully justified," remarked Perrin. "I have felt that shock, and I can assure you that its effects are anything but pleasant."

"I assure you that I had nothing to do with that, Mr. Perrin," said Rushburton earnestly. "I only heard of the attempt on your life this morning, when Brimstoke and Hardcastle were convinced that it had succeeded. I can only say how deeply thankful I am that you escaped."

Perhaps the man really meant it, thought Perrin. Anything must be preferable to the mental agony which he had endured since the murder of the Prime Minister. He must have known that before he could take a step towards betraying his confederates the same mysterious death would overtake him.

After a pause Rushburton continued: "On Saturday, the first of this month, Brimstoke came to see me. He told me that there was every possibility of the government securing a majority on the War Debts Bill, and that if this happened he would be completely ruined. He gave me to understand that an investigation into the affairs of the London and Provinces Bank might result in his arrest, in which case he would not be in a position to exploit Hardcastle's discovery. The only way to avert disaster was to secure the rejection of the bill. And the surest way of doing this was to remove Wedderley, the one man who was keeping the government together.

"I did not understand at first what he meant. It was not until he told me that Hardcastle had provided him with the means for this removal that I realized that he intended murder. Wedderley was to be killed by means of the active substance which Hardcastle had shown us, and in such a way that the means of his death could never be discovered.

"Brimstoke showed me the device with which the murder was to be accomplished. Hardcastle had taken a piece of ordinary pencil, of grade B, which it was known the Prime Minister favoured. He had bored out a quarter of an inch at one end of the so-called 'lead' which as no doubt you know is not lead at all but a graphite composition, and had replaced it by a composition of his own, containing a proportion of the active substance. Brimstoke showed me the pencil. In appearance it was utterly unchanged. The closest examination could not have revealed the fact that it had been tampered with. Only the point was blunt, and the first instinct of anybody who wished to use it, would be to sharpen it.

"Hardcastle had explained to Brimstoke what would happen then. At the first contact with the steel of the sharpening blade, a galvanic action would be set up which would lead to the instant disintegration of the active substance. Everything in immediate contact with it, that is to say, the rest of the pencil, would be reduced to dust, and consequently no vestige of the pencil would be found. The shock would be sufficient to kill anybody holding the pencil, without leaving any traces, except probably an injury to the hand in which the pencil was held."

"Mr. Hardcastle's predictions were correct in every detail," remarked Perrin grimly.

"I know," replied Rushburton dully. "I read every detail of the inquest, with a horror which I cannot express. Brimstoke's scheme was simple. As soon as possible he would contrive a pretext for seeking an interview with Wedderley, which he knew would readily be granted. He would take the prepared pencil with him, and also another which he would use in Wedderley presence. Then, on his departure, he would leave the prepared pencil behind him. Wedderley's trick of picking up pencils and putting them in his pockets was well known. He would be certain to pick this one up, and, sooner or later, seeing that it was of the grade that he preferred, he would seek to use it. But, before he could do so, it would require sharpening."

Rushburton paused and Perrin nodded. "Very well thought out," he said. "I guessed that something of the kind had happened when the same sort of trick was played on me!"

"In your case you were given a match-box, the metal of which had been alloyed with a minute quantity of the active substance. It was intended that you should strike a match on the box, when it would have been utterly destroyed, and you would have been killed by the shock."

"The match-box was certainly utterly destroyed," replied Perrin. "Fortunately for me, it was only just within my reach at the time, so I escaped with a shaking up and a damaged hand. My experience was very similar to that of Mr. Durrant. May I ask to whom I am indebted for this delicate attention?"

"It was Hardcastle who insisted upon the necessity of killing you," replied Rushburton. "He said nothing to either Brimstoke or myself until after the event. Then he explained that you had become too inquisitive. He was not in the least afraid that you would discover anything about Wedderley's death. But you were still trying to discover the facts about poor Solway, and he was afraid that you might prove troublesome in that direction. So, as he informed us, he had taken steps to ensure your silence."

"I appreciate the compliment," said Perrin gravely.

"Now, inspector, if you are quite satisfied, I think we are ready to take the steps agreed upon?"

Inspector Philpott nodded, and left the room. He went to the telephone and rang up the assistant commissioner at Scotland Yard.

His message was the signal for the arrest of Hardcastle and Lord Brimstoke.

CHAPTER XXI

PERRIN left Inspector Philpott at Oldwick Manor to take charge of Rushburton, who had completely collapsed on conclusion of his confession, and seemed in need of a doctor rather than a policeman. Perrin himself drove straight back to Scotland Yard, where he was at once admitted to the presence of the assistant commissioner.

"Well, Mr. Perrin, I must congratulate you," said the chief of police. "I gathered from Philpott's message that your deductions were correct. Unfortunately, one of the criminals has escaped us."

"I'm sorry to hear that!" exclaimed Perrin, anxiously. "Which one?"

"Hardcastle. As we arranged when I last saw you, I had men shadowing both him and Lord Brimstoke. Hardcastle was located in Harley Street, and Lord Brimstoke at his house in Park Lane. As soon as I got Philpott's message I sent out orders for their arrest. Lord Brimstoke was apprehended without any trouble."

"And Hardcastle? According to Rushburton, he was if anything the more guilty of the two. He didn't slip through your men's fingers, did he? Once at large, he will be a terrible danger to the community."

"No fear of that," replied the assistant commissioner gravely. "He slipped through our fingers, certainly, but not in the sense you mean. When our men entered the house to arrest him they found him in his consulting-room, apparently making entries in a book. Two of them went in, produced their warrant, and warned him in the usual form. Two others were waiting on the landing outside. We were taking no risks, you see.

"Hardcastle was smoking a cigarette. He smiled, said that there must be some extraordinary mistake, but that he was quite ready to go wherever the men chose to take him. Then he leaned over the desk, took the cigarette out of his mouth, and pressed the lighted end on a small metal ash-tray as though to extinguish it.

"At that moment the two men on the landing who could see through the open door what was happening inside the room, heard a sharp but not very loud report. At the same time Hardcastle fell forward on the desk and the two men beside him staggered and collapsed on the floor. The other two rushed in and found Hardcastle dead, with the flesh torn off his right hand, but no other sign of injury. The two men who had been in the room were unconscious, but still alive. They haven't come round yet, but the doctor who was called in has every hope of their recovery. The queer thing about it, is that the ash-tray seems to have disappeared."

"I think I can explain that," said Perrin thoughtfully. "So Hardcastle was prepared for all emergencies, was he? I might have guessed he would be. Was anybody else found in the house?"

"The house belonged to Hardcastle. The other specialists who rent consulting-rooms from him had gone home. The only people besides Hardcastle found on the premises were two men-servants who have been detained for the present."

"I'm glad of that," said Perrin. "I may be able to identify at least one of them. Now, I expect you'd like a full account of what Rushburton had to say for himself. He's an accessory all right, but I don't think he took an active part in any of the murders."

"Well, that's comprehensive enough," said the assistant commissioner when Perrin had finished. "From what you say, he won't have any objection to earning a free pardon by turning King's evidence?"

"My own opinion is that he'll be so relieved when he hears that Hardcastle is dead, and Lord Brimstoke safely under lock and key, that he won't have the slightest compunction in giving away the whole show," replied Perrin.

It was not until the following morning that Perrin had the chance of a word with Inspector Philpott. "I've left Rushburton in charge of Doctor Martlock with the couple of my chaps to keep an eye on him," reported the latter. "He's suffering from what the doctor calls a nervous breakdown, and isn't likely to give trouble. Now, look here, Perrin, I want to know how you tumbled to the fact that Hardcastle was the villain of the piece, and that he had murdered Solway? It was that that broke down Rushburton's resistance, in the first place."

"Deduction, my friend, pure deduction. That and the fact that I remembered where I had heard the Admiral's voice before. That hairy apparition was no other than the melancholy-looking individual who had opened the door to me when I first called on Hardcastle. I hope he's one of the chaps who were detained last night. I'm going round to have a look presently."

"That's all very well," persisted the inspector. "But it's a long step from there to deducing that Hardcastle was the chap who murdered the Prime Minister."

"Not such a very long step if you follow my reasoning. An attempt had been made to murder me, and the circumstances were remarkably similar to those found after Wedderley's death. The Admiral, I felt sure, was Hardcastle's man, most artistically disguised. Leighton Grange was in the occupation of Hardcastle. I, like the ass I was, never suspecting that Hardcastle, the respectable specialist, was implicated in the business, had opened my heart to him.

"Given all that, it wasn't very difficult to guess what had happened. When I gave my name the first time I called at Harley Street, Hardcastle recognized it and must have wondered what I was after. That's why he saw me so readily, of course. He saw through my yarn about looking for the missing attaché-case, and guessed that I had my suspicions about Solway's death. As soon as I left him, he put that chap in the hall on to follow me.

"He had an easy enough job. I walked slowly to Oxford Circus, lunched there, and then took a taxi to Southwark Bridge Road. I purposely hung about there for some minutes, which gave the fellow, who probably followed me in another taxi, plenty of time to catch me up. Then he saw me talking to Ben Hammerton in the North Star and transferred his attentions to him. He reported to Hardcastle, who issued orders that Ben should be knifed that evening and the post-card put in his pocket."

"Who did the knifing, do you suppose?" asked the inspector.

"I can't tell you that, but I expect the job was kept in the family. Probably the chap that followed me disguised himself, and did it. He's pretty good at disguises as I've seen for myself. But probably you won't get evidence enough to hang him. The point is that as soon as I realized that the Admiral was really Hardcastle's man, it became clear that Hardcastle was in some way concerned with Solway's death and that he had engineered a pretty good attempt to murder me. But this attempt had been made by the same means that had been employed in

Wedderley's case. Therefore Hardcastle, since he had supplied the means in one case, had done so in the other.

"But, even then, I couldn't prove anything. I could only conjecture that if a metal match-box could be made to produce a shock which laid me out, a pencil might be made to produce a similar shock which had actually killed Wedderley. I had never forgotten the curious fact that the pencil described by Durrant had never been found. Nor had you, for that matter. The difference between us was that I believed Durrant's story while you didn't."

"Well, you'll admit that the fact that the pencil he talked about couldn't be found, made things look a bit fishy?"

"I do admit it. I couldn't understand it until I discovered that the match-box had also disappeared. That set me thinking, and I took the ablest scientific advice I could find. Hardcastle himself had told me that he made a hobby of trying to solve scientific problems. You mentioned to me that there was a laboratory at Leighton Grange. If what I suspected was correct, Hardcastle was the man who held the secret.

"My scientific informant confirmed my suspicions to this extent. He told me that if it were possible to produce instantaneous disintegration of the atoms of any substance, he would expect the effects which I described to him. Nothing would remain of the original substance. The atoms would disappear in an electrical discharge, causing a local disruptive effect and shock.

"This was sufficient evidence to me that my theory was correct. And it was a pretty safe guess that if Hardcastle had discovered the secret of controlling the disintegration of the atom, this was the bond between him, Lord Brimstoke and Rushburton. Why, just think of it, man! A secret that must revolutionize the world, controlled by its discoverer, an astute financier and a member of the Cabinet. It's impossible to estimate the enormous sums which they might have made out of it!

And if the conspirators had only waited until the government fell in the ordinary course of events, they would have brought it off! But it's time we went to see those two fellows who were found at Hardcastle's place last night."

As soon as Perrin set eyes on them, he recognized them at once. The first was the misanthropic man who had opened the door to him on his first visit. As soon as he heard him speak, Perrin was prepared to swear that he was the man who had masqueraded as the Admiral. He controlled his astonishment at seeing Perrin, however, and refused to make any statement.

But the second man, whom Perrin recognized as the so-called under-gardener who had given him the matchbox and released him from the cellar, was seized with almost supernatural terror at the sight of Perrin. He eventually made a long and detailed statement, in which he accused the Admiral of having murdered Ben Hammerton. He also gave information which led to the arrest of the false Quentin, who, on learning that his confederates were in custody, also confessed.

His story was this. He had been waiting at the door of Hardcastle's house in Harley Street when Solway was brought out. At that time Solway was just capable of movement, but not of speech or resistance. A man in such a condition coming from a doctor's house was not likely to attract much attention. He had driven him straight to Leighton Grange, where the "under-gardener" was waiting for them. Between them they had carried Solway, who by then was unconscious, upstairs, and put him to bed. Hardcastle had come to see him every night.

On Friday evening Solway was evidently sinking fast, and "Quentin" received his instructions. As soon as it was sufficiently dark, Solway was put into the car, accompanied by the under-gardener, and was driven to Oldwick Manor.

From the entrance he was taken to the pavilion in the wheelbarrow as Perrin had suspected, and there deposited for Rushburton to find in the morning.

The removal of Perrin had been carefully planned. Quentin's story of the man who had spoken to him in St. James's Square was entirely false. As a matter of fact the grey sedan had not been out since the Solway episode. He had received his instructions from Hardcastle, who had coached him in what he was to say. As soon as he had deposited Perrin at the gates of Leighton Grange he had taken the car to where it was normally kept, a garage hidden in the woods which surrounded the estate and reached by a separate entrance. Then he had slipped into the house before Perrin reached it, through the open window.

He had there joined the "Admiral" and the "under-gardener" in the library. Perrin had not recognized him as the third man because he never had a chance of looking at him properly and because he had removed his chauffeur's livery.

These three alone were in Hardcastle's confidence. Mrs. Clarke and the staff of servants at Leighton Grange, and the receptionist and the man who had taken the "Admiral's" place at the house in Harley Street, were entirely ignorant of the plot.

Unfortunately for the cause of science the most meticulous examination by experts of Hardcastle's papers, and of his laboratory at Leighton Grange, failed to reveal his secret. The essential clues had died with him, and his method of controlling the disintegration of the atom was never discovered.

Rushburton's evidence and certain documents found in the private office in Lombard Street, were sufficient to condemn Lord Brimstoke. The "Admiral" was also convicted of the murder of Ben Hammerton and these two paid the penalty with their lives. "Quentin" and the "under-gardeners" were sentenced to terms of penal servitude.

Millicent Rushburton and Durrant were married very quietly directly after the conclusion of the trial. Osmond Rushburton produced a play which ran very successfully for some months in London. But, though the Government, as had been generally expected, was defeated on the second reading of the War Debts Bill, and a General Election ensued, Sir Ethelred did not offer himself as a candidate to the electors of Coalborough.

He had left the country, leaving his family to dispose of Oldwick Manor and the Berkeley Square house as best they could.

"And a damned good riddance too," was Perrin's comment.

THE END